Tom Joad and Me

A NOVEL
BY
Owen O'Neill

THIRSTY BOOKS
EDINBURGH

© Owen O'Neill 2024

Published by Thirsty Books 2024
www.thirstybooks.com

The author has asserted his moral rights.

British Library Cataloguing-in-Publication Data.
A catalogue record for this book is available from the
British Library.

ISBN 978-1-7393181-1-6 paperback

Design and typset
derek.rodger21@outlook.com

Cover
Tangletree Designs

Printing
Severn Print

For San, Ollie and my grandparents Joe and Sadie

'Happiness is having a large, loving, caring, close-knit family. . . in another city.'

George Burns

'I wrote it is midnight. The rain is beating on the window. It was not midnight. It was not raining.'

Samuel Beckett

PART ONE

RAINDROPS ON THE WINDOWPANE

ONE

THE PLASTIC BUCKET that sat at the top of the stairs should have been much bigger. There were eight of us children using it after all so it wasn't long before it was full to the brim. I knew, we all knew, that when Drunken Daddy came home from the pub the bucket would be knocked over. It happened with sickening regularity. He would get his foot stuck in it and invariably fall backwards down the stairs. Even so, none of us wanted to use the outside toilet. It was fifty yards from the house and the winter of 1963 was one of the coldest to hit County Tyrone in two hundred years.

The toilet was a badly constructed clinker-block building with a rusted tin roof and a cracked wooden door. The cracks were stuffed with paper to prevent people from spying. I thought no one in their right mind would have ever wanted to do that. It was pitch dark, the wooden toilet seat had a screw loose and swivelled as I tried my best to shit straight. Wet clingy cobwebs brushed my face and something always scuttled across the floor under my feet. Neat cut out squares of the *Mid Ulster Mail* hung on a nail on the wall and my ass was wiped in a hurry. If there wasn't any newspaper, a cold dock leaf picked on the way back to the house would have to do the job.

My mother, Maureen McCrudden, is five-foot-three and weighs eight-and-a-half stone. A wiry, quick-witted woman with spidery eyelashes and big green eyes. Her hair is black as coal. In the summer, when the sun shines on it, it takes on a dark purple sheen and her skin goes leathery brown. Her people, going way back to the 1700's, were the 'Dark Wards' from County Galway, also known as the 'Black Irish', they had Portuguese blood. My mother's great grandmother was Costello, from the Portuguese *Castelo*. My father, Frank McCrudden, is a six-foot ginger-haired seventeen-stone slab of Northern Irish snow-white flesh. He has enormous ears and when he was a teenager, tried to glue them back, which resulted in them becoming infected, taking the ailment glue ear to another level. He eventually had to be taken to hospital. After that he became known as 'Sticky Lugs' but God help anyone who called Frank McCrudden that to his face. The McCrudden family coat of arms hung proudly on a nail by the front door in a large wooden frame. It was an odd design of a coat of armour with a little tree trunk on the head, surrounded by an ornate red and white leafy border with the Latin phrase *Nec deficit alter*. No one fails. That never failed to make me smile.

Carricktown is a mile-and-a-half long and boasts the widest main street in Northern Ireland. It is set in a valley surrounded by the Sperrin mountains. It has two factories, a cheese factory and a carpet factory, both of which employ very few Catholics. It is a busy market town with a Shambles

Yard where cows, pigs, and sheep are sold on a Saturday. At the end of the day the pubs, all seventeen of them, are rammed with red-faced farmers covered in pig shit and cow dung. If anyone is brave enough to stomach the smell, and sing a song for them, they can make a few shillings. I do this with my friend Mickey Peach. Mickey only knows Irish Rebel Songs, which could go either way depending on which side of the political fence the farmers are on, so to be on the safe side I would belt out 'non party' songs like 'I'll Take You Home Again Kathleen' and 'The Wild Rover'. Sometimes the farmers would make us drink a bottle of Guinness. I was seven-years old, Micky was eight.

In the early 1900s, on a desperately cold, frosty, morning, a wandering poet was passing through the town, when he was attacked by two dogs. In an attempt to defend himself, he went to pick up a rock and throw it at the dogs, but the rock was frozen to the ground – and he wrote, *Long hungry Carricktown, where the stones are tied and the dogs are let loose*. This introduction to the town was proudly painted in giant white letters on the gable of an old barn and the first thing everyone saw as they approached from the north end at Gort Hill. We lived at the south end of the town, or the hem as my grandfather called it, in the townland of Tullybern, a scattering of small farms and cottages, snuggling within the shadow of the Burren, an ancient Celtic Fort.

We can hear our father coming. Everyone in the area can hear Frank McCrudden coming.

'Fuck you all! Fuck you anyway! Fuck the fucking lot of you! You don't love me do you? None of you love your fucking father! Your father that fucking reared you!'

The front door is hammered and kicked open and here comes Frank, up the stairs, breathing hard and murmuring death threats. We visualise his foot going straight into the bucket taking his right leg from underneath him, and there he goes, backwards down the stairs hitting every step as he tumbles like a circus clown. There is always a silence that follows, and I would often pray that the silence would last forever, that we would find him in the morning at the bottom of the stairs, stiff and silent and stinking and dead, but that never happened. Frank howls like a trapped animal and chases us from our beds, insane with rage shouting, 'I'll kill all of you outside-toilet-scared cunts.'

We would try to escape, some of us heading down the stairs slipping on the putrid, sodden, threadbare stair carpet. A madhouse of shit covered people running for their lives in all directions, my mother standing in the far corner of the room with the 'good knife' as she called it, which meant the sharp one.

On one occasion Jem Patterson rang the police. Jem, our next-door neighbour, actually lived at the bottom of the road but Frank had a powerful actor's voice, he could really project but he wasn't an actor. In fact, he wasn't anything except a professional drinker. When the police arrived neither of them were brave enough to come anywhere near this man who was roaring like a bull, covered in his loving children's urine and faecal matter. The sergeant wrote 'Domestic dispute' in his little black book and they both disappeared into the foggy night.

Sobriety repaired Frank to a shy, gentle, caring, intelligent man with quiet hands and a soft voice. A man with humour and an overwhelming generosity of spirit. We loved this man. This man who baked bread, made beautiful soup out of scrag ends of meat, potatoes and barley. Who made us laugh until we wept, with his stories and impressions of the neighbours and the local parish priest. The man who taught me how to catch salmon with a gaff hook in the quiet pools where they rested before trying to leap the river dam at Adair's End, how to take the tyres off a bicycle with a spoon, how to snare rabbits. The man who told me I should read *The Grapes of Wrath* by John Steinbeck. This was the man my mother fell in love with. But this man only existed when he was sober – and that was rare. The other man was always waiting in the wings. But I had a plan to escape and that's what kept me going, kept me sane.

I was brought up by my paternal grandparents and lived with them in Tullybern Cottage until I was nine years old. It was never fully explained to me why this was the case. I was the second child, the first boy and apparently the spitting image of my great-grandfather, my grandmother's father, Emmet Divenny. A few doors down from my great-grandfather's house in Scutchers Row, Tommy Heaney ran a barber shop from the front room of his terraced house. The story goes that Heaney and my great grandfather had a long-standing feud about a woman called Teresa McKenna. There was also a debt of money involved, I can't remember who owed what to whom. Heaney was a binge drinker. He would drink for six months and stop for six months, then start again drink for three months and stop for three months. This was a pattern throughout his life.

When he was drinking he became morose and extremely violent. This was the effect that alcohol seemed to have on most men when I was growing up. These men were frowned upon by other men, other men who could drink for twenty-four hours and not vomit, or stagger, or beat their wives, or have a hangover, or miss work the next day. These were the men who could 'hold their drink', drink like gentlemen it was said. These were men who had spilled more drink on their ties than those other useless bastards would ever drink in all their lives. I wished with all my heart that my father could have been one of those Gentlemen Drinkers.

On the 16th August 1936, my great grandfather, Emmet Divenny, was having his hair cut by Tommy Heaney in the front room of Heaney's terraced house in Scutchers Row. As they had grown older, a kind of an odd peace treaty had developed between them, a cessation of hostilities.

Although they never spoke, or recognised each other's existence, my great grandfather did allow Tommy Heaney to cut his hair and Tommy Heaney would cut it in a begrudging silence with a frown on his face. When it was done my great grandfather would grunt and throw a half-crown into the tin as he left.

On this particular day John McCormack, the famous Irish tenor was singing 'The Rose of Tralee' on the radio when Tommy Heaney grabbed a cut-throat razor and sliced open my great grandfather's throat, ear to ear. He then ran out into the street covered in blood shouting. 'I did it for Teresa! I did it for my love. He had it coming.'

My grandmother was the first on the scene, slipping on her father's blood and hitting her head on the stone floor. Three months later Tommy Heaney was hanged for murder. He was 70 years old and had waited fifty-four years to wreak his brutal cowardly revenge. My grandmother hadn't shed a tear for her father in twenty years but on the day I was born she came to the back room of the Chapel Hospital, took me gently in her arms, and couldn't stop.

Tullybern has three small bedrooms, a tiny kitchen, a scullery, a living room a front room. No bathroom or hot running water. Every room in the house has an open fireplace apart from the living room, which has an enormous Victorian cast iron range that burns coal and turf. It is lit most of the day in the winter and banked up at night, so only needs a little whiff of air to get it going again in the morning. My grandmother cooks on it. It's where she boils the water for washing clothes, which are hung on a wooden rung contraption strung up above the range and dries in no time.

It's where she 'warms her arse' on a cold day and has a large pot of tea on the go at all times. It is the beating heart of the house. My grandfather keeps it stoked up and polished with black lead until it is almost shimmering. 'I'm the engine driver,' he shouts and makes a noise like a train, 'Boooop! Boooop!'

There is an outside toilet and an acre of field at the back. Tullybern is one of the 'Soldier's Cottages' given to ex-servicemen who had served in the British Army during the World Wars. My grandfather was nineteen when he was gassed and blown up at the second battle of Ypres in 1915, which left him with a two-inch piece of lead embedded in his head. He would show me this when he was drunk. 'Look at that, feel it!' And I would stroke it gently. 'I used to be able to stand on my hands son and write me name with my head on a piece a paper.'

By the time I was four years old my grandmother had taught me to read the newspaper.

NORTHERN IRELAND QUALIFY FOR QUARTER
FINALS OF WORLD CUP.

EAMON DE VALERA ATTENDS CORONATION OF
POPE JOHN THE XXIII.

She always had a Raspberry Ruffle in the pocket of her apron and after I ate the Raspberry Ruffle, I would look at everything through the purple shiny paper and imagine this was a secret world that only I knew about. She read me stories about the giant Fionn Mac Cumhaill chasing Grainne and Diarmuid across Ireland. Grainne had eloped on the night of her engagement to Fionn with the handsome young warrior Diarmuid. Fionn hunted them for ten years over mountains and valleys, until he finally caught them. By then Diarmuid had been gored by a wild boar and was dying but Fionn refused to heal him with his magic water and Diarmuid died in Grainne's arms at the foot of Ben Bulben Mountain in County Sligo. Even though I knew the end of this story it always made me sad to hear it. I desperately wanted Diarmuid and Grainne to escape.

My grandmother baked bread on a griddle and I was the only one allowed to have first taste of it. She taught me how to churn soured milk into butter, using a wooden staff and plunger-churn with a hole in the lid. The staff is plunged into the hole for at least an hour until the butter separates from the milk and floats to the top. In the beginning this would give me blisters, my grandfather told me to pee on them, wait until it dried then wash my hands in the river with Lifebuoy soap. This seemed to do the trick. When the butter rose to the top, I'd scoop it into a dish and wash it with cold water.

My next job was to salt it, pat it into squares with two wooden butter-paddles and lay it out on grease paper. The butter went on the hot bread after it came off the griddle. I poured the left-over milk, the 'buttermilk' into a large glass jug, covered it with a wet tea-towel, stretched an elastic band around the rim and placed it gently on the stone sill of the small window, the coldest part of the pantry. I loved that pantry, the shelves stacked with all manner of spices and jams. The bottles and jars were neatly labelled: Oregano, Rosemary, Coriander, Holy Basil (For Ringworm and Bronchitis), Ginger, Cinnamon, Cloves, Caraway seeds, Chives, Lemon Balm. Home-made jams:

Blackcurrant, Strawberry, Plum, Gooseberry. A heavy black cauldron, its inside white and speckled with blue dots, filled with cooking apples all picked from my grandmother's garden. Sometimes I would stand in the pantry reading the labels out loud over and over like a prayer.

Then suddenly my grandmother was always in bed, and her bedroom took on a strange unpleasant smell. It was a smell that frightened me and every time I went in to see her, I hoped and prayed that the smell wouldn't be there. I wanted my grandmother to smell like she always did, of freshly baked bread and sweet Wilson's snuff. But the smell only grew worse, and her voice became hoarse and weak. There was yellow in the whites of her eyes and her smile was sad. Neighbours and relatives that I'd never seen before, started visiting the house. Then Father Hurson, the local parish priest, turned up. She was alive when he went into her bedroom at 9am and dead when he left at 11am. I overheard my grandfather saying that Father Hurson had been delivering Extreme Unction to my grandmother. I didn't know what that meant, but it sounded horrible. Father Hurson could shove his Extreme Unction up his arse. Father Hurson, that bastard, in his rustling black cassock. His shock of white hair. His Players Navy Cut cigarette breath. The two brown fingers on his right hand. The red pimples on his bulbous nose and his weeping left eye, which he dabbed at constantly with his grubby handkerchief. I hated the sight of him. I always thought there was something unpleasant about him, something I could never quite put my finger on. But now I knew, he was the bringer of death, he ushered it in, and that smell still lingered. It never really went away.

My grandmother, Sadie Imelda McCrudden, was the first dead person I ever saw. I couldn't understand why she was kept in the house lying in her coffin for three days. I kept thinking maybe everybody thought she was eventually going to wake up. I prayed to God every night for her to wake up, but then I learned that God was in on it. It was explained to me that it was God's will. God had decided it was her time to be taken to Heaven and from that day forward my relationship with God was over. Never again would I get down on my knees and pray to him or ask him for anything. He could go to hell for all I cared.

People I'd never seen before were coming and going. Strangers, telling me they loved my grandmother. I resented all of these people. I didn't want to hear how much they

17

loved my grandmother. I knew that none of them could ever have loved her as much as I did. I was told I could kiss her. I didn't really want to but my father said the coffin lid was going on and this was the last time I'd ever see her. When my lips touched her forehead I was shocked at how cold she was. She didn't look real. She looked like she was made of candle wax. Blood-red rosary beads wrapped around her joined hands. I had never seen her use rosary beads. When no one was looking I slipped a Raspberry Ruffle into her coffin. After the funeral I climbed the birch tree in the acre field, cursed God, shouted at the sky and cried until I was exhausted and all I had left were dry angry sobs.

After my grandmother died my grandfather, Joseph Patrick McCrudden, turned into a ghost, disappeared inside his clothes, became a negative photo of himself. I could never quite see him properly after that. Couldn't recognise him. I wanted to hold him up to the light so as I could see his lovely smiling face and broken nose, but he finally faded from sight and ended up in the Old Soldiers Care Home at Helen's Bay on the north coast of County Down, handing over Tullybern Cottage to my father. Our white-washed cottage, with black shiny roof slates and wild roses and ivy growing around the gable. Our cottage, with the wrought iron gate, that never squeaked because my grandfather oiled it every day. The privet hedge that he clipped once a week, the wavy path of shingle that led to the dark red front door.

My fairy-tale home. A cottage than Hans Christen Andersen would have been proud of. My haven now invaded by the McCruddens and my stupid drunken useless father. The world I knew and felt comfortable in, had fallen apart.

TWO

THE SUPPLEMENTARY dole benefit set up by the British Government fed and clothed all my family until we were of school leaving age. The Stormont Government, on the other hand, were determined to rid us from the face of the Earth. There were no council houses or jobs to be had for the likes of us. We were dirty lazy, thieving, Fenian gypsy bastards who didn't deserve anything. According to Sir James Craig, the first Prime Minister of Northern Ireland, his was a 'Protestant Government for a Protestant people'. We could all die in a ditch as far as Craig was concerned and most of the prime ministers who followed in his wake were of a similar mindset. Being brought up in the caring bosom of the British Government made it hard for me to feel patriotic about Ireland. As far as I could see, Ireland had given me nothing except ridiculous theatrical Catholicism, songs about dying rebels and a stupid language that no one ever spoke or cared about. Irish was impossible to learn and sounded pathetic when spoken with a Tyrone accent. The equivalent of English people trying to speak French. Those brave Irish rebels used to anger and frustrate me.

They were continually being caught and shot, or hung, or blown up, or drowned in a bog. I could never understand how anyone could be bothered to write songs about such incompetent bastards.

How were they ever going to get rid of Stormont?

Mickey Peach was my best friend. He had a mop of copper hair and a face that was permanently dirty. He had a blue eye and a green eye and was skinny as an eel. Our headmaster referred to him as Urchin. For years we thought he was saying Urgent which became Mickey's nickname for the rest of his life. We would go to the town dump every day after school and hoke around in the steaming rotting heap for beer bottles. It was the first time I ever saw seagulls. We washed the bottles in the river and returned them to Lenny O'Brien who ran the Brewery Tap pub.

The Brewery Tap was in the middle of Carricktown and had the added advantage of attracting customers from both the north and south ends. Lenny would pay us thruppence a bottle and shout, 'Stay where yez are don't come into the bar, yez are fuckin stinkin.'

Mickey's family weren't as poor as ours but not far off. There were five of them and they lived on the Gort Hill housing estate: rows of small red bricked terraced houses that had been built originally by John Gort, a Catholic mill owner, to house his workers. Mickey's father, Sean, ran a stall in the town on a Friday and Saturday selling all kinds of stuff, most of it stolen. Sean wasn't 'a big drinker; gambling was his problem and he spent all of his time in the bookies. Mickey's 'mother Carmel cleaned houses for rich people.

21

Mickey would follow her, watch where she put the key and then Mickey and I would break into the house at night, steal whatever we could lay our hands on and eat all the food we could find. That came to an end when we broke into a house owned by Judge Randolph Johnson, drank a bottle of his port, vomited everywhere and fell asleep in his living room. The Judge didn't press charges. The fact we were eight years old probably helped. He even let Mickey's mother keep her job but she had to take us back to the house to apologise and promise we would mend our ways. That lasted for about three weeks.

The *Carricktown 100* was a much-anticipated motor bike road race held every year. There was a festival atmosphere, everything closed down for the day and thousands of people lined the route. The programmes for the race were delivered to the offices of the *Mid Ulster Mail* and stored in a room at the back of the building. The night before the race Mickey and I broke into the office through a tiny toilet window. Mickey was the skinniest so he wriggled through. Using the same cloth sacks we had used to gather the beer bottles, we managed to get away with just over a hundred copies. We sold them in under an hour at two shillings each, half the normal price and made £13, an absolute fortune. We could barely walk, every pocket weighed down with coins, the two of us jingle-belling along the road with two double 99s bought from Willy Coulton's ice cream van. This purchase helped to rid us of some of the halfpennies and pennies.

'Jaysus boys did yez rob a bank?' We hid the rest of the money in bean tins found at the dump and buried them in the Burren Fort.

Nat Harkness was always good for a few bob. Nat was obsessed with fishing, he was never out of his waders. His heavy waterproof jacket was glazed with dirt, green with ingrained moss and glistening with fish scales. The lapels of the jacket and his trilby hat peppered all over with flyhooks which made him look like he had just walked out of a biblical plague. His grey beard was nicotine-brown from chewing War Horse tobacco. He spat when he talked, long streaks of black spit shooting from his mouth like liquorice sticks. His catch rate wasn't great. He used to say 'Give a man a fish and he'll ate for a day. Teach him to fish and he'll fuckin' starve to death'. He lived alone in the Graveyard House, a thatched cottage on the edge of the Old Graveyard. There was a rumour that he fiddled with some boys who went fishing with him. Paddy Larkin who was in the class below me said he went with him once to Lower Lough Erne and Nat suddenly opened his trousers, showed Paddy his penis and said, 'Look at the size of that one, you wouldn't catch that in a net. Do you want to have a feel of it? Come on show me yours. How big is yours?'

Nat used to pay me to have a shit. 'Every bottle of bluebottles you can give me when ye shite young McCrudden, I'll give ye four shillin. The trout will ate them for their breakfast, tay and dinner.' It was a skilled job.

Bluebottles are sensitive and could smell me from eight hundred yards away. They also have big eyes and can see behind them. I'd go into the woods, do my business, wait for twenty minutes or so until the shit was covered and humming black with bluebottles. Then I'd creep up on them with the stealth of an Apache warrior, a McVitie's biscuit tin with a hole in the side held carefully upside down in both hands, my milk bottle ready in the coat pocket of my jacket. The trick was to dive on to the mound of bluebottles and then quickly place the milk bottle over the hole, tap the side and fill the bottle, plugging it with a twist of newspaper. A bottle of bluebottles buzzing in my pocket was a lovely feeling and sometimes if Nat was in a generous mood, he'd give me two big half-crowns. Five bob a shite was not to be sniffed at.

THREE

ON THE 14TH AUGUST 1969 the day before my fourteenth birthday, British troops arrived in Derry and were welcomed by the people with 'wee buns and cups of tea'. It looked like the RUC had been stoned and petrol bombed into submission and the British cavalry had arrived to protect the Catholics. Harry Lagan, the Bread Man, said that in his opinion, 'Derry people were all fuckin hypocrites making thon cunts cups of tea'. I was a year away from my fifteenth birthday the legal age to leave school, but I couldn't be bothered to wait a year, knowing that I wouldn't pass any O-Levels. The only subject I enjoyed or knew anything about was English. One O-Level wasn't going to do me any good. I hated school, was fed up not having a school uniform. Ashamed to have to wear brown corduroy trousers, a blue jacket with green patches on the elbows, a grey shirt belonging to my father which was three sizes too big and a pair of black hobnailed boots. I also had to attend gym assembly in the morning in my socks as I didn't have the regulation white Dunlop plimsolls. My parents had managed to send me to one of the best Catholic boys' school in the county but then couldn't, or wouldn't, fork out the eight pounds ten shillings to buy me a uniform.

I had fights every day before and after school with the same group of middle-class boys in their pristine striped blazers, starched blue shirts, olive green ties, black trousers and brown brogues. Jackie Westwood was their gang leader. I hit him with half a paving slab, breaking his nose and fracturing his cheekbone, putting him in hospital for two days. Westwood had cut my face with his locker key and blackened both my eyes.

Every day they would tease me singing 'Dedicated Follower of Fashion' by The Kinks. They really spoiled that song for me, I grew to hate it. Jackie's father, Maurice Westwood, owned almost every shop and pub in the town and was on the school board of governors. The headmaster, Master Gerald McKenna, a distant relative of Teresa McKenna who had indirectly caused the slitting of my great grandfather's throat, was Maurice Westwood's drinking and poker-playing partner and he made an 'example' of me, caned me in the school yard in front of four-hundred-and-twenty pupils. Ten whacks of the bamboo on each hand. McKenna took off his coat to do it, rolled up the sleeves on his checked shirt. Little white flecks of spit forming in the corner of his ugly mouth. And every time he hit me I would whisper, 'Fuck you' under my breath, determined not to cry. The pain, physical and emotional, skewered like razor wire through my body to the very centre of my heart. McKenna aimed for my thumbs and slapped me hard around the face if I tried to move my hand away, 'Don't try and be clever wee sonny'.

I knew that McKenna was fucking Miss Flannigan, our English teacher. Nobody ever missed double English on a Thursday. Aoife Flannigan looked like Linda Ronstadt and we were all in love with her. She would always pick me to read poems in front of the class. I was one of the few pupils who knew the poems off by heart. A habit left over from reading the labels in my grandmother's pantry. *Do not go gentle into that good night. . . Rage, rage against the dying of the light.* She smiled at me all the way through the reading. The next week she brought in a recording of Dylan Thomas reading it himself. 'Listen to where he pauses Emmet, listen to the words he emphasises. The emotion in his voice. It will help you to understand the poem better.' Jackie Westwood and his uniformed arsehole friends were green with jealousy.

Miss Flannigan was twenty-eight and dating an IRA man who was on the run. McKenna was fifty-two and married with four children. After I knew about her and McKenna, Miss Flannigan went down in my estimation. How could she let that horrible bastard anywhere near her? Tommy Forbes, the school caretaker, had spotted McKenna and Miss Flannigan in the apparatus room of the gymnasium at eleven o'clock one Sunday night. Tommy had gone back as he had forgotten to switch off the heater in the changing rooms.

McKenna, his trousers around his ankles, had Miss Flannigan
bent over the leather pommel horse, her skirt over her head
and was apparently telling her what a dirty girl she was.

Tommy had let this slip to my father when he'd had a
few drinks and then begged him not to tell anyone. I knew
it was the truth as Tommy was a born-again Christian and
would never have made something like that up. Anyway, I
had already noticed how McKenna used to openly flirt with
Miss Flannigan, putting his hands on her shoulders and waist
when there was no need to do so. My father didn't tell
anyone, not because he could keep a secret but because he
was so drunk he didn't remember. But I had heard everything
and had noted it down in my little green book of revenge.

I found myself a job delivering Cantrell and Cochrane
lemonade with Norman Greer, the Lemonade Man. I then
obtained a post office book. I had plans. I told Norman I
was sixteen. Norman had a severe case of cleft palate. I think
he must have sacked me at least three times, but I had no
idea what he was saying, so just kept turning up on Monday
morning and Norman eventually gave in.

The education authorities made a few pathetic attempts
to force me back to school, but I intercepted any brown
envelopes that came to the house, and they eventually
stopped coming. Master McKenna was probably glad to see
the back of me. I enjoyed being driven around the country-
side, loved the smell of the red leather seats in the Bedford
TK lorry, the diesel fumes, the rattle of the crates and the

sound of the engine as Norman changed gear on a steep hill. Children waved at us. I felt special. We went to villages and townlands I'd never heard of: Cluntydoon, Ardvarnish, Ballysudden, Sullenboy. The green wooden crates held nine large bottles of Cantrell and Cochrane lemonade and it was my job to carry the crates down narrow lanes to the houses that the lorry couldn't get to, or Norman couldn't be bothered to tackle. 'Aham net huckin divin jown yon cunty a place.'

Six pounds ten shillings a week. It wouldn't be long until I would have enough to board the ferry to Stranraer. This was so much better than school.

Shortly after the British Army had arrived in Derry there was rioting. Harry Lagan was laughing from the window of his bread van, as he turned the corner he shouted to my father,

'Jaysus Frank that welcome didn't last long. The tay they made them is still fucking warm in the pot.'

Emmet McCrudden, even my name sounded preposterous. I hated it and promised myself that when I finally escaped from my decrepit and pointless life, I would change it to Tom Joad. Tom Joad had escaped. He had fled from the dust bowl poverty of Oklahoma to the orange groves of California – but he took his family with him and to my mind that was his big mistake. No way would I be taking the McCruddens with me. That was damn sure for certain. Individually they were tolerable, I could handle one bee at a time, but a swarm of the bastards was a whole different prospect and Drunken Daddy bee was the biggest, most dangerous bastard of the lot.

It took me three hours to cut the message out of newspapers and magazines and paste it on to a sheet of A4. I put it in a brown envelope and posted it to Brendan Cassidy c/o Her Majesty's Prison. Crumlin Road, Belfast. Brendan had been caught hiding in a disused church on the Irish border between County Monaghan and County Down and was given a life sentence for shooting dead a member of the Ulster Defence Regiment.

DEAR BRENDAN. YOU DO NOT KNOW ME. BUT I KNOW THAT YOUR GIRLFRIEND MISS FLANNIGAN IS GOING OUT WITH MASTER GERALD MCKENNA. THEY HAD SEXUAL INTERCOURSE AT MY SCHOOL. IF HE IS FOLLOWED YOU WILL KNOW I AM NOT TELLING LIES.

I wrote the address carefully, using my left hand. This was my going away present for Master McKenna. I had no idea if it would ever reach Brendan Cassidy. Mickey Peach assured me that the prison authorities read all the letters before they were handed out to the prisoners. Mickey had also been on the receiving end of McKenna's brutality; he once grabbed Mickey's cheek in his fist knowing full well he had a large abscess on the inside of his mouth. He squeezed his cheek until the abscess burst which left the right side of

Mickey's face looking like half a red balloon. Mickey swallowed some of the puss from inside the abscess and was sick, throwing up for two days solid. Mickey said the warders would be falling over themselves to give Brendan this message. So I was hopeful that Cassidy would receive it.

It was about two months after the Johnny Mackle missing leg incident that my mother finally left us. She had been threatening to do this for years, but no one had ever taken her seriously, especially my father.

'Stop talkin nonsense woman sure ye wouldn't survive ten minutes on yer own.'

My father arrived home late one Saturday night in September 1971 with three members of the Fuckme Paddies, a folk band lead by the notorious Johnny 'The Peg' Mackle. As they became more popular, they finally had to change their name to Riders in the Ditch as none of the Catholic dancehalls, mostly run by priests, would book them, but everyone still referred to them as the Fuckme Paddies. Mackle had spread the rumour that he'd lost his leg fighting for Ireland against the British Army.

They had him trapped in a barn and were torturing him. They threatened to cut his leg off if he didn't give up the names of his IRA comrades, but 'brave' Mackle refused and the commanding officer in charge of the battalion amputated his leg with a bread knife which apparently took two hours.

Mackle said it would have been quicker but the fucker kept stopping to slice bread and make sandwiches. According to my grandmother, and she knew everything, Johnny Mackle lost his leg in a chainsaw accident. He had stolen the chainsaw to cut down Christmas trees belonging to the Poor Clares convent. The chainsaw kicked-back, he fell on it, his hand got trapped in the trigger throttle and he sawed through his right leg just above the knee. Not a British soldier in sight.

Mackle's leg was made of wood with a hinge on the knee. It was held in place with a padded leather pouch that fitted snugly around the stump and was tightened by pulling the laces like a corset. The leg was pitted all over with small indents caused by him drumming on his leg during Fuckme Paddies performances. Earlier in the night, Mackle had gone outside to use the toilet. When he came out, my twelve-year-old sister, Noreen, was waiting to go in. Mackle suddenly grabbed hold of her, pinned her against the wall and tried to kiss her, put his hand up her skirt, ripped her panties and thrust his fingers inside her. Noreen was no pushover. She bit him, scratched his face and managed to escape, but said nothing to anyone. In the middle of the night when Mackle had fallen asleep on the sofa, unconscious from drink, Noreen and my other sister Maeve removed Mackle's trousers, undid his leg and set fire to it in the brazier beside the compost heap. It burned for quite a while until all that was left was a red-hot metal hinge.

The trouble started when Johnny Mackle woke up and quickly noticed that his leg and trousers were gone. He hobbled around the house in his baggy grey underpants shouting for my father. 'Frank. . . come on now what the fuck? Where's me leg?' He began to mount the stairs hopping from step to step. 'Frank! This is no joke now, where the fuck is me leg? Fraaaank!'

When he was nearly at the top of the stairs, my mother was waiting for him. All of us children including Noreen and Maeve, cowering behind her. She waited until he was almost on the landing, gripped the newel post of the banister to secure some purchase, jumped up and rammed him in the chest with both feet sending him crashing back down the stairs. She quickly followed his contorted body and began slapping him hard across the face, forehand-backhand, forehand-backhand, slap-whack-slap-whack, his black quiff flying from side to side.

She pulled out her 'good knife' and held it between his legs. 'If you think you can molest my daughter and get away with it, you can think again. You have twenty seconds to get out of my house otherwise I swear to God I will cut the balls clean off you.'

Mackle scrambled to his foot pleading his innocence. My mother grabbed the broom from under the stairs and gave it to him. 'Put this under your arm and fuck off. I won't tell you again!'

Mackle put the head of the broom under his armpit and

staggered out of the front gate mouthing obscenities and revenge, like some lewd version of Long John Silver. Noreen opened the bedroom window and started shouting, 'Per-vert! Per-vert!', and we all joined in, 'Per-vert Per-vert Per-vert Per-vert!', laughing and jeering as loudly as we could.

My youngest brother Fergal was shouting the loudest and later on that day asked my very hungover father, 'Daddy, what's a per-vert?'

I loved that little fella, had a connection with him that I didn't have with any of my other siblings. Fergal was as sly as a fox for his age and always made me laugh with the things he would come out with. Once Father Hurson came to visit and asked him what he wanted to be when he grew up and Fergal said, 'Six-foot-six'. The Johnny Mackle Carryon, as it became known, was probably the last straw for my mother and deep down none of us could blame her for bailing out. We never spoke about it but secretly hoped that she would return home soon.

It was the first news item on BBC's Scene Around Six and made the headlines of all the local and national newspapers. HEADMASTER OF CATHOLIC SCHOOL KNEECAPPED AT POKER GAME. The poker school took place every Sunday night in the Hibernian Hall on Church Street and went on into the small hours. Towards the end of the night two men in balaclavas burst in through the back door, trailed Master

Gerald McKenna into the car park at the rear, pistol-whipped him to stop him screaming, then shot him in both knees. The Provisional IRA issued a statement claiming responsibility for the shooting and the reasons behind it: *Sleeping with the partner or wife of a volunteer imprisoned for the cause.*

It had taken the IRA nearly a year and a half to mete out the punishment. I had forgotten all about it but my message had obviously reached its destination. Two days later I met up with Urgent Mickey Peach in the Hog and Chicken chip shop. We bought a Super Supper takeaway with double chips and a bottle of Blackthorn cider from Westwood's off license. Mickey had brought his Sobell transistor radio. We walked up to the Burren Fort with Rosie Byrne and Imelda Ryan and had ourselves a party. I had been going out with Rosie Byrne for about eight months, something that I couldn't really get my head around. I never referred to her as my girlfriend or admitted to myself or anyone else that we were a couple. I never wanted to say it out loud in case the spell be broken. Rosemary Anne Byrne was easily the most beautiful girl in Carricktown. I had to slap myself sometimes to make sure it wasn't a dream and when I say slap I mean slap. Mickey would crack up laughing, tears rolling down his cheeks at the sight of me slapping myself in the face whilst shouting, 'It's true it's true it's true fuck off it's true!'

Going out with Rosie was like winning the Irish Sweepstake every day. I couldn't believe it and neither could anyone else, especially Rosie's friends. It was the first time I'd heard the expression 'a bit of rough', that's how her friends described me, and I wasn't completely sure if I should take it as an offence or a compliment. Either way, when I was holding Rosie Byrne in my arms and kissing her soft lips, I didn't give a rat's arse what anybody said or thought.

Miss Flannigan emigrated to Canada. Apparently she didn't know Brendan Cassidy was in the IRA. Brendan Cassidy's mother and father and brothers and sisters and cousins also claimed they didn't know which was strange as every other person in the County of Tyrone knew. McKenna's wife left him and moved to Scotland with the four children. McKenna spent three weeks in hospital followed by four months of rehab where he learned to walk again. He made a remarkable recovery, even taking up cross-country running – but then hung himself from a tree in his back garden.

I imagined McKenna tying the rope around his neck, crying as he did so and whispering *Forgive me Emmet for making your life a misery. I'm doing this for you in the hope that someday you'll be able to forgive me.*

I didn't really know why but I had a sense I might need to go to confession and also get rid of my little green book of revenge. I thought I was going to confess to the school priest, Father McGuire, but when the grill slid back it was Father Hurson. I didn't want to talk to this bastard and began desperately trying to work out how I could make my escape. Father Hurson leaned forward, 'You'll have to speak up.'

Before I could think straight, the words, which had been drilled into me started to tumble out of my mouth. 'Bless me father for I have sinned. It's. . . two years since my last confession. These are my sins.' After I told Hurson about my drinking and masturbating and having impure thoughts every minute of the day and hitting Jackie Westwood with a paving slab, I took a deep breath and told him the whole sorry tale of how I sent a letter to Brendan Cassidy informing him about his girlfriend's infidelity and how that led to McKenna being shot in the Hibernian Hall and eventually hanging himself. A heavy ominous silence fell upon the confession box.

I hated the confessional, that musty smell of other people's sweat and guilt. The claustrophobic closeness of the priest, hidden like a spy in the darkness. His nearness wasn't comforting, it felt sinister. The light from the candles flickering through the louvered cross in the door, rippling occasionally across his purple stole. His hand cocked behind his ear, listening, like an executioner. I always imagined the priests had guns under their vestments and were about to blow my face off.

The silence seemed to go on for an eternity. I began to think Hurson hadn't heard a word I said or had fallen asleep. Then he started making little whispery sounds. 'Hmm huh huh ahhh. . .'

I tried hard to interpret what they might mean 'Ahh himmm. . . huh huh. . . ' but they made no sense. Father

Hurson eventually spoke. 'I know about the death of Mr McKenna. I can't divulge anything, but I can assure you, his death was not your fault, of that I am certain, so I will lift that burden from your shoulders today. Two years is too long to be without the holy sacrament of penance and absolution. If you turn away from God's grace and forgiveness it will only lead you down the path of temptation and sin. Do you understand?'

'Yes Father.'

'Good boy. Have you anything else to tell me?'

'No Father.'

'Are you truly sorry for all of your sins?'

'Yes Father'

'Good. Say five decades of the Rosary and promise me you will attend Mass once a week at least. Will you do that?'

'Yes Father.'

As he recited the act of contrition Father Hurson lowered his white head, dabbed his left eye, and dissolved me from all my sins, *'Diende, ego te absolvo a peccatis tuis n nomine Patris et Filii et Spiritus Sancti.'*

At Mass the next day, the body of Christ was placed upon my tongue and melted slowly against the roof of my mouth. My slate was clean. I was out of the woods and if I died this very instant I knew I could walk straight through the gates of Paradise. There was only one problem. I didn't believe a word of it. After what God had done to me, I couldn't be a believer. I knew that God was just a wicked human thief and I was determined not to give him the time of day.

Even at primary school I had refused to say my prayers and was made to stand out in the landing with Ronnie Ferguson. Ronnie was the only Protestant boy in the school and his parents probably thought the landing was the best place for him during prayer time in case he became infected with Catholicism. Our teacher, Mrs Flannery, said that the class must pray for Ronnie to save his soul from damnation. I wished that I too was a Protestant and then everyone could pray for me as well. If prayers worked then me and Ronnie had nothing to worry about.

Bridie Rooney, who sat between Ronnie and I, said that God hated Protestants because they had big ears but didn't use them to listen to him. All they did was eat hairy bacon, say bad words and fornicate on Sunday. My father had big ears. I wondered if he used to be a protestant and that's what was wrong with him. I liked the sound of the word fornicate and asked Bridie what it meant. She screwed up her nose and tapped it with her finger. I was none the wiser and got into trouble when I asked Mrs Flannery what it meant. She blushed and clipped me around the head scratching my ear with her diamond rings. Father McGuire had a quiet word with me after school about not praying. He said that my grandmother had been chosen by God to sit at his right-hand side in Heaven and what a privilege it was for her to be there and how she would be looking down on me and be very sad that I wasn't saying my prayers. Father

McGuire had funny blinky Tully eyes that pointed in different directions. They flicked about like ping pong balls and I couldn't take anything he said seriously.

I was sure that what Father McGuire was telling me was a crock of shite. My grandmother never liked sitting about, she was always on the go. She was forever scolding my grandfather, 'Is yer arse welded to that sofa?' I never once heard my grandmother praying. There was no bible in her house, she never went to mass or spoke about God. She always said that my grandfather did enough praying for the both of them. I had a feeling that my grandmother got to Heaven because she was a good woman and very smart. God wanted her to sit beside him so as he could ask her advice on stuff.

I suppose I went to confession because I needed to tell someone about McKenna. Mickey Peach knew about it, but Mickey was a cog in my wheel and we spun together in the same direction. I needed someone I could open my heart to. Even though I despised Father Hurson, I knew he would go to his grave rather than divulge to anyone what I had told him. The more I thought about that, the more I realised how profound it was. To be able to leave the darkest part of my soul in the hands of another person, knowing that it would be safe, and I would be welcomed back when I sinned again. In fact, everyone was urged to come back. I thought maybe that's why confession existed. It was the only thing that made sense. My slate wasn't clean. I'd just been given a new one.

My mother left in the middle of the night on the 10th November 1971. She took her small brown suitcase. Everything she had in the world was in that case. She left us a note. *Gone to London. Look after the little ones. I won't be back this time. Love you all. Mum xoxo.* I was jealous that she'd managed to escape before me, and very hurt that she hadn't taken me with her. She was thirty-six, had been pregnant almost every year since she was seventeen and given birth to eight children. As my sober father read the note his face began to twist and change shape. He shook his head, breathed in deeply and read it again. He read it over and over, big pools of tears welling up in his eyes. He gave it to Maeve. Maeve was eighteen and the eldest. 'Am I reading this right Maeve darlin. . . what does it say? Read it out to me there will ye?'

Maeve read it out loud. My sober father began walking around the room in circles hitting his forehead repeatedly and violently with the palm of his right hand. Maeve suddenly hugged him. 'It was the drunken you she left Daddy. . . if you could get rid of him, she'll come back. She's probably only gone to Auntie Fiona's in London.'

I went to the post office to close my account and draw out my hard-earned savings which came to nineteen pounds and seventy-five pence. I had begun saving in old money which had now been converted into new decimal currency. Harry Lagan said the whole country was being conned by the British Government and decimal currency wasn't worth the paper it was printed on. I hoped Lagan was wrong. I asked Madge McGuckian about it. Madge McGuckian had been the postmistress for twenty years. She told me that Harry Lagan was a gobshite eejit and not to close my account, my money was safe and I should continue to save. Saving was sensible, there would always be times when I would need savings and it was something I should always do. I was relieved that I didn't have to hide it anywhere in the house and was certain that Drunken Daddy would have snuffed it out like a pig in a truffle bed.

I took Fergal fishing down to Adair's End. There was a flood on. Relentless brown fast flowing water. Nat Harkness had told me that if I was ever fishing in a flood I was to use bread and spam or corned beef squashed into a ball and to use as big a hook as possible. Nat said chubb and roach loved this kind of bait. The river was noisy. Fergal shouted, 'If we catch any fish Emmy can we make a fire and cook them on it like cowboys?' I promised him we could. After two hours I could see Fergal was getting bored and then as luck would have it, I caught a fair-sized roach. I soon got a fire going, gutted the fish with my mother's 'good knife'. She wouldn't be needing it now.

I let Fergal slide a wet stick through the fish and hang it over the flames. I had never seen him so excited. It took ages to cook. I picked out most of the bones and we sat by the fire and spoke to each other in the best cowboy fashion.

'I tell ya pardner this fish is rootin tootin.' Fergal laughed and said, 'Sure thang. But we gotta keep our eyes peeled fir injuns!'

On the way back Fergal suddenly looked quite red in the face. At first I thought it was the heat from the fire, but when I pulled up his shirt it looked like measles. Fergal couldn't really walk much further so I carried him the rest of the way and pretended he'd been shot by a Comanche. 'Don't you go dying on me now! If ya do I'll kill ya!'

Later that evening Drunken Daddy swayed quietly out of the misty rain with a rock in his hand. Stood looking at Tullybern Cottage for a moment then hurled the rock through the front window missing Fergal by a matter of inches. Fergal did have measles and was sleeping on the couch near the range as the bedroom was too cold. The door was kicked in. Drunken Daddy had lost the belt of his trousers and was holding them up with the fingers of his left hand twisted around the front loops of the waistband.' Yer mother would still be here if it wasn't for you bastard cunts! She would never have left me! Nev-verrrr! It was you lot that drove her away, yappin and shittin and cryin and tormentin the fuckin life out of her and now she's gone! I hope yer fuckin happy!'

He punched a hole in the studded plaster wall under the stairs. Fergal began to scream and cry, his little face flushed and terrified. 'I'll kill the fuckin lot of you!' Something suddenly broke inside of me it felt like I had become two people. One half of me, the shit-scared half, stayed on the stairs whilst the other half attacked my drunken father. I ran at him smashing my forehead into his face. He staggered back against the front door, shocked and bleeding from the mouth.

He came at me, both hands outstretched and grabbed my throat. His trousers had slipped around his arse. My sister Maeve jumped on his back and began to pull his hair. Noreen hit him on the shins with the leg of a stool. Aisling, Sean, Robert and Connor grabbed his arms and between us we pulled him to the ground. He roared like he always did. We were used to that sound, it meant nothing to us anymore. Noreen then hit him on the back of the head with the ceramic vase that contained the dead cactus. He was immediately quiet. We held our breath and waited, frozen in time. He lay there with his arms outstretched. The cactus embedded in his forehead, blood trickled down his face, reminding me of Jesus Christ on the cross. Fergal, his face bursting with red spots, stopped crying, looked down and said, 'That was Mammy's best vase.'

Maeve ran down the hill to Jem and Mandy Patterson's, the Beatniks, and rang for an ambulance. Jem told Maeve that our father's bad Karma had finally caught up with him.

It was rumoured that Jem Patterson's grandfather once owned Carricktown Castle and when all the land was sold off, Jem, being the only grandson, was left thousands of pounds in a trust fund which matured when he was twenty-one. Mandy's family also had money. Her grandmother owned a chain of betting shops and when they were sold Mandy also received a small fortune. The two of them were the richest beatniks in Ireland. They travelled the world and their house was full of weird stuff which Mandy was always showing off. 'Oh, this is the shrunken head of the chief of the Aguarana tribe we picked up in Ecuador.' I always thought it was horrible and looked like a big bucked-tooth black rat. Mandy used to chase me with it when I was younger.

'And this is a crucifix we got in Mexico City made from the shin bone of Saint Cristobel Magallanes Jara. He was executed for hearing confessions.' The house was full of candles which Jem made himself out of Paraffin, soy flakes and beeswax. The Pattersons were strange people but their house was always open to everyone.

Maeve, Noreen and I visited Sober Daddy in the hospital, brought him Fig Roll biscuits and a flask of tea. Sober Daddy had a bandage around his head and a crusted bloody split on his lip where I had headbutted him. There was a pole on wheels with a bag of liquid and a tube coming from the bag leading into his arm. He said he didn't remember what had happened, but he loved us all. Maeve asked him again to get rid of the Drunken Daddy and everything would sort itself out. He cried like a child and asked about Fergal's measles, 'Is Fergal alright?' Maeve said Fergal was over the worst and was staying with Uncle Brendan in Kildress. Sober

Daddy said he was praying to St Jude, the patron saint of hopeless cases, to have his drunken self removed and taken away for good and then our ma would come back. We all knew that St Jude would have a job on his hands, but this was the first time that Sober Daddy had acknowledged there was a Drunken Daddy. It was a breakthrough of sorts but had come too late. My mind was made up, I'd soon be on my way to London.

FOUR

CHRISTMAS 1971 was by far the worst Christmas any of us could remember. On the 23rd December, a man in a yellow hard hat wearing Northern Ireland Electricity Board overalls and holding a pair of wire cutters, climbed up the electricity pole outside Tullybern Cottage and plunged us all into darkness. The electricity had been cut off for non-payment of bills.

Sober Daddy had been sober for the longest time I could remember. Saint Jude was doing a great job. Sober Daddy assured us that everything was going to be alright. He found a tilly lamp, put the wick in lit it and hung it on the ceiling where the electric bulb used to be. It hissed a bit but gave out a fairly good light. He cut down two old trees in the back field, chopped them up into logs, got the fire roaring, put up a crooked Christmas tree and baked four apple tarts. Later that evening Joe McKernan pulled up in his coal lorry and delivered three-hundredweight bags of coal, carried them around the side of the house, high up on his shoulders which were protected by a thick leather wetback that hung down almost to his waist. His steel toe capped boots crunching on the gravel, he shook his head in disgust, 'I heard what them fuckers did Frank, cuttin ye aff at Christmas and you with a house full of childer, sure you wouldn't do it to a dog. Fuckin Black Orange bastards. Ye'll come down to the Hibernian with me now sure and have a wee lemonade.'

Sober Daddy nodded his head in agreement. 'Aye, a wee Lemonade. I'll be back in a couple of hours.'

Maeve looked at me, a look that said, Well, it was good while it lasted.

Drunken Daddy came home seven hours later, threw the Christmas tree across the room and smashed the Fada Bullet Bakelite transistor radio that had belonged to my grandmother. Some of the children had been listening to Christmas hymns on Radio Athlone. *All glory be to God on high and to the earth be peace; to those on whom his favour rests goodwill shall never cease.* Obviously our favour didn't rest well with this particular God. He really seemed to have it in for us. Maybe he had taken up a post in Stormont Government.

Drunken Daddy took off his coat and threw it at the tilly lamp which swayed on its attachment throwing the dim light from one corner of the room to the other. He was suddenly everywhere on every wall, becoming bigger and wilder within his own shadows. 'I fuckin told youse about leaving the fuckin light burnin to all hours of the fuckin night. I told ye didn't I? But youse never fuckin listen, and now look where we are. Serves ye all fuckin right! '

I fantasised about cutting his throat while he slept or driving the 'good' knife many times deep into his fat gut.

Imagined myself walking along the landing of Crumlin Road Prison and all the other cons whispering, 'Yeah that's Mad Dog McCrudden. No he's not a political prisoner, he killed his old man. Stabbed him twenty times in the chest. He's completely mental.'

It rained all Christmas day. We ate the remains of a pot of soup Maeve had managed to throw together. All that was left after that was the hard cold crusts of the apple pies. But at least it was warm. Joe McKernan's coal glowed in the range. I watched the raindrops on the windowpane. One raindrop in particular seemed to be trying to escape from the rest. I knew how it felt and wondered where my mother was, how she was spending Christmas day? Hungover Daddy stayed in bed, his head under the blankets. A little woman called Alice Coyne from St Vincent De Paul called to the house and left three large boxes of food. The boxes were wrapped in silver tinsel with *Happy Christmas* written on the side in red lipstick. This was Catholicism at its best. *Glad tidings of great joy, I bring to you and all mankind.* I was glad to see the back of Christmas. I'd always hated it. Christmas was only for people with money. I was hoping that 1972 would be the year that I could finally get to hell out of this dump.

I had never been to Derry. Our MP, Bernadette Devlin, had made an impassioned speech from the back of a lorry urging people to go on the civil rights march. Luke Kelly from the Dubliners was with her, singing and playing the

banjo. Everyone was excited because he was famous. I had
really no idea who he was and hated the kind of songs
he sang. I didn't know what a Croppy Boy was and had no
interest in finding out. She was the only politician I listened
to. She made sense and what she said was true. I was made
to feel like a foreigner and a second-class citizen, not only
by the Stormont Government but also from within my own
community, my own school. So the only *civil rights* I was
interested in, were my own and all the *troubles* I had
experienced took place in the house I lived in.

Mickey Peach went to the march with Imelda Ryan. I said
I might go but knew I wouldn't. Two days later, Mickey was
still shivering. His mother said Micky was in shock and I
wasn't to stay longer than half an hour. Mickey's knees were
badly cut, his palms looked like they'd been grated with a
cheese grater and there was a big half-moon bloody scrape
on his chin. He had a haunted look on his face and kept
peeking out from behind the curtains in his bedroom. He
said that him and Imelda had been somewhere at the back
of the march when it stopped for a moment. A bald-headed
man on the trailer of a lorry was shouting something through
a loudhailer but Mickey and Imelda didn't know what he
was saying. Some of the marchers headed down William
Street away from the main march.

Mickey said he didn't know Derry that well and wasn't
sure what was happening, so him and Imelda just tagged
along. He could hear some commotion up ahead, people

shouting and jeering and then the pop-pop of rubber bullets. Someone said there was a battle going on, a crowd of lads throwing stones and bottles at the soldiers who had put up a barricade to stop the marchers from reaching the Guildhall in the city centre and that's when they used the water cannon and tear gas. Mickey said he and Imelda were drenched and then they thought they heard two or three shots fired.

'At that stage the people around us thought the Brits must be shooting into the air to scare the rioters. Then someone shouted that the Brits were coming, running at us on foot. Me and Imelda and a load of other marchers ran like fuck back down William Street we didn't know where we were running to. We ran for ages and that's when I fell, slipped on the wet street flat on my face, all I could hear was shots being fired. It wasn't like in the fillums. These were dull cracks. Crack! Crack! Crack! Crack! Everyone running everywhere, and not knowing where to run. Some people were shot right in front of us, it was fucking crazy man I couldn't believe it was happening. I managed to get up, grab Imelda's hand and we just kept running.'

Thirteen people were shot dead and many more injured. I was now more determined than ever to get away, would have to save harder, every single penny and even then, it was going to take at least another six months. Two weeks later, Mickey and six other lads from my school, including Jackie Westwood, joined the Provisional IRA.

I'd been going out with Rosie Byrne for about eighteen

months. She was my first real girlfriend. We had sex for the first time when we were fifteen. Rosie was babysitting for Marlene Dixon. Marlene's boyfriend, Petey McFadden, was in the UVF. Petey shouted out things at random, it was a mental disease that I could never remember the name of. Petey was particularly fond of shouting 'ACK ACK! SUCK IT SUCK IT!' and 'CUNTYCUSTARD!'

Some people in the town wondered how he managed to join a paramilitary force like the UVF. Harry Lagan said, 'Sure none of them boys is right in the head. One more would make no difference.'

Then Petey was sent to prison for trying to rob the sub post office. Madge McGuckian jabbed him in the face with the steel tip of her umbrella and he shot himself in the thigh. Madge said he was the foulest mouthed robber she had ever encountered. Her sub post office had been robbed four times in three years. Marlene didn't go out much after that, so we lost our 'love nest' as Rosie called it.

I didn't enjoy my first time having sex with Rosie. I'd never used a condom before and realised much later that I'd had it on inside out. That sick rubbery chemical smell on my hands for days afterwards. Washing didn't seem to do any good. I was convinced everyone could smell it on me so I kept my hands in my pockets as much as possible. We did it in Marlene's double bed and Rosie bled a little, leaving a couple of bright red spots on the white sheet. Rosie panicked, ripped the sheet from the bed and told me to get rid of it. I folded the sheet into as many squares as I could, put it up my jumper and walked through the Old Graveyard with the intent of throwing the sheet into the skip used to take away dead wreaths. As I entered through the gates I was stopped by two RUC men who had been hiding in the bushes. it was obvious I was concealing something. One of them pointed his Sterling sub machine gun at me and shouted, 'HALT!' They searched me and found the sheet. 'And what's this for? Where are you going with this? You'd better tell us the truth or you'll end up in the cell for the night.'

I told them I was going to run around the graveyard, pretend to be a ghost and scare people. It was the first thing that came into my head and as I said it I thought it was brilliant. I was so pleased with myself.

'You could get yourself shot. Is that what you want, eh, a bullet up your ass? You could become a ghost for real if you don't watch yourself. Now clear off before we arrest you.'

When I told Rosie she laughed for half an hour. I was going to miss that laugh so much. Rosie laughed like a donkey, big hee-haws followed by a braying sound. It was the least sexy thing about her, but she had so many other sexy things it didn't matter. The way she piled her long jet-black hair on top of her head with one hand, twisting it around and then inserting some kind of invisible clip into it. How her dimples appeared as if by magic when she smiled. The way she prodded me gently on the nose for no reason.

The smell of her skin, a mixture of vanilla ice cream and wild roses. The feel of her soft lips on mine. The fact she was kissing me and only me was unbelievable, almost too much to bear. What if she left me and went with someone else? It was unthinkable. Yet, I had made the decision to leave, but it wasn't her I was leaving. It was the confines of my terrible life. I was making my getaway, going somewhere where I would have my own identity. Someplace where I would cease to be seen only as the son of drunken Frank McCrudden. That was a death sentence. When I thought about not seeing Rosie again my stomach cramped up and I wanted to cry. I tried to cry but the tears wouldn't come. I was hoping I could cry at some point. I knew I needed to, otherwise I was going to do damage to something or someone. I knuckled down for the next few months of the year, made sure I wasn't late in the mornings or missed any days on the lemonade round. I couldn't give Norman an excuse to sack me. Norman laughed when I asked for a rise. 'Yiv sum huckin neck on ye Macudden amp in a payin ye fa too mulch as it is.'

The next time I saw Mickey he didn't seem the same. He had become much more cautious, didn't get drunk like he used to. I didn't ask what he was up to, didn't want to know, and I doubt he would've told me anyway. But I did know I was now on the Provos' radar. Mickey said he had told them about the letter I'd sent to Brendan Cassidy and that I might get a visit from someone. I played it cool, didn't want to

arouse Mickey's suspicions that I might be about to clear off
to London. Harry Lagan had dropped by Tullybern on a few
occasions hoping to talk to me but I'd always managed to
avoid him. It had recently become common knowledge that
Harry was now heavily involved with 'the cause' It wasn't
only bread he was delivering.

They were waiting for me at the end of the road. My
schoolyard sparring partner Jackie Westwood, Harry Lagan
and Mickey. I knew by their unusual stance which was stiff
and awkward that they were preparing for something,
something they weren't used to. Like people waiting in line
to receive an award or make a speech. Westwood was smiling
at me, a smile that looked like it had been drawn on, a smile
that didn't have any connection to his dead eyes. 'Aright
Emmet, what about ye?'

I wanted to kick Westwood in the balls then follow up
by kicking his teeth out. Westwood sticks his hand out. I
shake it. It's like shaking a deflated balloon. 'Look mate I
know we've had our differences in the past. I have the scars
to prove it.' Westwood smiles his fake smile and points to a
small scar on his cheekbone. 'But I think it's time to put all
that behind us, because you and me Emmet, have a bigger
enemy to fight.' Mickey is looking at the ground, he can't
meet my eyes.

Harry smiles at me. All of a sudden, it's all smiles. 'We
thought we might have a wee word with ye Emmet.' I nod,
giving nothing away. 'Let's go sit in the van.'

We walk towards Harry's bread van parked up on the grass verge. The van smells great, freshly baked bread and what I think could be raisins. We squash in beside each other. Harry drums his dusty floured fingers on the steering wheel. 'It's like this son. Me and Mickey and Jackie here have all volunteered to fight for the cause. Now, there's more than wan way to fight. It's not all about bombs and bullets. Mickey here tells me that you're good at the writin.'

Harry looks at me for confirmation. I give him none. I look at Mickey who is staring out of the window. Harry clears his throat and continues. 'So I was wonderin if you'd like to write for the Republican News. Propaganda is very important in this war against the Brits. In fact, I'd say it's. . . crucial.'

There is silence in the van, total brutal silence. I let it hang for as long as I can. Harry's jawbone begins to tighten. Westwood pipes up, 'I loved those stories that you used to write in Miss Flannigan's class. Remember the one about the man who didn't believe in Fairies? He tied his wife to the fairy thorn tree and when he woke up the next day he had two horns growing out of his head. That was brilliant and Miss Flannigan chalked the whole story up on the blackboard. She called it an old-fashioned morality tale for the modern age.'

Westwood smiles his dead smile. Harry's jaw is working overtime. 'So, what do ye say Emmet are ye in?' Mickey looks at me for the first time.

I look directly at Harry and with as much sincerity as I

can muster. 'This would be a lot to take on Harry and if I'm to do it right then I need to think about it.'

Harry drums on the steering wheel with his short stubby fingers leaving white fingerprints. 'Absolutely son, you think about it. But don't take too fuckin long because this war has well and truly begun. We'll be seeing you around.' I nod, open the van door and walk away. I can still smell the baked bread and raisins. I think of my grandmother and realise it's time to leave.

The McCruddens tended not to celebrate birthdays. Sometimes Sober Daddy would bake a gooseberry crumble or a sponge cake but there was never any money for presents. My mother would make party hats out of newspaper, and we would all sing Happy Birthday but more often than not birthdays passed relatively unnoticed. I actually forgot my birthday. Forgot I was seventeen, and so did everyone else. I checked my post office book. Thirty-eight pounds and seventy pence. It wasn't much but it would have to do.

Norman Greer wished me well, handed me a P45 form and some cards with a few stamps on them. I had no idea what they were. Norman explained as best he could. 'Ess yer P foy five an inhurince cad an nasinurince umber. Yill nee all at when ye snot wok.' He shook my hand, pumped it firmly up and down. His grip was strong. It was the first time an adult had shook my hand. 'Gluck now ung Macudden. Eff ye cum bick ell be a jab fe ye.' Norman jumped in the Bedford TK and drove off, all the crates rattling. I had no idea I'd been employed legitimately by Cantrell and Cochrane. I watched the lorry until it disappeared over Gort Hill.

Rosie makes no crying sound, she has tears in her eyes but they don't run down her face they just stay there, getting bigger by the second, her bottom lip trembling. I had never seen her upset like this before. It breaks my heart and when she finally speaks it's in a different voice from the one I know, 'Why Emmet. . . why didn't you tell me you were leaving?. . . You knew for months! You should've told me. . . '

I desperately want to say, 'I'm not going, I've changed my mind.' But I know I can't do that, there's no turning back. I tell her I'll come back for her next year, save enough to pay her fare and we can get a flat together.

Rosie shakes her head wildly from side to side, chews the inside of her mouth. 'Don't be so stupid! I have exams! You think I can just run off with you like in some fucking fairytale!'

I try to hug her but she pushes me away and runs off. I'm crying now but I still want to do untold damage to something or someone.

PART TWO

THE FUTURE IS FEELGOOD

FIVE

I LEFT AT FIVE THIRTY in the morning. In all the books I had read people always did their leaving early in the morning. Jim Hawkins. . . *A little after dawn the boatswain sounded his pipe and we had begun our voyage.* Tom Joad . . . *Jesus Christ it's near sunrise, we gotta get goin.* As I crept down the stairs, my holdall gripped to my chest, Fergal appeared on the landing and peed into the bucket. Fergal was the last person I wanted to see.

He looked up at me. 'Where ye going Emmy?'

I put my finger to my lips. 'Can you keep a secret?' He nodded, still peeing. 'I'm going away for a while to find a job and when I've enough money I'll come back and buy you a big new fishing rod.'

He didn't look that impressed. 'Could I have a rifle instead, a Winchester like the Rifleman?'

'OK, it's a deal.'

'Emmy?'

'What?'

'Can I come with you?'

'No Fergal. You'd just get bored. I'm only going away for a wee while. I'll be back soon.'

For a split second he looked like he was going to cry. His eyes full of panic and fear but that only lasted a moment, and his next expression was way beyond his years, a look that said I know you're bullshitting me but I'll go along with it for your sake. He nodded without any conviction, a nod that made me feel like the biggest arsehole on the planet, pulled up his pants and went back to bed. I climbed on the bus outside the Town Hall at 5.45 am. I knew the driver, Arnie Harris.

'Jaysus, you're out and about early young McCrudden. Did ye shite the bed?'

'How are you doin Arnie. I'm just headin down to Larne for the day to see a friend of mine.'

Arnie threw the bus into gear, the air brakes hissed and we were on our way.

'Aye well, I think it's goin to be a quare day anyway.'

It definitely was a quare day. A day I'd been planning since my grandmother's funeral. As we drove through the town I had a memory for every place we passed. The Burren Fort, Westwood's off licence, St Malachy's Catholic Boy's School, the other half of the paving slab that I hit Jackie Westwood, with still not replaced. I felt a pang of guilt that I hadn't told Maeve I was leaving. As we passed the Hibernian Hall I imagined I could hear Master McKenna screaming as the bullets tore into his knees. My stomach turned over, I slunk lower in my seat and when I closed my eyes, saw Fergal's face staring up at me.

I boarded the *Antrim Princess* at Larne Harbour at 7.30 am on the 15th of Sep 1972 paying £4.50 for a single second-class ticket. There was an announcement that the sea was calm and the duration of our journey to Stranraer would be approximately two hours and thirty-five minutes. The 2nd class cafeteria was now open for breakfast and hot drinks. Alcoholic drinks would be served in the bar from 9 am. The *Antrim Princess* was much bigger than I had imagined. It was more like a ship, and I didn't know it took cars and lorries as well. This was the first time I'd been on anything like this. Once I was rowed out to the middle of Lough Neagh with Bandy Quinn to catch eels and I didn't enjoy that. It was death by a thousand midges. Bandy was paralytic drunk and crying about something, it was raining and cold and we didn't catch any eels. This was a much better affair altogether. I could hardly contain my excitement as we eventually moved off, the propeller blades chomping and churning at the waves, and Larne Harbour disappearing from view. Emmet McCrudden was no more.

Tom Joad had hitched a lift from prison without a cent in his pocket. I had thirty pounds left which I was determined to hold on to for as long as I could. Disembarking in Stranraer I waited on London Road for all the lorries to emerge out of the belly of the *Antrim Princess* and hooked my thumb out with a hopeful grin on my face. Two hours later it started to rain. When you are hungry there is nothing like the smell of fish and chips to break your will. I was about to enter the

Starfish Chip Bar when a large blue Scammel lorry pulled up. I ran towards it, my holdall banging against my leg and climbed up into the cabin. The driver was a red-faced man with a bright woolly cap and hardly any teeth.

'Am only gan as for as Car-lisle, ahreet?'

I had no idea where that was and I didn't care so I just nodded and smiled. During the journey I found out that the driver was from Newcastle. I said I knew where that was in County Down. The driver laughed, 'Na man nought that wan, Newcastle upon Tyne in England like!'

His name was Clem and although I didn't really under-stand half of what he said, the time flew by. It was just like being back on the lemonade lorry with Norman Greer and it seemed like no time at all until he had dropped me on the outskirts of Carlisle and told me where to stand if I wanted a lift to London.

I didn't have to wait long for that second lift which was straight to Birmingham. The driver had a blonde perm and a tanned smiley open face. He looked a bit like a white Jimi Hendrix. 'Hi, I'm Ambroos.'

I told him my real name as I had forgotten that I was now Tom Joad. I'd have to try and remember that in future. He told me he was from Rotterdam. I stared blankly at him and smiled.

'Holland!' he shouted, 'you know Holland?'

Of course, I knew Holland. 'Johan Cruff!', I shouted back. It was loud inside his cab and he had the radio on.

He laughed and corrected me, 'No Cruff! Ker-roiff! Yo-han Ker-roiff! You like Football?'

'Yes, I do. Ajax! European cup. They beat Arsenal in the quarter finals.'

He laughed again. 'Yes, by Arsenal scoring in their own goal. I hate Ajax. My team is Feyenoord. Van Hanegem you know him?' I'd never heard of him. 'He's fantastic. Best left foot in all football.'

We stopped at a motorway cafe. I'd never seen such a selection of food. I liked the sound and smell of something called Deep Fried Kentucky Chicken, so I ordered that with baked beans and a Pepsi Cola. I was famished and it was absolutely delicious. Ambroos had hamburger and chips. When we were back on the road Ambroos burped loudly and said, 'English food is so terrible shit!'

The Rolling Stones came on the radio with 'Wild Horses'. We talked about all sorts of things, music, football, Tulips. He told me his second cousin, Pierre van der Linden was the drummer for a band called Focus, luckily the only Dutch band I'd ever heard of and I told him I loved the song 'Hocus Pocus'.

He looked impressed. 'Yeah, da only bend to make yodelling sound cool.'

He told me how Tulips were brought to Holland from Turkey in the 16th century and if I ever got a chance I had to sleep with a Dutch girl because they were the best, the most beautiful and the dirtiest. Before Ambroos dropped me off he asked me if I was running away from home. I said I thought I probably was. 'Make sure you contact your family,' he said, 'and be careful OK?' He waved at me as he drove off. I liked Ambroos. Would have liked to have hung out with him for just a while longer.

The last leg of my journey was in a McAlpine's tipper lorry driven by a man who hardly spoke a word during the two-and-a-half-hour journey. I fell asleep for most of it. I think he was Irish, he looked Irish. He had a big head of corrugated red hair and a constant surprised look on his freckled face. If he was Irish then he was the quietest Irishman I'd ever met. He grunted something and dropped me off in someplace called Harrow on the Hill. It was 10.15pm. I counted my money, thirty-one pounds and eighty pence. One pound eighty more than I thought.

Auntie Fiona wasn't really our Auntie. She was my father's cousin, but that's how she always referred to herself, *Och come here and give yer Auntie Fiona a wee kiss*. She used to live in Belfast and sometimes came to visit us when we were kids. She moved to London in 1965 to work as a nurse in Charing Cross Hospital. She may have come back sometimes at Christmas, but I couldn't really remember.

The address I had for her was on a letter she had sent to my father. Perfect cursive handwriting in black ink, *498 Dalling Road Fulham*. She was the only person I knew in London and I hoped with all my heart that she still lived here, and maybe there was a chance that my mother was here too. After getting lost twice on the tube trains I finally arrived at 498 Dalling Road. It was well after midnight and the house was in darkness. There were two bells on the door, one of the names in the white gap below looked like Rajah or Hajah the other was faded. I rang the faded one. I could hear the shrill of the bell going off in the distance like an annoyance. I waited for a respectable amount of time and then rang it again holding my finger on it for just a little longer this time. I hated what I was doing, hated the nagging ring of this bell but what choice did I have now? I waited, my heart beating. My mind raced away with itself. What if she didn't live here anymore, what would I do, where would I sleep tonight? I was dog-tired and starving with hunger. I could always sleep in a hedge, thumb back to Stranraer and get the ferry back home. This thought calmed me for a moment before panic set in again and I imagined being raped and murdered in the hedge by a madman. I rang the bell again three times in quick succession. A strip of light appeared under the door, someone approaching, a nervous cough. The door was opened a fraction, held back by a chain. I could see a set of eyes I didn't recognise.

'Yes! Who is it you're looking for?' I knew the voice.

'It's me Auntie Fiona, Emmet, Emmet McCrudden.' That stupid name again. 'Frank's son.'

The door opened, she was a lot thinner and looked old. I had never seen her without makeup on her face. She stared at me.

'Mother of sweet Jesus son, what are you doing here, what's wrong?'

'Nothing's wrong Auntie Fiona I've just come to London. I'm going to get a job. I was wondering if I could stay with you until I find somewhere?'

She shook her head and made huffing sounds. 'Come in come in!' She shuffled along the hallway in green fluffy carpet slippers. 'Come in here'. She showed me into a small front room with the biggest TV I ever saw. 'Sit down.' I sat on the sofa. She sat opposite me, her arms folded tightly across her chest her eyes opening wider as she looked me up and down. 'Why didn't you let me know you were coming? You just can't turn up on someone's doorstep in the middle of the night.'

At that moment a woman popped her head around the door and stared at me. She looked Chinese. 'Everything OK Fifi?'

Auntie Fiona waved her away.

'Go back to bed Patti. It's a relative of mine turned up out of the blue.'

The woman grinned at me flashing a mouthful of big teeth. 'At this time of night? Maybe you are on the run. The policemen are chasing you yeh?'

'No, I thumbed here from Scotland. It took a long time.'

She chuckled to herself and sucked through her teeth, 'Scot-land?' And then left us to it.

Auntie Fiona lit a cigarette. 'You can stay here tonight,

sleep on the sofa, but then I think you should go home son. You're far too young to be in London on your own. Does your father and mother know you're here?' She obviously didn't know my mother had left. I wanted to lie, but I knew she'd find out so I told the truth.

'No, I didn't tell anyone I was coming.'

Auntie Fiona blew smoke hard out of her mouth. 'Jesussss.' She stubbed out the cigarette in a glass ashtray.

'I'll get you some blankets. We'll talk about this in the morning. I need my sleep.' She stopped at the door. 'There's no room here. I have a lodger.' She was about to leave, I plucked up the courage.

'Auntie Fiona...'

'Yes?'

'Could I have a sandwich? I'm really hungry. I can make it.'

She sighed loudly almost a hiss. 'You bloody well will make it, in here.' The kitchen was almost twice the size of the front room with the biggest fridge I'd ever seen.

'There's bread in that bin, butter and cheese in the fridge. Make sure you put it all back and switch out the light. We need to have a serious talk in the morning young man.'

'Thanks Auntie Fiona.'

She came close to me and whispered, 'And stop calling me Auntie Fiona, you're not four years old anymore. Everybody here calls me Fifi.' I nodded. 'OK.' She disappeared upstairs and was back immediately with blankets and a pillow.

The bread was brown with bits in it and the cheese had red skin, but I was so hungry I didn't care. I found a tomato and that helped. I ate hungrily, hardly giving myself time to chew. I had to slow down, poured myself a glass of milk. The milk was called UHT and tasted like sweat.

Ambroos's voice came back to me. *English food is so terrible shit.* I suddenly started to laugh. I couldn't stop myself. The thought of calling Auntie Fiona Fifi suddenly seemed hilarious. I imagined myself saying it in a posh English accent, *Good morning, Fifi I trust you slept well?* I almost choked on the sandwich. I was lightheaded and a little hysterical, maybe it was the hunger, or I was giddy at being in London? I coughed and sprayed the fridge with chewed bread cheese and tomato, which made me laugh all the harder. I got down on my knees and covered my mouth with both hands. I was now choking and laughing at the same time. I had to spit out the remains of the sandwich. I eventually regained control of myself and cleaned up the mess. I found a black banana and ate that as well.

The sofa was very comfortable. I'd never been so tired in my life. I was about to drift off when someone said, *Wee cup of tea.* I thought Auntie Fiona had come back into the room. I switched on the lamp. The room was empty. *Wee cup of tea!* Was I so tired that I couldn't see Auntie Fiona? *Wee cup of tea!* I tried to focus on where the voice was coming from. I went into the kitchen switched on the light. Nobody there. *Wee cup of tea!* There was no question in the voice. It was more of a statement and definitely coming from the living room. *Wee cup of tea!* I didn't believe in ghosts but this was getting very weird. I stood in the middle of the living room, my heartbeat the only sound. I waited, hardly daring to breathe. *Wee cup of tea!* The voice was coming from an old-fashioned folding screen that people used to use to get dressed behind. I pulled it across and saw a cloth covering a square shape. I removed the cloth to find a parrot in a cage. I'd never seen a parrot up close before. It was a beautiful looking thing, black and white face with a turquoise head, bright red body, deep blue wings and yellow tail. I whispered to it. 'No, I don't want a cup of tea Polly, now shut up, I'm knackered.' I put the cover back and it was quiet, switched off the lamp, climbed under the blankets on the sofa and fell asleep immediately. *Wee cup of tea!*

I was awoken by the six pips preceding the news on Radio 4. My grandmother always used to listen to it in the morning. A sadness swept over me. I still missed her. Auntie Fiona entered the room dressed in a blue nurse's uniform.

'Morning. Did you sleep alright?'

'Yes thanks.'

She whipped the cover from the cage. The parrot squawked. 'Did this bad boy keep you awake?' She put her face near the cage. 'You're a bad boy aren't you, Oscar?' The parrot squawked again. 'The world is full of bad boys this morning.' She gestured to me. 'I've tea in the pot, come into the kitchen.'

Wee cup of tea, said Oscar.

I followed Auntie Fiona into the kitchen. She poured tea from a big flowery teapot. I sat at the table, suddenly nervous. 'I'm going into work now. I'll be back at eight tonight. When I get home we can phone your Mum and Dad, let them know you're safe and then we can talk about trying to get you a flight from Heathrow. I'll pay for it. . . OK?' I stared at her. I didn't know what to say. She said it more forcefully, 'OK?', emphasising the *kayyyy* the way people do when they want you to answer them.

'I'm not going back home Auntie Fi. . .Fifi.' I felt a giggle coming on but I fought hard against it. 'We don't have a phone and my ma isn't there anyway. She left us last year. I thought she might have come here. My da's drinking a lot. There's nothing there for me. I'm not going back.'

Auntie Fiona blew on her tea and supped it silently. 'Still the same old Frank then. That man will never have sense. I wonder your mother stuck him as long as she did' She sighed into her tea. 'There's no room here for you. Do you have money?'

'I have.'

'How much?'

'Thirty pounds.' She rolled her eyes. 'Mother of Jesus. How long do you think that will last you?'

'I'll get a job.'

She banged her cup down on the table a few drops of tea flew out. 'Doing what? You're still a child for Christ's sake!'

Patti entered with a towel, turban-wrapped around her head. 'Hello Scottish boy. You causing trouble?'

Auntie Fiona sat beside me at the table, looked at her watch. 'I haven't time to talk about this now.' She rose from the table, took a few quick sips of her tea, put on her coat, grabbed a bag hanging from the back of a chair. 'Patti, give him the spare front door key for now and we'll sort this out tonight.' She looked at me again and was going to say something else but said nothing and left.

Patti dried her hair with the towel. I drank my tea. Patti shook her head the way a dog does when it comes out of the river. She sniffed the air. 'You need to have a shower, it's upstairs on the left. Do you have a towel?' I shook my head. 'You can use the brown one hanging on the back of the door.'

The shower wasn't anything like the ones we had at school. It took me a while to work out how to use it and then it almost scalded me. I washed with a bar of 'wild rose' pink soap I found on a saucer on the bathroom shelf. The smell reminded me of Rosie. I wished I could talk to her, explain why I had to leave. I began a conversation with her in my head. She cried but was very understanding, told me she loved me and would wait for me. I kissed her soft lips. When I came back down Patti had made me scrambled eggs on toast. She was dressed in the same blue nurse's uniform that Auntie Fiona had on.

'Here you are Scottish boy.'

'I'm not Scottish.'

She smiled with all her big teeth. 'I know. What's your name?'

I hesitated. 'Emmet.'

She laughed.

'Helmet? What kind of name is that?'

'Em-met.' I said it louder. She shook her head and laughed again. I was determined to change my stupid name first chance I got.

She shook some keys at me and removed one. 'This is the front door key, don't lose it. I'm going to work now. If you are determined to stay in London, then you need to find a job and quickly. Get the *Evening News* and find where it says 'Vacancies'. The paper comes out early just after lunchtime on Hammersmith Broadway. You'll see a man selling it outside the tube station. There's a phone box across the road beside the George pub. You'll also need to get a couple of bags of ten-pence pieces from the bank or post office. You'll have to phone, phone, phone and keep phoning. Take a notebook and pen. You understand?'

I nodded. 'Yes, I understand, thanks.'

'You can't stay here you know that don't you?' I nodded again. She smiled.

'I'll ask at the hospital if anyone has a spare room. Sometimes they put rooms to let on the notice board.' Before she left she turned back quickly and said, 'You can't stay here because Fifi and I live to-gether.'

'Yes I know she told me, you're her lodger.'

'No, we only have one bedroom, and we sleep in the same bed, you understand?'

Hammersmith Broadway was the noisiest place I had ever been to in my life. It had six major roads leading into it with buses, cars, lorries, taxis, motorbikes, cyclists, coming nonstop from every direction. People running across the road but not in a nervous way, in a way that looked practiced and confident. I didn't have the nerve to chance it so I used the tunnel which went under the road. So many different people, Black, Chinese, Indian, an Arab in a long white dress and head-towel with a black band around it, three women behind him their faces covered in masks. There was a tramp with a dirty beard and long brown overcoat. A boot on his left foot and a shoe on his right, playing an accordion and singing 'I'll Take You Home Again Kathleen'. A group of lads with very short hair and sideburns all wearing the same black Crombie coats and big shiny boots, their jeans held up by braces, hung around the entrance to the tube station laughing and smoking. One of them mocked the Arab as he walked past which the rest found hilarious. Two policemen appeared walking together and the lads disappeared into the tube station. These were real London policemen wearing those black pointy hats with the silver badge on the front. A flutter of excitement ran through me, I was actually here! I had made it and none of these people knew me or my history. I now had the chance to be whoever I wanted to be. Tommy Forbes, our school caretaker, used to talk about being born-again, about being given a second chance by God to be a different person, a better person, a person with a new lease of life. No one really ever knew what he was going on about or took him seriously. We all thought he was just a bit of a headcase, but now I completely understood what he meant.

SIX

'COME ALONG IN THE MORNIN at half-seven to the MJ Gleeson's site on North End Road Fulham.' The Southern Irish voice shouted at me down the phone. I scribbled furiously on my notepad. 'It's a two-in-one gang. Do ye have yer own hod?'

'Yeah sure,' I lied.

'It's a five-minute walk from West Kensington tube station. Ask for Fast Eddie, he'll sort ye out. Twelve quid a day in the hand fourteen quid for a Saturday until two o'clock.'

Considering it had taken me over two-and-a-half years to save thirty-eight pounds the prospect of earning seventy-four pounds a week made my head spin. The other four jobs, plumber's mate, trainee barman, road sweeper and library assistant had been too far away. I would've been travelling twenty-five stops on the tube or an hour-and-twenty-minutes on a bus to get to any of them. North End Road in Fulham was fifteen minutes from Dalling Road, although I had no idea how much longer I'd be allowed to stay there. But this was the least of my worries. My real problem was where was I going to find a hod and learn to carry bricks in fifteen hours?

It was almost six o'clock in the evening by the time I found a builder's merchants that sold hods. ROBERT GRIMES AND SONS, Brentford was on the river, a half-hour bus journey from Hammersmith. The hod was made from hard plastic and cost two pounds and fifty pence. It was a lot lighter than I had imagined. The man in the shop also put the wooden shaft on for me which cost an extra eighty pence. I had fish and chips in the cafe next door. On the way back to Dalling Road I counted my money twenty-two pounds and forty pence. In my *Evening News* I could see that bedsits cost around ten pounds a week with most of them asking for at least two weeks' deposit. I needed this job.

I wanted to leave it as late as possible before returning to the caring bosoms of Fifi and Patti so I went into a pub on Dalling Road called the Anglesea Arms. My first English pub. I ordered a pint of bitter. It was what the man in front of me ordered so I asked for the same. The woman behind the bar leaned on the counter and looked me over.

'How old are you?'

'Eighteen.'

'What's your date of birth?'

'15th of August 1954' I had rehearsed that date in my head for occasions like this.

She brought her fat top lip down over her bottom lip,

stared at me some more. 'You don't look eighteen.'

'Well, I've only been eighteen for one month.' I lifted up my hod. 'I'm starting work tomorrow as a hod carrier.' She shook her head and smiled, then poured the pint. 'That'll be nineteen pence, please.'

I found a corner and sat with my back against the wall and listened to Marc Bolan on the jukebox. *Metagaroo is it you yeah yeah yeah.* I didn't know what a Metagaroo was, in fact I never knew what Marc Bolan was singing about. *Ride a white swan?* But I still liked his songs, they always made me want to dance. The bitter tasted like a mixture of nettles and disinfectant. Jesus, how could anyone drink this stuff? The woman behind the bar watched me as I supped and gurned into the pint. I was still there an hour later and had only managed to drink half of it. When she was busy serving, I made my escape.

The first thing I heard as I opened the front door to 498 Dalling Road was a howl of grief. 'Oh my God nooooo! How did it happen?' It was Auntie Fiona. Patti was trying to calm her. 'Shoosh now Fifi'.

'Are you sure he's dead Patti? He still feels warm.' More howling. 'Ohhhh God. . . He looks dead. . . he's dead Patti! He's gone, my poor wee Oscar.' I stood back in the hallway not quite knowing where to go. I thought about going back out when Patti stepped into the hallway. 'We think Oscar has died.'

I followed Patti into the front room. The parrot was lying

79

on the coffee table. Auntie Fiona wiped her eyes and stared at me. 'Was he OK when you left? Did you feed him anything?'

'No. I didn't feed him anything. He was fine when I left.'

Patti stroked Auntie Fiona's back. 'Maybe we should call the vet?' She looked at me for help. 'Do you think it's dead?' The parrot was obviously dead, stiff as a board on the table and suddenly I was in the Monty Python parrot sketch. I knew I desperately needed to get out of the room otherwise I was going to start laughing. I could feel it creeping up on me, the *devil's tickle* as my grandfather used to call it. Laughing when you're not supposed to. I pretended to cough, held my breath. I couldn't speak.

'He's dead!' Auntie Fiona screamed.

'I know he's dead!' Patti hugged her. 'We should call the vet.' She looked at me again. 'Can you feel him. Is he dead?' I approached the parrot and all I could hear was John Cleese shouting, *He is an ex-parrot!* Tears were in my eyes, my chest started to vibrate. I looked at Auntie Fiona but didn't trust myself to speak. I turned and ran upstairs to the bathroom, buried my face in the brown towel and stifled my laugh as best I could. *Get a grip, come on!*

There were footsteps on the stairs, a knock on the door. Patti's voice. 'Are you OK Emnet?' Emnet? I removed the towel and took a deep breath, tried to compose myself.

'Yes. . . yes, I'm OK. I'll be down in a minute.' I sat on the toilet bowl and tried to think of something sad. I thought about Rosie, and it suddenly occurred to me that I should write to her. I also started thinking about Maeve and how she was coping.

When I walked back into the front room, the parrot was still on the coffee table covered with the cloth that had been over the cage. Auntie Fiona was crying softly into her hankie, Patti sat holding her hand.

'I'm sorry about Oscar Auntie Fio. . . Fifi.'

Auntie Fiona looked up at me. 'You're a sensitive boy I can see that.'

Patti stroked her hand. 'We can take him to the pet cemetery in Ealing. Or you can bury him in the garden?'

Auntie Fiona sniffed and blew her nose. 'I think the garden would be best. He would be closer to me then.' Patti nodded and left the room quietly. Auntie Fiona sighed deeply. 'Oscar was given to me the first week I moved here in 1965. He belonged to a lady who I was looking after in hospital. He kept me company. He was a great talker. She told me he'd been with her for forty-five years, so he must have been at least 52. He died of old age.'

Patti entered the room with a shoe box with Sling-backs written on the side. She put the box beside Oscar. 'Do you want to put him in?' Auntie Fiona picked up Oscar gently in her hands and laid him in the box, put the lid on. I thought for a second about my grandmother and lost any inclination to laugh.

It was a neat long narrow garden with a hedge on one side, a fence on the other side covered with ivy and what looked like a plum tree in the far corner. Dusk was descending. I stood and watched as Auntie Fiona dug a hole with a small gardening spade. The hole didn't really seem deep enough, but I thought it better not to say anything. She placed the box in the hole and covered it with about three inches of soil, patted it down with her hands and hung some wind chimes on a little bush. We all stood there for a few minutes and then went inside.

Patti removed the cage and put it in the hall. When she came back, she looked at me and asked, 'What is that thing in the hallway?'

'Oh that's a hod, I'm starting work tomorrow.'

'A what?' Auntie Fiona asked.

'A hod, for carrying bricks.'

She sighed. 'Carrying bricks? I don't think you're cut out for that kind of work. Where is this job?'

'It's on the North End Road. They're building a housing estate. It's seventy-four pound a week.'

Patti made a mock shock face. 'What? Seventy-four pounds a week? Can you get me a job there? I think you are fibbing with us Emnet.'

'I'm not. I spoke to the boss on the phone and that's what he told me.'

Auntie Fiona got up from the sofa. 'I'm going to my bed.' She looked long and hard at me until it became very uncomfortable. 'You can stay for another two weeks. But after that you must find somewhere. Do you understand?'

'Yes. I'll look for somewhere tomorrow thanks.'

'Is there a phone at home where you can ring your father, or one of your sisters?'

'Yes, the Patterson's live down the hill, they have a phone. I'm going to write to Maeve as well.'

She nodded and left the room. Patti called after her, 'I'll be up soon.' She turned to me. 'There's soup in a pot. Just warm it up if you're hungry.'

'Thanks.'

Patti suddenly put her hand on my arm. 'Were you really crying, or were you laughing?'

The question took me unawares and I began to blush. 'I. . . no, I was. . . shocked. . . it was a sad thing.'

Patti made a sucking sound through her teeth. 'I have my eye on you Emnet and done you forget it.'

I told Fast Eddie my name was Tom Joad. It felt great to say it at last. Eddie didn't look particularly fast. He was a small stout man with curly black hair, a beer belly and large round glasses which gave him enormous horse eyes. He kept pushing the glasses back on his face and on one occasion took them off to clean them with the front of his shirt. I was shocked at how small his eyes actually were. Two little black peas. He hadn't said anything since he'd asked my name. He put his glasses back on.

'Show us yer hands!' I held my hands out, he turned

them over palms up. 'You've never carried the hod in yer life.' My mouth opened and closed. I felt like an idiot standing there in my black hobnailed boots and corduroy trousers, my Wrangler jacket faded so badly I could see through it. Holding my hod awkwardly like a bunch of flowers for a girlfriend. The trousers just about still fitted me. 'Tell ye what I'll do son, I need someone to prime doors. There's over two thousand doors to do on Block 10 and then some of the houses on Block 8 need to be cleaned out so as the sparks and tilers can get in. I'll give ye £50 a week in yer hand and that includes Saturday morning. You won't get paid until the second week, but you can have a sub. Alright?'

My mouth was dry and my heart was on the run. 'Yeah thanks. Thanks Eddie.'

The housing estate was massive, over fifteen hundred homes, some almost completed, some in between and some still at the foundation stage. Block 10 was in between. Each house had ten doors which needed priming. I was put to work with another lad in his early twenties with curly auburn hair and a large red heart-shaped birthmark on his cheek. Fast Eddie introduced me.

'Strawbs, this is Tom, show him what the craic is, alright?' Fast Eddie looked at me. 'Give me that hod I'll put it in the storeroom for you. Who knows ye might even get to use it someday. . . and watch that Strawbs fucker. He's from

Limerick, he'd steal yer shite before it hits the ground and ride the arse off yer grannie!'

Strawbs laughed loudly. 'I wouldn't steal your shite Eddie, it's fuckin minging! I'd have a go on yer grannie though!' Fast Eddie was out the door and gone.

Strawbs was wearing white overalls covered in paint. 'My real name is Harper, but everyone calls me Strawbs because of me face. You'll need some whites, follow me.' I followed him outside, he opened a large wooden box and threw me a pair of white overalls covered in paint. 'We keep the gear in this box, our whites, tins of paint, scrapers, brooms, brushes, shovels. I'll get you a spare key at lunchtime. Make sure it's locked every night and your brushes are kept clean. Eddie is as straight as they come, he's the heart of corn, but if you don't do your work or try and fuck him around, like being late in the mornings or staying above in the pub at lunchtime, any of that fuckin craic, and you'll be down the road straight away.'

I nodded. 'I'll keep that in mind.'

Strawbs laughed. 'So you were going to chance yer arm at the hod carryin, wha?'

I smiled shyly, 'Yeah.'

Strawbs laughed loudly again. 'That's one job you can't bluff. I've never seen such a clean hod in all me life. That was a kind of a giveaway like. That and the fact you look about 15 years old. But fair fuckin play to you Tom. You have to start somewhere.' He handed me a brush and a tin of paint. 'And that would be here and now!'

By the end of the day I'd gotten the hang of it. All the doors needed two coats of primer. Strawbs told me to keep a wet sponge handy in case I got splashes on anything. The paint was water based, so it was easy to wipe away. He also showed me how to wedge the door half-open and how to tap the inside of the tin twice with the paintbrush after I had dipped it in the paint to keep it from dripping. I had to paint the frame first, then around the edges of the door before I tackled the door itself. I'd also been holding the paintbrush too tightly. 'Yer wrist is too stiff, it's not yer cock yer holdin, relax a bit.'

Strawbs played his radio all day long, a Sobell transistor, the exact same as Mickey Peach's. Don McClean's 'Starry Starry Night' echoed throughout the house. I missed Mickey. I wished he was here with me. I wondered did he really join the Provos? I couldn't imagine Mickey hurting anyone, but what happened in Derry had changed everything.

The canteen was a long purpose-built building with wooden benches and tables, a lively place full of men and steam and laughter and cooking smells. A large blackboard with the menu chalked up FRIED BACON AND POTOTOES. Some of the men teased one of the three women behind the counter. 'Ah Jaysus Maureen I'll try the Fried Bacon and PO-TO-TOES. I've never had PO-TO-TOES before.'

Maureen was back at him in a flash. 'I never listened at

school Brendan that's why I'm here feeding you feckin savages!' A great roar of laughter went around the canteen. Someone chipped in. 'He's a Mayo muck savage Maureen yer right there!' I liked the look of Maureen. Maureen was my mother's name. I also couldn't believe there was a dessert called SPOTTED DICK. The food was good and cheap. I had the fried bacon and 'pototoes'.

By half past four, Strawbs had painted six doors and I had painted four. 'Ye did OK today Tom, ye'll quicken up soon enough, but sure we don't want to go too fuckin quick like, otherwise we'll be out of a job. '

I felt it on the way home on the tube. My body ached all over, neck, lower back, wrist and a large blister on the inside of my thumb. But it was a tiredness I was proud of, one I had earned, a feeling of achievement. My plan was working out. All I needed now was a place of my own.

Dear Maeve
I'm in London and I've found a job painting doors
on a building site. I'm staying with Auntie Fiona.
Sleeping on her sofa. She's living with another nurse.
I thought she was Chinese, but she's from a place
called Manila. They sleep together. She wants me to
call her Fifi. It's all a bit mental. Me Ma never came
here. I can only stay for a week so I'm looking for
somewhere. My wages are £50 a week. How is Da? Is
he back drinking? London is all go. They have big
trees growing out of the pavements on a lot of the
side streets. I was on a red bus the other day. They

87

are great because you can just jump on them as they are moving off. I haven't been sightseeing yet, can't afford it at the minute but maybe when I find my own bed-sit.

Good luck. Emmet.

Dear Emmet

We were all worried when you didn't come home. But then Arnie Harris told Da you got on his bus at half-five in the morning going to Larne. So I guessed you went to London. You talked about it enough. I was very shocked to hear that Auntie Fiona is a Lesbian, or is that you joking? I can hardly believe that is true. Da is drinking again but he hasn't much money so hasn't been able to get plastered. His benefits were cut for some reason. He's going down to the brew today to find out what's happening. We are all well enough. Fergal and Connor had lice, but all the youngsters at their school had them. Mickey Peach called to the house looking for you. I told him you probably went to London. He looked sad. I saw Rosie in the Spar yesterday. She was with Tony Mulgrew. She pretended not to see me, as if I care who's she's with. I'm glad you found a job. £50 a week is great. I'm going for an interview at the carpet factory as a book keeper. The manageress is a Catholic so I might have a better chance. No point in asking you to say a wee prayer that I get the job for I know your a friggin heathen! hahaha! Take care of yourself. Write soon.

Maeve xoxox

The letter trembled in my hand. My heartbeat began to go out of whack, stopping and starting and scaring the shit out of me. I thought I was having a heart attack. I could feel the blood draining from my face. I felt faint. Tony Mulgrew! Why was Rosie with Tony Mulgrew? Tony Mulgrew was an idiot.

Patti looked across at me. 'Bad news Emnet?'

Patti was really beginning to get on my nerves. The quicker I was out of this house the better. I couldn't even read a private letter in peace. 'No, everything's fine. As soon as there's any bad news, I'll let you know!' I got up quickly from the sofa and went upstairs to the bathroom. Patti made the annoying sucking noise through her teeth.

I sat on the toilet and the name TONY MULGREW jumped up from the page. I had worried about this happening. I knew it probably would happen but not this quickly and not with that gobshite. I hadn't even looked at another girl and I'd been in London almost ten days. I had to write to Rosie, but what was the point? I wasn't going back, but I knew I would still write to her. Maybe she only met Mulgrew in the Spar. It wasn't like Maeve saw them kissing or holding hands. I read the letter again. *I saw Rosie in the Spar yesterday. She was with Tony Mulgrew, she pretended not to see me, as if I care who she's with*. 'Who she's with', what did that mean? It could mean anything. The only way to find out was to write and ask her. But even if she was, what could I do about it? I wanted to punch the wall.

Dear Rosie

I'm so sorry I had to leave. I didn't want to, but I couldn't stand living in my house any longer. I would have ended up killing my Da. I'm in London working on a building site. The money is good £74 a week. I'm staying with my Aunt for now but I'm looking for a bedsit and when I find one maybe you could come over in the summer holidays. I'd pay for everything. Maeve said she saw you in the Spar with Tony Mulgrew. Are you going out with him? I'd be surprised if you are, but I hope you're not. He's a moron. Do you remember the time he vomited into Imelda Ryan's handbag and then denied it. . . and that other time he stole the crate of beer from the Brewery Tap and got caught because he wrote his name on the wall and the time he killed the rabbit with a brick because it had Maxi ma tosis? (I know I didn't spell that right) but you know what I mean and I don't think it had Maxi ma tosis anyway.
I hope you did well in your exams. I'm sure you did.
Emmet. oxoxo

Fast Eddie handed me a brown wage packet with Tom Joad written on it. Tom Joad. It now felt official. I stared at the amount written on the slip: £58.50. Fast Eddie pushed his glasses back and hitched up his trousers around his paunch.

'Yez got a bonus for flying through them doors. Youse keep up the good work now and I'll look after yez. A few of us are going down to the Swan on Fulham Broadway tomorrow night for a few pints so come down and we'll have the craic.'

Strawbs checked his wage packet. He looked at me and laughed his big laugh. 'Didn't I tell ye Eddie was the heart of corn wha?'

'You did Strawbs.'

The Swan was easily the biggest and most crowded pub I'd ever been to in my life but the barmen and barmaids were amazingly fast and no one had to wait long to be served. It had a fiddly-dee Irish band playing. Not my kind of music and no-one seemed to be listening to them. Strawbs was chatting up a girl called Lyndsey. Lyndsey and her friend Veronica worked in the betting shop next door to the pub. She giggled every time Strawbs said anything. Fast Eddie had three pints of Guinness lined up on the bar in front of him and the barman was pulling him another. He put one of the pints to his lips and all of the black stuff disappeared down his throat leaving a white moustache on his top lip which he shaved off in one movement with the rim of the glass. He picked up another pint and did the same. Strawbs suddenly appeared over my shoulder. 'That's why they call him Fast Eddie. I'm away to the Jacks, go over and keep those two company til I get back.'

I ordered my first pint of lager, Kronenbourg and after taking my first sup knew immediately I had found my drink.

When I reached the girls, Keefer was already there, sitting between them. They called him Reefer Keefer. He was a six foot three Aussie, blonde and tanned and reminded me a little of Ambroos. He wore sandals and shorts and a bright red shirt. I had no idea why they called him Reefer Keefer, but I suspected it was because he came from somewhere near the Great Barrier Reef. Keefer was one of the brickies that I had originally applied to hod-carry for and he had teased me about it ever since. 'I'm still waitin on those bricks little Tommy boy. What the fuck is keeping ya?' Then he'd slap me on the back and roar at his own joke. 'I'll teach ya to lay bricks mate, ya don't wanna be on the monkey! Fuck that. You'll be old before ya toyime. . . by the way, Crash Test Trevor is using ya hod. I'll get him to pay ya for it.'

Crash Test Trevor was from Barnsley in Yorkshire.'He got the nickname as he kept getting run over by cars and motorbikes but survived every knockdown. For the first time in my life I felt I was part of something. Some of these men I'd only known for just over two weeks but I felt equal to them. I also realised that none of them used their own names. Which made it permissible for me to be Tom Joad, the second fastest door primer in the West and for now that would do me just fine. Strawbs arrived back from the toilet. 'Oh fuck bollox! When Keefer is sniffin none of us have a dog's chance. Women queue up for him like he's the fuckin Boxing Day sales. Looks like I've got the ugly one.' Strawbs was referring to Veronica who in my mind was very attractive and why would he want to go with her if he thought she was ugly? I didn't ask him any of this, as I had a feeling it was all bluster and part of some joke that I was yet to figure out.

It turned out that Keefer wasn't interested in Lyndsey and Lyndsey and Veronica weren't interested in anybody. They went to the Ladies together and never came back. Strawbs was moaning. 'Buying them drink all fuckin night and then they piss off! Typical!'

Keefer laughed at him. 'Maybe it's cos yer an ugly bastard, ever think of that?' Strawbs pretended he was going to hit Keefer but Keefer puckered up his lips for a kiss and Strawbs fell back laughing.

Keefer had a really stunning Norwegian girlfriend, Annouska and she arrived almost at closing time. The whole pub staring at her. She worked in a casino somewhere in the West End. We all ended up back at Keefer's place in Castletown Road, West Kensington, listening to King Crimson and Camel. It was the worst music I'd ever heard. There was one song that I did like called 'Roadhouse Blues' by a band called The Doors. I'd never heard of them before. It was also Keefer's favourite track and the two of us danced to it playing air guitar which everyone agreed I could do better than Keefer. I was introduced to tequila and after one mouthful had to run to the bathroom and be violently sick. I tried to make it to the toilet bowl but couldn't manage it and puked in the bath. Keefer cleaned it up. 'No worries mate, we've all performed the old pavement pizza at some stage of our drinking apprenticeship.'

I woke up early in the morning lying on Keefer's sofa with a warm cat on my chest purring in my face. Church bells tolled nearby, they seemed very clangy and out of tune. I'm not fond of cats and threw it off. It hissed at me and scampered under an armchair knocking over empty bottles. Apart from a horrible taste in my mouth and the smell of vomit on my clothes, I didn't feel too bad. On the way back to Dalling Road, I checked my money. I had taken £15 out with me and I was shocked to find that I'd spent almost all of it. I knew I couldn't keep doing this if I wanted to get my own place. I had looked at a few places that Patti had found for me but none of them were suitable. They were either with a family or sharing a bedroom which I didn't want.

'You can't be too choosy Emnet. This is London, it's all you can afford.'

SEVEN

IT WAS 8.30am on Sunday morning when I reached 498 Dalling Road and as I entered the front room Auntie Fiona and Patti were sitting at the table in their dressing gowns. The expression on their faces told me that this was the showdown I'd been expecting. I had prepared myself for this moment and was actually relieved the time had finally come to pack my bags. I would now be forced to look harder for a bedsit. I'd been at Nursie Towers over a month so I'd had a good run. Auntie Fiona was smoking, not a good sign. 'Sit down son.'

I sat at the table and decided to speak first. 'I went to a party with some lads from work and fell asleep on the sofa . . . I'll leave today. I might be able to stay with a fellah from work until I find somewhere. . . but thanks for letting me stay here.'

Auntie Fiona blew smoke softly at the ceiling. 'Your sister Maeve rang this morning. . . your Grandfather died yesterday . . . I'm sorry son. I always thought he was a decent man. She's going to call back at 9 o'clock.'

I heard what she said but it didn't completely land. My granda's pipe smoke suddenly drifted into the room.

Peterson's Irish Flake. A sweet earthy smell of aniseed and wood burning. I could see him polishing his Sunday black shoes. Spit and polish, spit and polish, the small brush a blur in his hand, 'The shiniest shoes in Ireland, son.' Lowering his head for me to feel the lead under his skull and the faint smell of sweat and Brylcreem on what was left of his hair. Meeting me from primary school with an apple and a piece of ginger cake. The way he used to grip my arm when he was talking to me and how he would drill up and down the back yard when he was half-drunk, using his walking stick as a rifle and imitating the English Sergeant Major. 'Bayyy da lift! Queeek Matchhhh!' and my grandmother watching him, smiling and shaking her head. 'That man's got a screw loose.'

I didn't know what to say to these two. It suddenly hit me that I didn't know them very well. I stood in silence staring at them and the longer I stared the stupider I felt. I began to blush. For some reason I wanted to tell the both of them to fuck off.

'I'm sorry son,' Auntie Fiona said again. I heard myself say. 'I'm going for a shower' and went upstairs. By the time I came out of the shower, I had made up my mind to leave Dalling Road. I didn't know where I would go but I knew I had to get away.

Maeve's voice was clear and calm. 'Granda died in his sleep. They think it was his heart. He was on tablets. Da has been drunk since it happened, everyone's buying him drink and he never refuses. He's really playing to the gallery. I just hope he doesn't show us all up and is sober for the funeral . . . which is on Wednesday.' There was a long pause and I knew the question was coming. 'Will you come home for the funeral, Emmet?'

'I don't know Maeve. I might not have a job to come back to if I do. That's the way it works over here.'

Maeve cleared her throat. 'I think you should come home. You were Granda and Grannie's favourite. They reared you for God's sake. The least you can do is carry his coffin.'

'I don't know. I'll have to see how it goes. I'm just getting started over here.' My voice sounded weak and pathetic. Why was I saying this? I wasn't convincing myself.

'Alright, you do as you please. You always do. But I'm telling you it won't go down well here. I've got to go. . . bye!' I listened to the dialling tone for a minute or so before I put the phone back on its cradle. Was I selfish? Maybe I needed to be.

I stood in the hallway with my bag packed. Auntie Fiona put her hand on my shoulder. 'You've nowhere to go son, you can stay til you find somewhere. I'm hardly going to throw you out on the street, don't be silly.'

'Thanks, Fifi but I'll head on over to a mate of mine in West Kensington and if he can't put me up, I'll come back if that's alright?'

Auntie Fiona shook her head in exasperation. Patti sucked her teeth. A sound I wasn't going to miss. I left my key on the table in the hall, opened the door and was gone. The street was Sunday quiet, and the sun had come out.

Keefer slapped me on the back, he had a habit of doing that. 'It's yer lucky day Teejay mate. Kadeem has gone back to Palestine, his brother got shot in the ass by one of those Israeli drongos. I doubt he'll be back for a while, so ya can have his room. It's at the front, you've got the traffic but it's bloody ripper for eleven quid a week. The Dunnie's upstairs on the right, same one you tried to redecorate last night!'

The room had two big windows, a wardrobe built into the wall, a massive thick rug on the wooden floor, a sink, a large bed with an iron bedstead and something called a Baby Belling, which turned out to be a small cooker. On the wall was a poster of someone called Yasser Arafat. He didn't look like a rock star. I almost cried with joy, my own room at last! I sat gently on the bed and stared at the four walls. I had only expected to sleep on Keefer's couch until I found somewhere, I couldn't believe my luck.

First thing on Monday morning, I went to see Fast Eddie and told him I wanted to go home for my granda's funeral but if it meant I might lose my job then I wouldn't go. Eddie had new glasses, brown ones with a thicker rim but his eyes were still enormous. He put the glasses on his head. 'Sorry to hear that, Grandad's can be great people. Of course ye can go home for the funeral ya fuckin eegit.'

'Thanks Eddie. I'll leave tomorrow and I'll be back on Friday.'

He nodded. 'Do ya need a sub?' Before I could answer he handed me a twenty-pound note, put his glasses back on his face and walked away quickly.

I was told by the inspector at Hammersmith tube station that I could go to Hounslow West on the Piccadilly line and from there I could get a bus direct to Heathrow Airport. He was a black man and his hair was made up of long plaits. He smiled a lot and I liked his accent, it was musical like he was singing. 'Ya can get a tube, to Hoonslow West or go rone da back der and hap an a one sevan four, to Hoonslow West and den ya get da bas straight to Heat row! Up to you which one you wan.'

This was my first time on an airplane. A stand-by ticket was almost 50% cheaper than a booked flight but it was hit and miss whether I'd get a flight or not. Fast Eddie told me to get there early and put my name down and if the first flight was full my name would automatically go on the next stand-by list.

I was lucky and managed to get on the first flight which was the 10.45am to Aldergrove Airport. The airplane was a lot smaller inside than I had imagined. The stewardesses were nice, they smiled at me a lot and said, 'Good morning sir'. I thought that was funny. I couldn't believe how quick the flight was. It seemed we had only taken off when the captain told us we would be landing in ten minutes. Apart from rendering me completely deaf, the flight was a bit of an anti- climax.

I was stopped at the security checkpoint by two men in suits. One was tall with a tired face and the other was shorter and fatter with blue veins in his nose. The tall one flashed his badge at me like the way they do in films. 'Could we just have a word please sir?'

His voice seemed to be coming from far away. I hoped my hearing would soon return. Being called *sir* twice in one day, what were the chances of that? But somehow this *sir* didn't quite have the same friendly ring to it. Being brought up as a downtrodden Catholic Fenian gypsy bastard in the North of Ireland meant that I had it drilled into me from an early age to be suspicious of men in suits, especially policemen in suits asking questions. Never sign anything, don't let them take your fingerprints – it's illegal – be polite, stay calm, say as little as possible. These people are the enemy and the only reason they are talking to the likes of you in the first place is they either want to plant something on you, torture you for information, kick the living shit out of you, or throw you in prison for having an Irish face.

'Where are you travelling to today sir?'

'I'm going home for a funeral.'

'Can we ask is that a relative sir?

'Yes, my grandfather.'

'Where's home sir?'

'Carricktown, County Tyrone.'

'Will you be staying at a private address or a hotel?'

'Private address.'

'And where would that be?'

'Tullybern Cottage, Burren Road.'

'And where are you travelling from today sir?'

'London.'

'Do you have an address in London?'

'Yep. 265 Castletown Road, West Kensington.'

'Could we see some identification please sir?'

'Em. . . like what?'

'Like a passport, driver's license, credit card.'

'No, I don't have any of those.'

'Do you have any form of identification on you sir?'

'No.'

'Can you tell me your name please sir?'

'Tom jo. . . Emmet McCrudden.'

'Sorry I didn't catch that.'

'Tom Joe Emmet McCrudden.'

'Are you saying Tom Joe Emmet McCrudden?'

'Yeah, but I eh, I don't use the Tom Joe anymore, it's just Emmet, Emmet McCrudden.'

The taller one sighed. 'Can you just come with us sir and once we've established who you are you can continue your journey.'

I was taken into a small windowless room with a table, two chairs and a green bench against the wall. Sitting on the table was a plastic jug of water and a plastic glass. They

101

didn't look clean. Veiny Nose told me to sit so I sat. The taller one took out a notebook and pen.

'Have you ever been in trouble with the police Mr McCrudden?'

'No.'

'Are you sure?'

'I think I'd remember that.'

Veiny Nose leaned in a little too close to me. 'Just answer the question!'

'No, I haven't been in any trouble with the police.'

The taller one handed me the notebook. 'I'd like you to write your name and address in London, the address you'll be staying in Carricktown, the name of your dead grandfather and the time and place of the funeral. I'd like you to write it in capitals.' I did what he asked. He stared at it for some time and then put it quickly in his jacket pocket.

'Have you ever been involved with any political organis-ation Mr McCrudden, civil rights movement, anything like that?'

'No.'

'Have you been on any marches?'

'No.'

'Do you know anybody who may have been on these marches, friends of yours maybe?'

'No.'

'What do you think of these marches Mr McCrudden?' I wasn't expecting that question.

'I think it's a free country, people can march if they want.'

Veiny Nose pulled up a chair and sat beside me. 'And what about the wanton destruction of property and the killing of policemen and soldiers, do you agree with that Mr McCrudden'

I didn't answer.

'I asked you a question.'

'I don't have an opinion on that.'

'I bet you fucking do!'

The tall one held up his hand to Veiny Nose, a gesture that said *Cool down*. Veiny Nose was obviously trying to intimidate me. Of course he couldn't have known how pathetic that attempt was compared to being throttled by my drunken father. Or having the crap kicked out of me on a daily basis by five well-dressed clever Catholic school boys. Or being rabbit-punched by Master McKenna. Veiny Nose got up and lit a cigarette. The tall one poured a glass of the dirty water and pushed it towards me. I ignored it.

'Why did you leave Northern Ireland and move to London?'

'To find work.'

'How old are you Mr McCrudden?'

I hesitated. 'Seventeen.'

'What's your date of birth?'

'15th August 1955.'

Veiny Nose left the room like he suddenly needed the toilet. The taller one opened the door slowly and looked at me.

'We'll have to check all this out and if it all adds up you

can be on your way. We can't be too careful Mr McCrudden with all the shite that's going on here. Sit tight.'

After an hour I tried the door, it was locked. I sat there for another hour and ten minutes. My deafness had gone but had been replaced by a ringing in my ears. Eventually the taller one opened the door and beckoned me with a jerk of his head. 'On your way! And if I was you sonny, I'd get myself some form of ID. Save yourself a lot of trouble in the future.'

There was something about his accent, the pronunciation of *sonny* and the way he twisted his mouth that reminded me of Master McKenna. McKenna was the only other person ever to call me sonny. I must have been staring at him. His face darkened. 'Is there something you'd like to say to me Mr McCrudden?'

There was a lot I wanted to say to him, like how come it took you over two hours to find out who I was? And how about an apology? 'No. There's nothing I want to say to you.'

I had only been away from Carricktown for less than six weeks but it seemed far longer. As the bus rose over Gort Hill and the town came into view, everything seemed smaller and grubby, and an inexplicable sadness washed over me. I had the odd experience of being familiar with everything I saw, every building, every face, even the dogs in the street, but also feeling like a stranger.

Drunken Daddy was asleep on the sofa, he stank of stale drink, dried piss and tobacco. One eye was closed, the other fluttering and half open. There was a soft whistling sound coming from his chest like a child's toy and a little bubble of snot blew in and out of one nostril. He had aged in six weeks, the skin red and blotchy bulging around his neck and chin. I wished this was his funeral and not granda's. The younger kids Fergal and Connor were excited to see me. I had bought them sweets at the airport, bags of Liquorice All Sorts and packets of Spangles that had been in the half-price bucket.

Fergal stared at me. . . 'Liquorice All Sorts? Where's me rifle?' I said they didn't sell rifles at the airport, but I would buy him one before I left.

'Promise me Emmy.'

'I promise.'

Robert, Sean and Aisling had been farmed out to different aunts and uncles and were now at an age where they could fend for themselves. The house was spotless. Maeve and Noreen had cleaned the place from top to bottom and bought some bits and pieces of furniture, they had also bought food for the reception: sausage rolls, pork pies, ham and cheese sandwiches which was all laid out neatly on a table in the front room. I joked with them that I had never seen so much food in this house before. It had been decided that granda's coffin was to be taken straight to the church and people could pay their respects there. There was to be no wake. Maeve said she didn't trust Drunken Daddy not to make a show of us.

Maeve smiled at me. 'I got the job at the carpet factory by the way, thanks for asking.'

I had completely forgotten she had applied for the bookkeeping job but I was genuinely happy for her and told her as much. If anyone deserved to better herself it was Maeve. Noreen had also found herself a job in Anderson's shoe shop and between them they had paid the electric bill and got the lights back on. So despite the useless heap of shit snoring on the sofa, things had improved. When my father woke up he was still groggy-drunk and had that shaky nervous bloodshot look about him that meant he was desperate for another drink.

'So yer back,' was all he said in my direction. It wasn't a question so I didn't answer. Maeve told him to have a wash and get dressed. There was hot water simmering in the big pan on the range. The funeral was in six hours. He searched all his pockets, his eyes scanned the room, he looked behind the sofa pulling the cushions up, and started opening cupboards. Maeve grabbed his arm.

'There's no drink in this house. You promised me.'

He pulled away roughly. 'I'm not a fuckin child to be scolded. My father is dead. I need a drink. Where's that naggin of whiskey?'

Maeve told him he'd already drank it although if I knew Maeve, she had poured it down the sink. He caught me glaring at him. 'What the fuck are you gawpin at?'

I didn't respond or avert my gaze. I knew I had the

measure of him now and I thought if he makes a move towards me or any of the girls, I'll break his neck. I could feel the anger rising within me, years of pent-up rage and resentment. He stared at me, picked up the boiling water in the pan and stormed off to fill the tin bath in the scullery. We could hear him banging around in there, talking to himself.

'1972 and I'm still washing meself in a fucking tin bath! Them Orange cunts in Stormont will all rot in hell!'

What?. . . What the hell?. . . The Union Jack? Was that the Union Jack? The British flag, that emblem of triumphalism that had been flapped in our faces for over a hundred years? Yes it was and it had been draped across my grandfather's coffin. Three old men wearing black berets with war medals pinned to their chests stood to attention beside the coffin. One of them produced a bugle and began to play what I assumed was supposed to be the 'Last Post' although it sounded nothing like the 'Last Post', more like Willy Coulton's Ice Cream van. I looked at Maeve, her expression was a mixture of shock and hilarity. I knew she was about to crack up laughing. I had to look away from her otherwise she was going to start me off. This was ridiculous. I stared at the floor and whispered 'Maeve, what's going on?' She held her hankie over her face, pretending to cry (*the devil's tickle!*). The strangled cat version of the 'Last Post' floated slowly and painfully up towards the rafters.

'They're Granda's friends from The British Legion,' said

Maeve when she'd composed herself. 'They asked could they come to the funeral but they never said anything about this!' The church began to fill slowly with people, my grandfather was well liked in this town. The priest arrived, a young priest I didn't recognize, and began the funeral Mass. He concluded by saying a few nice words about my grandfather and then it was time for me, my father, my Uncle Brendan, my two cousins on my mother's side, Daniel and Martin Ward and Paddy McGee, the landlord of my granda's local pub, to carry the coffin down the aisle to the hearse. I grabbed my father by the arm. 'We have to get rid of that flag.' My sober father put his hand over mine. It was amazing the change that only a few hours off the drink had on him. The red blotches on his neck and cheeks were gone. His voice was calm. 'This is what your grandfather wanted. I'm not happy about it either. But it's staying on.'

The undertakers manoeuvred the coffin onto our shoulders. A recording of my granda's favourite song the 'The Flower of Sweet Strabane' sung by Maggie Barry played as we began the slow march towards the hearse. He was heavy, the weight of him, a sadness crushing down on me. The sun was shining outside the church doors and far in the distance I could see the tops of the trees surrounding the Burren Fort, which made me think about Rosie – and then there she was to the right of me. I caught her eye and she smiled, a sad *I'm sorry* smile. My heart leapt inside my chest and I felt guilty at this sudden feeling of elation.

As we approached the back of the hearse, two men in balaclavas came out of nowhere and whipped the Union Jack from the coffin shouting the IRA slogan *Tiocfaidh ar la! (Our day will come)*. I got a good look at the eyes of one of them through the wonky holes in the home-made balaclava and I couldn't believe it. My father suddenly broke away from me and grabbed hold of the flag. We were all unbalanced and the coffin lurched to my left crashing into the side of the church door. Someone, I don't know who, placed both hands on the coffin and managed to stop it from falling off my shoulder. I could hear people shouting, 'Fuck off ye bastards!' And more shouts of *Tiocfaidh ar la!* Through the melee I could see Maeve and my father in a tug of Union Jack war with the balaclava men and then a ripping sound as the flag tore down the middle. Noreen jumped into the affray punching one of the balaclava boys on the side of the head, other mourners joined in the fight and eventually the Balaclava Two leapt over the church hedge and ran off.

The rest of the funeral was a bit of a blur. The last image I have is of one of the old soldiers, a tear in his eye, standing at the graveside carefully folding up the torn mud-streaked Union Jack. When we got back to Tullybern for the reception it was all anyone could talk about. I had one thing on my mind, and she was standing on the other side of the room talking to Maeve. Such an easy unselfconscious beauty, those dimples and the way she tossed her hair back. Maeve saw me coming, smiled and left me alone with her. I tried my best to be cool. She made a funny puzzled face, 'Is that a suit?'

I looked down at my black jacket and trousers. 'The jacket might be from a suit and the trousers might be from another suit but no, bought them in a rush.'

Rosie looked around to check no one was listening. 'What the hell was Mickey Peach thinking?'

This took me by surprise, so she had spotted him as well. But I had to be sure, so I played it by ear. 'What do you mean?'

She made a face. 'Oh c'mon Emmet you saw him as well as I did. Him and that eejit Jackie Westwood. God help us if that's all the IRA can recruit.'

I didn't really want to have this conversation in the front living room. 'Do you want to go for a walk up the Burren?'

'No. I'm in my best dress. Let's go to my house. All our lot are in Donegal.'

I didn't believe in Heaven, but I knew that being naked with Rosie was better than being there. She placed her hands on my chest and pushed me back gently, 'Not so fast. . . not so fast.' My face was buried in her long black hair. 'Take your time. . . kiss me.' I kissed her and as we made love, I felt myself leave my body and I never wanted to come back from whatever place she had taken me to.

After it was over, I felt I was coming down slowly in a parachute. I wasn't sure if I was really feeling this or if I was purposely creating the feeling to prolong the moment. I noticed that dusk had crept into the room. We lay entwined and a sudden wave of sad happiness engulfed me, it was so overwhelming I started to cry. I couldn't stop myself. I kept apologising, 'I'm sorry. . . I'm so sorry'. I felt like such an idiot. What the hell was wrong with me? Rosie just stroked my hair and shooshed me like a baby which made me feel worse.

After an interminable silence, she turned to me and said, 'How are we going to get Mickey Peach out of the IRA?'

I was more than a little annoyed at this. I wasn't expecting her train of thought to be focused on Mickey Peach. 'I don't think it's any of our business. It's his choice.'

She leaned up on her elbow. 'I thought he was your best friend?'

I didn't want to talk about Mickey Peach, especially not here, at this glorious unforgettable moment in my life. 'Do we have to talk about this now?'

She lay back down. 'No. OK, sorry.' She smiled and ran her finger down my nose. Another long silence but this one wasn't awkward. 'When are you going back?'

This was something else I didn't want to talk about but knew I couldn't avoid the question. 'Tomorrow.' She sighed, turned towards me wrapped one leg over my side and kissed me like her life depended on it. . . and we were off again, to that special place.

Before I left we agreed that I would come back later that evening and spend the night with her. She would cook me breakfast but wouldn't walk me to the bus stop. She didn't want to say goodbye. She promised she would try and come to London in the summer. She wanted to be a journalist. Everything felt a little too calm, too reasonable. I think we both knew that if this wasn't the end of the relationship, it was the beginning of the end. Even if she came to London, there wasn't any road for us to walk down in the future. She never mentioned she received my letter and I didn't ask. Tony Mulgrew's name never came up which suited me down to the ground.

The Rifleman Winchester came with a cowboy hat, a holster and a handgun. Eamon Rafferty owned the toy shop which also, for some inexplicable reason, sold wallpaper and oilcloth. He also sold fireworks which were now banned because of the troubles. He said the rifle was the last one he had in stock, as the Government were now considering banning toy guns as well and he sold it to me for half price.

When I got back to Tullybern Cottage, Mickey Peach was waiting for me at the front gate. I held up the box with the Winchester rifle emblazoned on it. 'Here I've brought you something for the arms struggle.'

Mickey was in no mood for jokes. He looked different, I wasn't sure in what way, couldn't put my finger on it. He got straight to the point. 'Why didn't you tell me you were goin to London?' His tone and body shape was aggressive and pushy, not the Mickey I knew.

'Mickey, I didn't want to tell anybody in case they tried

to talk me out of it. I mean, they wouldn't have been able to talk me out of it, but I didn't want any hassle. I just wanted to go!'

He shrugged his shoulders. 'You coudda said somethin. I wouldn't have tried to talk you out of it. I'm not yer fuckin girlfriend. I'm yer mate. . . at least I thought I was. If ye didn't wanna write for *The Republican News*, then you shoudda said. Instead of just running away like a baby!' He spat on the street, stuck his neck out like a cheap gangster, grabbed his lapels and pulled on them, shifted inside his jacket like the way you do when you first try it on in the shop.

This was Mickey Peach. We went to primary school together, had our first drink together. He was the only one who never laughed at my hobnailed boots or took the piss when I had to do PE in my vest and underpants. We knew everything about each other. He had fought my corner and I had fought his. But today he had tried to ruin and disrupt my granda's funeral and now here he was being intimidating, trying to play the hard man. I was hurt and a sudden anger took hold of me.

'Well, I thought you were my mate as well, so what the fuck were you doing today at my granda's funeral. What was all that about?'

'I was following orders.' I burst out laughing. Sat down on the wall beside the gate and just laughed.

'Jesus Mickey. Can you hear yourself?'

'Don't laugh at me, Emmet. What's goin on in this country is no fuckin laughing matter. People are dyin and some of us want to do something about it and then there's other people who just want to fuck off to England.'

I stood up from the wall and we faced each other. 'He was my granda. He wanted a Union Jack on his coffin and you or nobody else had the right to rip it off!'

He started poking me in the chest with his finger to emphasise every point. 'Emmet, you know as well as I do what the Union Jack represents. It's everywhere like a fuckin plague, so there's one place that it definitely shouldn't be and that's inside a Catholic church!'

I took a deep breath. 'Mickey if you poke me one more time, I swear to God. . .' He stepped back, looked at me and then sat on the wall. 'I took an oath Emmet. I joined this organisation because I want to change things. I saw what happened in Derry. I was there. . . they shot people down like dogs. . . we tried marching. It's no use, everybody knows that. I promised I would do whatever they asked me to do. They knew I was yer mate and that's why I was chosen to do it. It was a test. I didn't want to fuckin do it and I know there's going to be other stuff that I don't want to do. . . but I'm in this thing. . . and I can't be half in it.' He looked at me almost pleadingly and suddenly I had my Mickey Peach back. We sat for a while and I let the moment pass. Mickey stood up.

'Do ye fancy goin up to the Burren. I hid a few cans and a half bottle of wine up there. A farewell drink?'

It was great to be back with the Mickey Peach I knew. We got drunk and I told him all about Keefer and Auntie Fiona and Patti and the dead parrot and Fast Eddie. I exaggerated a lot of it, especially how much I was earning. I did this to try and tempt him to come back to London with me. But the experience in Derry had affected him deeply and I knew he was lost to the cause. Before we parted he gave me a drunken hug, called me a Union-Jack-loving-cunt and staggered off towards Gort Hill. He never could hold his drink.

I sat at the large wooden table in Rosie's kitchen and marvelled at how shiny it was. The dark swirly natural knots of wood looked like they had been specially designed. There were table mats, the milk was in a jug. The knives and forks placed neatly beside white napkins. Two glasses of fresh orange juice. Salt and pepper in small crystal containers. Rosie wore a plastic apron with Heinz 57 written on it. In our house we usually ate everything on our lap. I watched her cook the breakfast, turning it carefully in the pan with a wooden spatula. For some reason the smell of the bacon made me sad. I knew that everything about this moment was perfect, but also a kind of fantasy. Even if I stayed in Carricktown I would never be accepted into this family. Rosie's father Henry Byrne was a solicitor and her mother Marie May taught the harp at a posh girl's school in Belfast.

Rosie's brother Ben was already at Queen's University doing a Structural Engineering degree. Once as a joke, or maybe he wasn't joking, Jackie Westwood had said to me, 'Well, I know what you want from Rosie Byrne, but what the fuck does she want from you?'

Westwood was cruelly talented at zoning in on everyone's doubts and weaknesses. But it was something that had crossed my mind many times. I had been going out with her for two-and-a -half years and this was the first time I'd been inside her house. I had only met her parents once and that was with lots of other people at one of Rosie's birthday parties. I wasn't even sure if her parents knew I was going out with her. There was an embarrassing incident between Rosie's father and my father, when my father had shat himself outside Loughran's bakery. He had been drinking for three days and wasn't eating anything. As he passed Loughran's he almost passed out and had to hang on to the side of the awning which began to come apart with the weight of him. His legs slowly splaying as he desperately clung on. Rosie's father left the queue and went out to help but quickly backed away covering his face with a hankie as the smell overcame him. My father started shouting at him. 'What are you looking at Byrne? I suppose you've never shit yerself before ye swanky cunt ye!' I was also in that queue and wished I was dead.

Jimmy Loughran looked down at me and said, 'I think you should take yer father home son.'

I walked out of the bakery, my face scarlet with shame to

the sound of my father's loud voice bellowing after me, 'I'm as good as any of them cunts! Don't walk away from me. I'm yer fucking father!'

Rosie suddenly turned away from the pan and looked at me. 'A penny for your thoughts?'

'I was just thinking, what would your parents say if they came back now and found you cooking me breakfast?'

Rosie adopted a perfect southern American drawl. 'Whale ma Diddy wid git his shatgun and blow yir pretty head ride off, fer de-filing his daw-tur!' She was very good at accents and it always made me laugh when she did it. I waited a moment.

'I'm serious, what would they think?' She dished the breakfast onto two plates that had been warming in the oven.

'I love my parents. I really do. But they're snobs and think that no-one in Carricktown is good enough for me. They call you 'that McCrudden boy'. Even though I've told them your name a hundred times. I think the fact you passed the test to get into St Malachy's means something. They know you can't be an idiot. My mother used to keep asking me if it was serious. I always played it down Emmet. That was the easiest way for me to deal with it. . . She doesn't ask any more now that you've gone to London. . . Do you want brown sauce?' I nodded. Rosie bent and rummaged in a cupboard, came up with a bottle of Daddie's, unopened.

I couldn't help but laugh. 'You keep it hidden in the cupboard and bring it out when a peasant arrives?'

She laughed but I could see she was also stung. 'Oh fuck off Emmet!'

We ate our breakfast in silence. I couldn't figure out what kind of silence it was. Finally I said, 'What do you see in me Rosie?'

Rosie puffed her cheeks in exasperation. 'Jesus, Emmet, you need to get rid of that chip off your shoulder! It's not your fault you come from a big family and your Da's a lunatic. You're smart Emmet, you helped me with my English essay and I got an A-minus. You should never have left school. You're not like that Westwood lot. You're sensitive, you know when I'm in a mood and you let me be. . . You make me laugh with your stupid jokes. . . and. . . I love your dark curly hair and blue eyes. . . It's not too late to take your A levels and try and go to University. Do an English degree.' She chewed her bacon and glared at me. 'OK, is your ego massaged enough now?' I was about to say something but she interrupted. 'Just eat your breakfast!'

She said she wasn't going to walk me to the bus stop but changed her mind. A *saft rain,* as my granda used to call it, had begun to fall gently. I could smell chimney smoke and hear cows mooing in the fields behind the church. Two things I would never smell or hear in London. I could see the familiar blue and white of the Ulster Bus in the distance. Rosie grabbed me and hugged me tightly. We kissed. I didn't know if the salt was her tears or mine. Some gobshite blew his horn and let a *Yeoooo!* out of him. His fellow passengers guffawing from the rolled down windows, cigarettes sticking out of the side of their mouths, hair slicked back. Farmers all of them, that was for sure. Rosie squeezed my hands, 'Safe Journey' and off she went in that little half-run that girls do with their arms folded across their chests. I watched as she rounded the side of Faulkner's the Chemist and was gone.

I left a note for Fergal to check under the stairs, apologised that I couldn't find a rifle, but had bought him a pair of woolly socks to keep his feet warm in bed. I imagined his little face lighting up when he found the Winchester.

EIGHT

KEEFER WAS AS GOOD as his word. During the lunch break he began to teach me how to lay bricks. All I had to do in return was, every other day, go one stop to Earls Court on the tube from West Kensington and buy him four packets of Tasty Toobs and two packets of Tim Tams. These, he assured me, were local delicacies only eaten by Aussies.

'Go to the little Thai grocers opposite the Kings Head. They do all things Aussie. They never have anything left by the time I get there after work. You do that for me mate and I'll teach you to build the fuckin world!' Tasty Toobs were tube-shaped chicken-flavoured crisps and Tim Tams were malted biscuits with a sweet creamy filling in the middle. That seemed like a fair enough deal to me.

For the first few days all I was doing was learning how to spread the mortar – or *muck* as Keefer called it – along a row of bricks. Slicing and rolling the muck off the muckboard onto the trowel and then dragging it along the row of bricks drawing the tip of the trowel back along its length, all in two flowing movements. This created an even dip for the brick to sit in. Too much muck and it wouldn't work, it had to be just right. This was a lot harder than it looked but I persevered and after a week or so I could do it. Then came the *buttering* of the brick. Which meant putting the muck on the brick itself. This was done by picking up just enough muck on the tip of the trowel then flicking my wrist so the muck would stay on, next I had to hold the brick so it pointed downwards at a forty five degree angle and butter all four edges of the top of the brick. Keefer taught me how to read a tape measure and the difference between centimetres, millimetres and metres. 'Feet and fucking inches, that's Victorian. You can forget that shit! Two bricks laid together should measure no more than 470 mil and ya bed should always be 10 mil. Keep to that and you can't go wrong.' After about six weeks, I was allowed to *jump on the line* which meant going in between two brickies who were building a straight wall. There were probably fifty bricks in a row and the others would have laid twenty-three bricks each to my four bricks. I kept hitting the string line with the tip of my trowel, this was called *banjo playing* and I got stick for this every day from Keefer who kept doing the tune from 'Deliverance', *Der der lit dit dit dit dit dit dern.* But four months later, I was up to fifteen bricks, and by December I was learning to lay face bricks and build corners. Fast Eddie also used to give me shit as he walked past. 'Don't ye think there's enough fuckin chancers in this game Keefer?'

Rosie never came in August. She wrote to say that things weren't great between her parents. She thought they might separate. Her father decided they should all go to France for the half-term holiday and try to patch things up. She said she missed me and hoped I was happy. She wrote again in November and told me how much she was enjoying university, asked if I was coming home for Christmas? She never mentioned her parents. My eighteenth birthday came and went. I never told anyone, there didn't seem much point.

Keefer, Annouska and I spent Christmas day and Boxing Day at the flat in Castletown Road. Annouska bought a Christmas tree and decorated it with stuff she cut out and painted heself. They were better than the decorations you could buy in the shop. She told me that the Norwegians had invented the Christmas tree and gave the idea to the English and the rest of the world. She also cooked a turkey with roasted potatoes. It was the first time I had tasted turkey but I didn't let on. I thought it was OK but not half as good as Kentucky Fried Chicken.

Annouska was probably the most physically perfect woman I had ever seen. Her hair was blonder than blonde and reached to her waist. She had evenly tanned skin, but it didn't look like she got it from the sun, it looked like she was born that way. Her lips were pink and full and her teeth perfect and white, big deep-blue eyes. I don't think she ever wore a bra; she liked Tee shirts or blouses and it was hard for me not to stare at her nipples. She wore tight-fitting jeans or sometimes black slacks that accentuated every curve of her body below the waist. She wore some kind of perfume that made me lightheaded. I was shy around her and tongue-tied. Keefer would tease me, 'Hey Nooski. Teejay's in love with you! I'd better watch it cos he's gonna clean my clock any day now!'

Annouska would laugh, grab hold of me, swing me around in a dance and say, 'Yes! Maybe Teejay and me, we will run away together.' And I would redden like a tomato. I hated the fact that I blushed, my stupid face was always betraying me.

I hadn't consciously decided not to go home for Christmas, I just didn't plan anything or write back to anybody. I drifted in my mind and let Christmas arrive. It seemed the easiest thing to do. It was a certainty that my father would be drunk for the whole time. I had reached the end of my tether with him and I was seriously concerned that I may actually kill him. I knew there was no future with Rosie and I felt it was less of a heartache not to see her than see her, make love to her and then have to leave her again. I also didn't want to know what Mickey Peach was up to. I hated the fact he was politically involved. I didn't really know what Ireland was supposed to mean to me. It was my home of course, my place of birth. I didn't agree with the British being there, but it was a place that I'd always wanted to get away from. It felt like a prison.

Fast Eddie made a comment to me once about Ireland when he was drunk which really chimed. He said, 'Ireland to me is like being at a best friend's wedding. You know you have to be there. You know the craic is good and you can act the bollocks and make a fool of yerself, but by the end of the day you've had enough and want to get as far away from these people as possible.' That summed it up for me. I had come to London to become someone else, and I was never going to be able to achieve that if I kept going back every five minutes to be reminded of who I was.

The three-day week that had been imposed on the country didn't affect Irish sub-contractors in the building trade. We were all still working six days a week. Fast Eddie informed me it's the Trade Unions' fault. 'They're all lazy fuckers who want something for nothing and that Ted Heath is a cunt. Just because he likes it up the ass he wants to fuck the country up the ass as well. The sooner Wilson gets back in the better although he's a cunt as well, they're all cunts!' I'm not sure how well-informed Fast Eddie is about the political situation; he tells me all the time that he doesn't listen to the news or read a newspaper. 'I don't listen to them lying fuckers on the news or read all that propaganda shite! I make up me own mind about these things son!' England does seem to be in a mess. There was a power cut on Sunday night, all the lights went out in Castletown Road and we had no heating for three hours. Brought back some lovely memories for me. And now there's rubbish bags beginning to pile up on the streets.

Letters arrive from home. I recognise Rosie and Maeve's handwriting but I don't read them. It's unbearably hard to throw them in the bin but I know I have to. I'm well aware that my heart strings are still very tuggable and I have to guard against that if I want to achieve my goal. Spring is here and my wages have gone up to £70 per week. I'm taking Madge McGuckian's advice and putting away money in my post office book. I wasn't as fast as Keefer or any of the other brickies on site but my work is neat and precise. Fast Eddie, Strawbs, Keefer, Crash Test and about eight or nine more of us have been transferred from the North End Road site to another site two miles up the road near Kensington Olympia. The canteen is clean and new with chrome tables and heating and a very varied menu, although I am going to miss Maureen who used to give me extra slices of bacon and the biggest piece of sponge cake. There are showers also. We're building offices and it's my first time laying concrete blocks. It's hard work but I take to it like a duck to water and actually think it's technically easier than laying bricks.

The nearest pub is imaginatively named the Kensington. It has jazz music on a Friday and Saturday night. We all bring a set of clean clothes, have a shower and go to Harry's Caff up the road for our dinner. I smoke my first joint in the toilets of the Kensington and finally find out what a reefer is. I thought Keefer was going to have a cardiac arrest when I tell him I thought he was called Reefer Keefer because he was from Australia and lived near the Great Barrier Reef. He reels around the toilet almost screeching with laughter, 'Fuckin hell Teejay! Oh my Good God! I don't need ganja when your around mate you've defo got a few roos loose in the top paddock!'

Dope makes me giggle at everything for a while, but I'm exhausted afterwards with bloodshot eyes and when I look in the mirror I see my father. So I quickly decide it's not for me and stick to Kronenbourg.

Jazz music isn't really my thing. Fast Eddie likes it but that's because he's nearly forty years old. But the band that played at the Kensington on one of those Saturday nights in April 1974 were an R&B outfit called Dr Feelgood and none of us had ever seen anything like them. The lead singer didn't say much, just got on with it, and the intensity of his harmonica playing was incredible. He sang with a gruff anger in his voice and had a *Fuck you* attitude that I could relate to. I also never saw any performer sweat so much. The lead guitarist walked up and down the stage staring like a mad bastard at everyone. They were also very down to earth and would have a pint with us after the gig. I became a fan. The lead singer was called Lee and the mad bastard was called Wilko. I learned later that wasn't their real names, my kind of people.

I would search the *New Musical Express* every week to find out where they were playing. Dr Feelgood were so popular at the Kensington that they moved the jazz to a Sunday and booked rock bands on the Friday and Saturday. Other pubs around the area started to do the same. The Red Cow and The Clarendon Hotel in Hammersmith. The

Nashville Rooms in West Kensington, Golden Lion in Putney and the Greyhound in Fulham Palace Road. I loved this music scene. I really knew nothing about the blues before I saw these bands. I thought Dr Feelgood wrote all their own stuff – in fact they did write some songs but mostly it was their versions of old blues numbers like 'Dust my Broom' and 'Mad Man Blues'. Keefer, Crash Test and Strawbs were more into Prog Rock which I hated, so quite often I would go off on my own to see bands like Ducks Deluxe, The Kursaal Flyers, Kilburn and the High Roads, and Bees Make Honey. I became an expert, knew every member, and could sing along to all the songs. I started to meet new people, other fans like Bingo Tidy and his girlfriend Lou Nelson. They published a music paper every week called *The Big Fret*. It was mostly for fans and they sold it at gigs for thirty pence a copy. I plucked up the courage and asked Bingo if I could write an article for it. Told him how English was my best subject at school. Suggested I could write about how I felt about the pub scene, which band was my favourite and why. He looked at me and grinned. *The Big Fret* was very popular and always sold out at gigs but I knew I could write as well if not better than some of the articles I'd read in there. 'Yeah, OK,' Bingo said at last, 'I'll give ya a shot. Five hundred words no more.'

I spent the whole of the next week writing it. Of course I got a lot of stick from all the lads. 'Oooh he's a music journo now boys. Hey Teejay, you know there's only one tit in pretentious.'

Bingo was from a Caribbean Island called Antigua. He was a very well dressed, tall rangy guy with a leather pork pie hat, short hair, a lisp and little round gold glasses. Lou was a small redhead from Glasgow. I could understand Bingo better than I could Lou, her accent was impossible. Bingo told me he really preferred reggae. I had no idea what reggae was. Bingo laughed and sucked through his teeth, exactly the same sound that Patti used to make. 'I will give you a record to listen to.' He reached into his bag and handed me an LP called 'Screaming Target' by Big Youth. 'You won't understand it at first but keep listening, and you'll soon get in the gawoove.'

I really wanted to like it. I tried my best to get into the groove with Big Youth and Screaming Target. I played it over and over on Keefer's record player. He wasn't happy. 'Fuckin reggae shit all sounds the same just like you Micks with ya fuckin fiddly dee.' I might as well have been trying to learn double algebra. I couldn't get into it at all.

When I told Bingo he laughed and said, 'Maybe you jus need to see some live?'

Bingo and Lou were very happy with my article. The heading read PROG ROCK IS DEAD. THE FUTURE IS FEELGOOD: *By the time some spaced-out Prog Rock fan had listened to the first elongated ass-numbingly boring first chord of Tangerine Dream's soundscape, Dr Feelgood had played five songs and each of those songs had taken my breath away and stopped my heart. . .* The article continued in this vein for another thousand words, double what Bingo said I could write. I took it home and read it twenty times. Keefer and the lads all read it and of course took the piss 'Shittin on our fuckin music? Who did you pay to write this for you, must have cost you a bomb?' I really wanted to send it to Rosie but I had ignored her for six months. She probably wouldn't want to speak to me and I wouldn't blame her.

The landlord installed a pay phone in the hallway which everyone got very excited about. There was a queue around the landings for the first few weeks until the novelty wore off and people started to complain about it ringing at all hours of the day and night. I decided I'd better phone Auntie Fiona and let her know I'd found a place. I realised it was bad manners just to ignore her. She asked me for the number which I gave her but I hoped she wouldn't be checking up on me all the time. She seemed pleased to hear from me and wished me well.

One evening on my way back from the launderette I could hear Keefer having an argument with his father on the phone, I could tell straight away by his tone that it was serious. The pain in his voice, trying to get past that lump in his throat. I knew that sound only too well.

'Why is she there Dad? What the fuck have you done?. . . That place will kill her. . . No. . . you had no fuckin right to make that decision without talkin to me and Julie about it first. . . Hello!. . . Hello!'

Keefer slams the phone down, 'Fuckin bastard!' Stomps back up the stairs, doors slamming.

I wait for a few minutes before I go up. On the way past his room I can hear Pink Floyd being played very loudly. 'Dark Side of the Moon'. The phone rings from the hallway, I let it ring for a few minutes. No-one is answering it so I go back down pick up the receiver.

'Tom, it's Bingo, listen man ya wanna come to a gig tonight with me and Lou? think ya might enjoy.'

'OK, where is it?'

'Stoke Newington, a club called Phebes. He spells it out P.H.E.B.E.S. Just ask for me at the door.'

Stoke Newington was a pain in the ass to get to from West Kensington and after nearly an hour and a half of messing around on tube trains and overground trains I was beginning to regret my decision. I finally find the place but have to get off at Dalston Kingsland station and then walk for another twenty minutes up Stoke Newington Road which seemed like the longest road in London. Bingo meets me at the door and takes me upstairs. The place is packed with mostly West Indians, there was a few white people but not many. Bingo hands me a cold bottle of beer and flashes a big smile. 'Ya got here just in time, Rye is about to pafam.' Lou gives me a kiss on the cheek and says, 'Yer gonnae huv a baw heir wee mon. Roy's fuckin stoatin a telt ye.' The only

130

word I could recognise was Roy. I had no clue about the rest so I just smiled and said yeah.

The Roy in question was someone called Roy Shirley. He sang with a five-piece band and was an extraordinary performer. I couldn't understand anything he said other than the chorus which was *Rocksteady* but what I did get from him and from the audience around me was the feeling of sheer joy. Everyone was smiling and shouting and cheering. The atmosphere was the complete opposite of a Dr Feelgood gig. Roy was on his back at one point scrambling around like a cockroach on its shell trying to get up. Then he was walking on his knees like one of those mad American Evangelist preachers. The crowd in the small room going completely mental. I couldn't help but get caught up with it and found myself singing along *Rockstay-eh-dayyyyy!* At the end of the evening Bingo gave me a lift to Victoria station and said I could write an article about Roy for *The Big Fret* if I wanted to. I really enjoyed the evening and thought I would go again, but I didn't get the same adrenalin rush as I did with a Feelgood or a Ducks Deluxe gig. My mind was open on the subject.

I step out of Bingo's green Volkswagen Beetle wave goodbye and head for Victoria underground station hoping I haven't missed the last train. As I enter the station, I think, just for a split second I can hear a voice in the distance calling 'Emmet!' I figure I must be mistaken and continue walking to the ticket machine. 'Emmet, Emmet is that you?' I turn around and see a thin woman in a black coat with a pink scarf around her neck coming towards me, she stops and loosens the scarf. 'Emmet?'

I stare at her. I know it's her, but I need to stare at her to gather my thoughts. 'Ma?. . . Jesus!'

She hugs me tightly, whispering, 'Oh my God. Oh my God' repeatedly under her breath.

NINE

MY MOTHER LIVES in Turnham Green in Chiswick, four stops from West Kensington. She works part-time in the kitchen of The Holiday Inn hotel in Victoria. We have the 'Isn't it a small world' conversation. She's surprised at how tall and muscly I've become, said she'd only recognised me by my walk. We just manage to catch the last train to Richmond. She cried a lot and kept apologising. Her biggest fear was that we would hate her for leaving us. I assured her none of us hated her, we all understood why she left. She said it was easier to cut all ties with us, she couldn't live with my father anymore and knew if she contacted us, she could be persuaded to come back and if she had come back, would probably have ended up either killing herself or my father. I could relate to that. Drunken Daddy was definitely an easy man to want to kill.

She wanted to hear all the news. I didn't say that I had also cut all ties with everyone, so told her what I knew about Maeve and Noreen's new jobs, Granda's death. How I had become a bricklayer, about Auntie Fiona and Patti. She said that had been common knowledge for years but no one had ever spoken about it. She scribbled her address on a tissue with an eyebrow pencil and then blurted out that she was living with someone, a nice man called Kenny McDonald. She asked if I would like to come around for lunch on Sunday? I said I would. We hugged again and I could feel her bones beneath the black coat. 'Oh. . . and Kenny calls me Molly I'm not Maureen anymore.'

I didn't sleep much that night. Stayed up and wrote another article for *The Big Fret* headed THE JOY OF ROY, my experience of a completely different musical culture and how it differed from a pub rock gig. In the piece I also thanked Bingo for inviting me, otherwise I may never have bumped into my long-lost mother.

On Friday afternoon after work Keefer, Strawbs, Fast Eddie and I all went to see Crash Test Trevor in Charing Cross Hospital. He had been run over by a Canadian on a pushbike. Crash Test said 'Fat fuck were eatin a fuckin pie and wayn't lookin where he were goin.' We all cracked up at the image of a fat man eating a pie whilst cycling and then running over Crash Test. 'Dunt nah why thee brung me here like, theers nowt wrung wey is.' He had been kept in as they thought he may be concussed, but he made such a fuss they finally discharged him. The Canadian was in another ward with a crushed ankle. Crash Test was, of course, unhurt, apart from a bicycle tread mark across his stomach. I thought maybe I might have bumped into Patti or Auntie Fiona at the hospital but I never did. Which was OK by me, I'd had my fill that week of bumping into people.

On Saturday, Crash Test insists I go with him to Portobello

Road market as he wants to buy a leather jacket. 'Come along Tum thas sum great ba-gans ta be had.' I'd heard a lot about the market and I'd never been, so I went. The street is lined with stalls selling everything from African Zulu warrior shields to rainbow-coloured tea cosies and of course leather jackets. Crash Test tries on at least a hundred jackets. The man who runs the stall has the patience of a saint. A small, neat man in a straw hat with a tape measure around his neck, he has an accent which could be Italian or Spanish. Each jacket Crash Test tries, the neat little man says the same thing, 'Yees thees a one look a very goat'.

Crash Test eventually chooses one, an American flying bomber jacket with a fur collar. I think it's too big for him but I keep that to myself. Another stall is selling platform shoes which are all the rage. I see a pair for £1.50. I tell Crash Test he can pay for them as he owes me for the hod. He grins. 'Hah! so thas the reason ya came wey us!' I try them on, they have six-inch heels and I like being six foot four so Crash Test buys them for me. 'Ah telt thee Tum didn't ah. One-fifty! Thas a ba-gan tha is.'

Bingo rings again and says he's pleased with the Roy Shirley article. He only had to amend a few spelling mistakes and take out the last paragraph, but apart from that it was great, and he liked how I made it personal, talking about meeting my mother. He said that really made it stand out and linked it neatly with the theme of joy. He then asked if I wanted to write for the magazine on a regular basis and he would pay me something. I didn't have to think twice and said yes right away.

The IRA had taken their bombing campaign to London. Starting with Madame Tussauds. The joke was that they couldn't get near the real people they wanted to kill so decided to blow up their lookalike wax models – apparently the Duke of Edinburgh had his ear blown off and the Queen Mother lost her handbag. They went on to plant one outside the Houses of Parliament and another one at The Tower of London. One person was killed and forty injured. I thought about Mickey and my heart sank. Keefer said that I should keep my mouth shut for a while and started to teach me to do an Australian accent. When I tried to do it he would cry laughing and say, 'Ya sound like a Sith Effreecan that needs a shit.'

I decide to take a night off from the pub rock scene and go with the lads to the Hammersmith Palais or to give it its full title, The Famous Hammersmith Palais de Danse. This is Fast Eddie's idea and Keefer looks out of sorts, so we all want to try and cheer him up. The Palais reminds me of an Irish dancehall with its big stage, glitter ball, sprung wooden floor and long bar at the side of the hall. It also has a balcony with another bar for 'courting couples' The Ken Macintosh Big Band have a residency. They play Trad Jazz and Swingtime. Although this isn't my kind of music I can see that Ken Mackintosh is a great musician as is the rest of his band and I don't mind some of the tunes, like 'Solo Hop' which he tells us is by someone called Glen Miller.

At the bar I see a girl in a blue dress standing alone, a girl that reminds me very much of Rosie. Raven hair and pale skin. Before I can think about it I'm beside her and asking her to dance. She smiles and sips her wine, raises her dark eyebrows.

'You like this music?'

I can't quite place her accent but I know she's not Irish or English. 'Not really, but I don't hate it. Do you want to dance?'

She sets her glass of red wine on the bar, bends down and removes her high heels. 'OK let's do it!'

Her name is Eva and she comes from Hartford in Connecticut. I know that's in America but I don't know where and then, as if reading my mind, she says Connecticut is on the East coast about a two hour drive from New York City. The music suddenly changes to a slow number and she casually puts her arms around my shoulders and casually, but with added excited panic, I hold her gently around the waist. She even smells like Rosie and my heart begins to race a little. She's smaller now that she has taken off her heels, she smiles, a kind of mischievous smile and stares up at me. 'Are you wearing Platforms?'

I smile back. 'Yeah, I bought them today. To be honest they're not very comfortable.'

She laughs. 'High heels are stoopid! I'm never wearing mine again.'

The music ends and Ken announces there will be a ten-minute break. We walk back to her high heels and wine. I ask if she would like a drink? She drinks the remains of her glass. 'Sure!'

At that point Fast Eddie, Strawbs, Crash Test and Keefer walk past, grinning at me like idiots. Crash Test is sweating in his flying bomber leather jacket and looks quite drunk already. He leers at Eva. 'Wud ya like ta see ma spare tyre luv?' Then pulls up his shirt and shows her the bicycle tread mark across his stomach. The guys fall about laughing.

Eva looks at me, 'Do you know that guy?'

I'm about to deny him like St Peter did with Jesus, *I tell thee I know not of this man*, but decide I should own up and say 'Yes, unfortunately.'

Luckily they move on. Eva and I find a booth to sit in. We talk for over an hour. She's twenty years old and is studying at the London School of Economics for a business degree and sharing a flat in Holborn with two Chinese girls and an Irish girl from Cork. She had come to the Palais with the Irish girl, who had felt ill and had to go home. Eva had offered to go back with her but the Irish girl insisted she stay, so she did but was just about to leave when I asked her to dance. I keep offering to buy her drinks and she keeps saying yes, then we dance again, another slow dance. I hold her a little tighter. The beer has loosened me up and then suddenly I lean in and kiss her. She goes up on tiptoes and grabs my hair. This was the first time I'd kissed anyone other than

Rosie in almost four years. In my mind I am kissing Rosie. I want this kiss to last forever. I know I'm probably being too passionate but I don't care. When we stop kissing, she looks kind of shocked and maybe a little puzzled, but then smiles and prods me on the nose. Jesus! That's what Rosie used to do. What was it about my nose that women wanted to push it like a doorbell?

We return to the booth and she buys the next round of drinks. Eva tells me that her full name is Evangelina Alejandro Membreves Copeland. She shakes her head. 'What a ridiculous name. My father is Spanish, so am I actually. I was born in Seville. My mother is English but emigrated to New York with her family when she was eight years old. My parents met in New York City in 1951. Dad worked as a chef in a hotel and Mom was on reception. Five years later they owned the place. I was born when my parents went back to Seville for my grandma's funeral. My mother's waters broke and I was born at the graveside. The locals said I was my grandma's reincarnation and it's spooky because I look just like her. The spitting image in fact. I'll show you a photo sometime.' I'm pleased there was going to be a 'sometime'.

I like Eva, her accent, how relaxed and open she seems. She smiles at me, that mischievous smile again. 'OK now it's your turn to bore me with your life story!'

'Alright, but I need the gents. I'll be back in a minute.' The toilets are at the back of the hall. Old-fashioned marble urinals, which were almost overflowing. I pee for a long time. I was drinking Harp lager. They didn't have Kronenbourg. Fast Eddie says that Harp is just piss and I'm now beginning to believe he is right.

I wash my hands and as I walk across the wet tiled floor I slip and fall on my back. There's a cheer from my fellow pissers. I find it difficult to get up and no one offers to help. I've had a few to drink but I know I haven't yet reached the falling over stage. It soon becomes clear why I'm having trouble getting to my feet, both heels on my platform shoes have broken off. When I take a closer look I see they weren't proper platform shoes at all. The heels had been glued and nailed on which was probably why they only cost £1.50. I try to walk in them but that's proving impossible as the nails have started coming through the soles stabbing my feet. I throw the shoes in the corner and on the way back to Eva I'm stopped by an eagle-eyed bouncer. A big meaty culchie with a crew cut, who sounds like he's probably from County Kerry. He's impeccably dressed in a grey suit which is worn by all the bouncers. 'Hey where's yer shoos boy?' I try ignoring him and keep walking which is a mistake. He grabs me by the arm. 'Arroo deaf like? I'm askeen ya weir's yer shoos? Ye can't be in here wid out shoos!' I look down at my feet, a small hole has appeared in the toe of my sock, it definitely wasn't there when I put them on.

'My shoes fell off in the toilets.'

Meaty culchie man stares at me, tightens his grip on my arm and ushers me towards the front door.

'C'mon smart fella out!'

I wriggle like a weak worm on a hook. 'Oh no, come on, listen! I'm with a girl! At least let me tell her I'm being thrown out!' He's not listening. Next thing I know I'm outside and the big glass doors are closing behind me. Fuck!

The air is chilly for July and I suddenly feel drunker than I was inside. I have to get back in. I'm desperate to get back in. I'm determined to get back in. I have to see Eva and explain. Meathead and his mate laugh at me and point at their shoes. Maybe there was a back entrance? I walk up a couple of blocks until I find a narrow alleyway just wide enough for me to walk up. At the end of the alleyway there's a brick wall with a drainpipe leading up to the next level and after that a fire escape. I think if I can reach the fire escape it may be possible to get on the roof of the Palais, climb back down and find a back entrance or a window? It's not easy to climb a drainpipe in wet socks. It really hurts my feet but I make it on to the next level and clamber up the fire escape. I go through a door which takes me along a fibreglass corridor between the buildings.

I can hear Ken blowing his saxophone, he seems to be urging me to succeed. The corridor takes me out onto a flat roof. I reckon I must be right underneath the stage as I can feel the vibrations. There's a skylight in the roof I grip the side of the wooden frame and begin to pull at it. I pull as hard as I can and suddenly the whole lot comes away, the glass splinters into pieces. I stare into the black hole can't see a thing. Ken and his Big Band are playing their hearts out. *Waow Wawwww! She's gonna cry until I tell her that I'll never roam. So Chattanooga choo choo won't you choo choo me home.* I lower myself into the hole in the roof, hold on to the side, hang there for a moment like a condemned man waiting on the trapdoor to open then drop into the room. I hit something hard on the way down, bounce off something else and wind myself. I have been winded once before when Mickey Peach had rolled a tractor tyre down a hill at me. I had my back to him at the time and when I turned around the tyre hit me full force in the chest. This was the same. The air in my lungs had been literally knocked out of me and all I can do is make a pathetic gasping attempt at breathing 'Waaaaarrrrggggggh! Warrrrragggghh! Ohhhhhhwarrrrgggggghhh!'

After several minutes of me imitating someone dying loudly of tuberculosis, the light in the room comes on and I'm surrounded by two policemen. 'What the hell? What are you doing, how did you get?. . .'

The policeman stops and stares at the broken skylight. I can still hear Ken trying to board the Chatanooga Choo Choo. The policeman looks back down at me and then across to his mate. 'Did he just fall through that roof window?'

'Warrrrrgggggghhh! Arrrrrrggggghhh!'

They drag me on to my feet, take me arm in arm down the stairs through some offices and finally to the desk sergeant. 'We got a live one here Sarge, he's only gone and broken through the bloody roof skylight into the Log room.'

The sergeant's mouth drops open. 'He did what?'

Just my luck that the Hammersmith Palais was right next to Hammersmith Police Station.

After I'd filled in a form with my all my details I'm taken into a smaller office by the sergeant. It's slightly bigger than the room I'd been taken to at Aldergrove airport but just as drab and soulless. My breathing is almost back to normal. The sergeant gives me a drink of water and sits behind his desk. He sighs heavily and shakes his head in disbelief. 'Can you speak now?' I nod. 'OK son, you've got some explaining to do and if you lie to me you'll spend the night in Wormwood Scrubs. Do you know what that is?' I shake my head. 'It's a prison! OK in your own time. What were you doing breaking into a police station?'

I tell the sergeant the whole story, about the platform shoes, meeting Eva, falling in the toilets, being thrown out of the Palais and trying to get back in. The sergeant drops his head slightly and holds his face in his hands. I think, Christ my story has affected him so much he's crying or maybe he's got other problems and this has tipped him over the edge. He takes a hankie from his pocket and dries his eyes and then he's off again those big shoulders shaking. He begins making little high-pitched sounds almost like squeaks. Takes a deep breath and looks at me and I realise he's not crying, he's laughing, 'Both heels?' His voice is choked with laughter. 'Both heels? One pound fifty. . . and they were glued on? Oh my God!'

Tears are on his cheeks. He's trying his best to control himself but is finding it difficult. He finally gets a grip, sniffs a lot, blows his nose, puts the hankie back in his pocket. 'What you did tonight son was very very stupid. You could easily have got yourself killed.' He took another deep breath smiled and shook his head. 'What size do you wear?'

I wasn't sure I'd heard him properly. 'Pardon?'

'Shoes son, what size?'

'Oh em size 9.'

The sergeant gets up from the table, opens a large cupboard which contains shelves full of police boots. Picks a pair of size nines and hands them to me. 'Try those on.'

I put the boots on, tie up the laces. I get up and walk around like the way I used to do in Andersons shoe shop. 'Fit alright?'

'Yes they fit me.'

'OK, now you listen to me young man. I'm not going to charge you for breaking and entering into a police station, because I believe your story, but that doesn't mean I'm a soft touch. I want you to bring those boots back here on Monday and if you don't I will charge you with breaking and entering and criminal damage. Do you understand?'

'Yes sergeant.'

'Good! Now clear off before I change my mind and with a bit of luck you'll still get the girl. Go on scram!'

I thank him and promise myself there and then that I

will never badmouth the police again. Not the London police anyhow. I stand outside the doors of the Palais until I manage to attract the attention of Meathead the bouncy boy. I point at my new boots. Meathead opens the doors. 'What is it?'

'Look, I've found some boots. Can you please let me in?'

He stares at the boots. 'Where'd due get dose?'

'A policeman gave them to me.'

Meathead laughs. 'You're some fuckin Latchico alright. In ye go but any fuckin messin and you know well how tings'll end up!'

I dart past him with one thing on my mind and that's to find Eva.

Eva isn't in the booth. Another couple have taken our place. I ask them if they'd seen her and they shake their heads. I scan the dancehall. The glitter ball twirls and sparkles over the heads of three or four-hundred smiling dancing people. Coloured shards of glass-light flickering momentarily on their faces, but not the face I want. I can't see any of the lads either but knowing them they've probably moved on for a pub crawl. This is impossible. She has obviously gone home. I check the time and work out I've been away for at least forty minutes. She wouldn't have waited that long, why would she? Arms around my waist and for a second I think it's Meathead come to throw me out again. I turn around and it's Eva.

'Oh my God you waited for me!'

She raises those eyebrows and frowns. 'What makes you

think I was waiting for you? I've danced with three other men since you ran out on me!'

I'm not sure how serious she is. 'I didn't run out on you. Look let's get out of here and I'll tell you all about it. The pubs will be open for another twenty minutes.'

The Laurie Arms is next door. A tiny pub full of locals, mostly old guys nursing a pint. We cram ourselves into a corner, knees touching. I tell her the whole story and when I'm finished she sips her half pint of Guinness and considers me for a long time. 'I'm not sure if I should be flattered that you did all that to see me again, or if I should be worried that I'm in the company of a crazy person?'

I take a good look at her eyes and notice they are blue but flecked with green and amber spots. It's the first time I'd ever set eyes on eyes like this but then I'd probably never looked this closely at anyone's eyes before. Not even Rosie's. She checks her watch. 'I gotta get my train at eleven fifteen. You want to walk me to the toob?'

I stand with her on the Piccadilly line platform at Hammersmith tube station. The big clock reads 11.15. She puts her arms around my waist. 'I know I shouldn't do this. I promised myself I wouldn't do this again'.

I don't respond. I'm not sure what she's talking about so I think I'll play it safe and say nothing. 'Take a guy home that I've just met.' She's looking at me, it seems to provide the answer. Her dark eyebrows working overtime.

'You don't have to,' I say, suddenly feeling all chivalrous

and then regretting it. 'We can meet another time. I'll give you my phone number.' I wish I could keep my mouth shut. A gang of skinheads appear on the platform being loud and skin-heady.

She holds me tightly. 'God, I hate those guys, they give me the Heebie Jeebies.'

One of them opens his fly and pisses on the railway line. The others do a countdown. '1. 2. 3. 4. 5. 6. . .' This really is a pissing contest. A light appears in the distance and the whoofy whooshing sound of a train approaches. Her train. She grabs my hand. 'Those guys are getting on my train. Can you ride with me?'

Thank God for skinheads.

Eva's flat is small compared to Castletown Road. She tells me the apartments in the road are only three months old and have been built specially for students which explains why everything smells new, the paint, the polish on the floors. I can even smell the concrete in the walls. There's three other rooms with names on the doors. NOREEN. YING YUE and HUI JING. At least I know which one is the Irish girl. I sit at Eva's small table in the shared kitchen. Everything has sticky labels attached with warnings like *Ying Yue's bread. Dont touch!* And stuck on a banana is *Noreen's banana please don't eat me. Hui Jings juice dont drink!* I can't see this working in Castletown Road. If I left a note saying *Tom's eggs don't touch,* there would be a note from Keefer saying,

Ate your eggs cobber fuck off! And that to me seems a better, more friendly system.

A redheaded girl in a bathrobe suddenly appears with a glass in her hand, fills it with water at the sink. Eva is in the middle of pouring me coffee from some complicated thing with a plunger in it. 'Oh, hi Noreen, feeling better?'

Noreen looks at me. 'I think so, yeah.' She continues staring at me.

At last Eva says. 'This is Tom Joe. We met after you left.'

I nearly correct her but decide I'd leave that for later. Noreen tucks one side of her hair behind her ear. 'Oh, hi ya Tom Joe.'

'Hello Noreen.'

She tucks the other side of her hair around the other ear, picks up her banana, peels it and throws the skin in a bin. Her face is wide and white with a bottom jaw that juts out slightly. She drinks the water and continues to stare at me as she chews the top of her banana. 'I'll see ya in the mornin Eva and. . .' she stops and ruffles the hair away from her ears, 'I'll probably see you as well, Tom Joe.'

Eva waits until she hears Noreen's bedroom door closing then whispers to me. 'She gets kinda weird when I bring guys back.'

I know I shouldn't ask what I'm about to ask but it comes out anyway. 'How often do you bring guys back?'

Eva sighs.

'Every night, Tom Joe! I just can't help myself!'

We drink our coffee in silence. Turk Khavesi Dark Roast. I have never tasted anything like it. I can feel every nerve in my body revving up for take-off. Eva tops us up with what is left in the pot. She rises from the table. I'll be back in a minute. She returns and places a black and white photo on the table. It's a picture of her dressed up in old fashioned clothes. I study it for a moment. 'That's my grandmother when she was twenty.'

I can hardly believe it. 'You're joking.'

She shakes her head, 'Nope.'

'Jesus you really are the spitting image of her, that's weird.'

She gets up from the table, walks to the door. 'Listen Tom Joe, it's my business how many guys I bring back here. I don't have to explain anything to you OK?' She suddenly has a different look about her and I'm not sure I like it. 'OK' I say and try not to blush, but I can feel my cheeks burning. I think it's a smile she gives me but I can't be sure. It could be a smug grin. She runs the fingers of her right hand through her hair. 'You wanna go to bed?' 'Sure' I say, but I'm not sure.

Eva has condoms in the drawer of her bedside table. I never knew they came in packs of twelve. She doesn't seem interested in taking things slowly. Eva likes to grab my hair, a little too hard at times. I don't say anything but think I might broach the subject at a later date, if indeed there is a later date. The twelve-pack of condoms could well have pointed to the fact that she wasn't joking about all the guys she brought back. I was very aware that this was definitely sex I was having. Unlike Rosie, Eva wasn't taking me to another place. This was happening here and now I wasn't going anywhere. When we finally finished it was four o'clock in the morning. I had used up three condoms in just under four hours. I once got Nat Harkness to buy me a packet of three from Faulkner's chemist. Faulkner's was the only Protestant chemist in the town. Catholic chemists didn't stock condoms. That was in 1969 and I still had two left in 1971.

TEN

I AWOKE TO THE SOUND of Chinese music. I had a dead arm which was under Eva's shoulder. I dragged it out with my good arm and beat it into life. I hated dead arms. It was always a moment of panic until I got the blood flowing again. The fleeting thought I might be left with a gimpy arm for the rest of my life. Eva stirred and looked at her watch. She had a cotton wool mouth. 'Wow ates leven o'clock.'

My stomach dropped suddenly as I remembered that I was meeting my mother and her 'nice man' Kenny McDonald. I guessed he must be Scottish. I wasn't looking forward to it. I got up and had a pee. My penis was shrivelled, bruised on both sides and my balls ached.

When Eva was making the tea and toast I wrote my phone number on one of the sticky labels and stuck it on the door of her cupboard. I thought this was a cool thing to do and put the ball in her court. If she really was seeing lots of other guys then I thought she probably wouldn't call.

I was introduced to the Chinese girls who giggled a lot. Noreen appeared still in her bathrobe. She stared at me. 'Hi Tom Joe.'

'Morning Noreen.'

Eva grabbed her coat from the back of the door. 'I'll walk you to the toob.'

I ate the last piece of toast and drained my coffee. Eva was in a rush all of a sudden. She waited with me until the train arrived. I wasn't sure what to say. I'd never experienced anything like this before, I was unnerved by her. She grabbed my hands. 'Do you want to say something to me?'

The train doors opened, I let go of her hands, stepped into the train and as the doors closed I shouted. 'My name's Tom Joad! I'd like to see you again. Call me!'

Eva turned and walked away leaving me even more confused. I also felt stupid as I didn't mean to shout so loudly and have so much panic in my voice but it seemed to amuse the people on the tube as I sat there with a big stupid red face.

As I opened the door to the Castletown Road flat, Annouska brushed past me and ran down the stairs. She looked like she'd been crying. I could hear Keefer still shouting after her 'Fucking two-timing lying Arab fucking bitch.'

Arab fucking bitch? I knew she wasn't an Arab, and then I realised he must have meant she fucked an Arab. Sometimes I was slow on the uptake. Keefer slammed the door of the kitchen. I jumped in the shower, washed the smell of condoms from my body and changed into some clean clothes. I slid my police boots under the bed, then took them out again and put them on the side table. I didn't want to forget to return them to the Laughing Policeman and end up in Wormwood Scrubs. I was relieved to get them off as two painful blisters were forming, one on the big toe of my left foot and one on the heel of my right foot. My Northern Irish Fenian Catholic feet were obviously not cut out for police boots. I decided to steer clear of Keefer. I wouldn't have known what to say to him anyway and if he wanted to tell me what was going on he would.

I read the address again on the crumpled piece of tissue. *135 Abinger Road.* I asked the flower seller outside Turnham Green station and she pointed me in the right direction. Abinger Road was one of those quiet residential tree-lined streets. Large red bricked detached and semi-detached houses with big bay windows and gardens. My mother had definitely found a nice area to live in, although the garden of 135 hadn't been attended to in a while. There was a dead tree in the middle of the crazy paving and weeds growing everywhere. The bedroom window was open, the curtains blowing like sheets on a clothesline. Bob Dylan was singing 'She Belongs To Me'. I knocked on the door and my mother opened it straight away. She must have been waiting in the hall. She hugged me tightly and I could feel her shaking. She was wearing denim jeans and a big green floppy jumper, two blue marbles hung down from her ears, exactly the same as the ones I used to play with when I was a kid. She had her hair up and was wearing glasses. Her perfume was a little overpowering. 'Kenny's looking forward to meeting you.' I followed her upstairs. Dylan was in full voice.

My mother showed me into a living room which, despite the windows being wide open, stank of cannabis. The blackest man I'd ever seen in my life jumped up from the couch. He had bare feet and was wearing a pink shirt and yellow trousers. He shook my hand firmly and laughed loudly. 'Amet! eet ease soooo good to meet with you! Yoa ma-ther has toll me a lotta bout you.' Kenny McDonald definitely wasn't Scottish. He laughed loudly again. 'Ah hop you like Bab Dee-lan. Ah heer heem on ma seesters ray-dio when ah aim twentee yars ol an he seenging bloween in da weend an ah like heem very match. Hah! Ah can see you wey nat expectin me to be a black man! Ken-nee Mac Don-ald? Ah believe ma great great gran-fathar was a slave owna and had sex-ual relay-shons weeth ma great great gran-mather who wok for heem. He was probab-ly a bad man!'

He opened his mouth wide and laughed again. I was already exhausted and I'd only been in the house five minutes. He switched off the record player and Dylan was silent. 'I was ban in Ni-geer-ria but all ma famillee now live in Ameerika you have to come some time.'

My mother said there was stewing steak and runner beans for lunch. I had no idea what runner beans were but I just nodded and smiled. 'It should be ready in about fifteen minutes.'

Kenny whispered to my mother. 'Half you toll heem?'

My mother shook her head. 'You half to tell heem?'

'I know I do of course I do but he's just got in the door.' My mother sighed and looked nervously at me. 'Come with me I want to show you something.'

I followed her into a small brightly painted bedroom. My mother reached down into a cot and picked up a child. A little brown boy with tight black curly hair. She held him up like a trophy, 'This is your half-brother Andre. Do you want to hold him?'

Well fuck me sideways! I'm Wile E. Coyote running off the cliff and plummeting to the ground in a silent puff of smoke. I took the kid in my arms. He was a lovely little fella but all I could think was, *Fucking hell Ma what is wrong with you? You've already had eight of these.* He gurgled and played with my hair. I handed him back.

My mother laid him in the cot. 'I know what you're thinking and you're right but he wasn't planned it just happened.'

I'm thinking, No Ma, you're not the Virgin Mary it didn't just happen! But I said nothing. I just wanted to get to hell away and clear my head.

I don't really remember a lot about the rest of the day. Kenny never mentioned the baby, he just smoked a large joint, told me he worked shifts at Heathrow airport, laughed a lot and talked shit most of the afternoon. My mother was quiet. She could see I was shocked by the whole affair. I made an excuse and left around four-thirty. My mother walked me to Turnham Green station.

'Kenny talks too much and laughs a lot when he's nervous.'

And I thought yeah, and also when he's stoned. We hug. She gives me her phone number. I say I'll call her soon. She suggests I can tell Maeve and Noreen about Andre but it probably wasn't a good idea, just yet, to tell anyone else.

On Monday evening after work I headed down to Hammersmith Police Station. In the cold light of day, I couldn't figure out how I ever thought I could get into Hammersmith Palais from that alleyway, it was at least four buildings away. I must have been a hell of a lot drunker than I thought. And it brought Eva sharply back into light. The sergeant was right. I could've killed myself and for what? It had been two days and she hadn't called. I had the boots wrapped up in brown paper and tied with string. I rang the bell at reception. I could see two people typing in an office, but not a policeman in sight. I rang the bell again. Stood there for another two minutes, rising on tiptoe waving at the typists, 'Hello, anybody here?' Then I saw myself on the CCTV camera high on the wall. I waved at it, 'Hello. Anybody?'

A woman looked up from her typewriter but just ignored me. I shouted as loud as I could. 'Hello, got a parcel here!'

I began to think it would probably be quicker to go across the road and dial 999. I decided to leave the parcel on the counter. I wasn't going to hang around here all day. As I walked back down the steps two policemen arrived behind me, one of them grabbed me in a choke-hold and I was flung against the wall. There was a lot of commotion and shouting. I'm trying to breathe and explain that I left a pair of fucking boots back! Then I heard a voice I recognized. 'It's OK Constable Simms I know him! Let him go! Let him go!'

It was the desk sergeant. He shook his head. 'You again?'

'I'm only doing what you told me sergeant. I'm leaving the boots back!'

'Yes I know. I'm sorry but unfortunately, it's your accent. We've had some bomb threats from the IRA and we can't be too careful. Everyone's a little on edge.'

My legs felt unsteady, jellified. I was furious. 'Do you really think I'm going to walk into a police station wave at the CCTV camera and shout that I have a parcel if it was a bomb?'

He smiled at me and I thought he was going to start laughing again. 'Listen young man, you broke in here through a skylight. Remember that? So nothing would surprise me these days. Anyway, sorry you got roughed up a bit. Thanks for bringing the boots back. I hope she was worth it?'

Maybe Keefer was right about my accent. I'd have to work a little harder at being Aussie.

ELEVEN

OUR PHONE RANG early on Saturday morning. I was going to answer it but Keefer got there first. 'G'day. . . who?. . . nah I don't sorry. . . what was the last name again? McCrudden . . . nah sorry I'm fairly sure there's no Emmet McCrudden here. Unless they've just moved in?. . . Listen leave your number and if there's anyone of that name just moved in I can leave a message here beside the phone.' Keefer writes down a phone number on the phone pad. 'OK, yeah gotcha . . . Auntie Fiona. OK no worries, cheers!' Keefer bounded up the stairs and I moved away from the door.

'McCrudden what kinda name is McCrudden, Scottish?'

I decided there was no point in blowing my cover. 'No idea.'

I was curious to know what Auntie Fiona had wanted. I thought I would call her back after breakfast. It was pissing down so we were rained off for the morning. I wasn't bothered. I never like working Saturdays. Keefer was still in a dark mood. I hadn't seen Annouska around so I guessed it was over between them. I had hoped it might have been Eva calling me. I knew I could always leave a message for her at the London School of Economics but I thought I'd bide my time.'It had only been a week.

I called Auntie Fiona from a call box at the end of the road. 'Hi Auntie. . . Fifi. It's Emmet.'

'Oh, hello son, you've just caught me. I'm off to work. They said they didn't know who you were when I rang.'

'Yeah sorry about that Fifi, there's a lot of people in my flat coming and going.'

'Well, listen son, you need to call your sister Maeve. I couldn't quite hear her properly, it was a very bad line, but something to do with your father. You're to call her as soon as you can, alright? I have to go now, I'm late for work. Come around some time.'

'OK Fifi. . . thanks for letting me know.'

Countless things ran through my mind. He had been jailed. Drowned in his tin bath. Fell into the range and burned himself alive. The IRA had shot him for not being able to hold his drink and giving the virile proud alcoholic men of Ireland a bad name. I was apprehensive at having to call her. I had no excuse for not having answered any of her letters. I had to call the Patterson's and leave a message and then wait by the phone for Maeve to call me back which she did fifteen minutes later.

'Oh my God, Emmet, why didn't you get in touch? I've been so worried about you. Why the hell didn't you write or call? You can be so bloody selfish!' I let her get it out of her system. 'Hello, are you still there?'

'Yes, Maeve, look I'm sorry I didn't write. I just wanted to forget about Carricktown for a while and Rosie and Mickey

Peach and my Da and the whole lot. I wanted a break from it.' There was a silence on the line.

'We're not Rosie Byrne or Mickey friggin bloody Peach! We're your family. Unless you think you're too good for us now. You've always thought that anyway, I know you have.' She was right about that, I had no argument against it.

'Maeve, I don't want to argue with you. I promise I'll keep in touch.'

She cleared her throat. 'OK, what I wanted to tell you is that. . . Daddy had a heart attack. It wasn't serious. He was only in hospital for three days. They've put him on tablets. Same ones that Granda was on I think? He's not supposed to drink with them, but I don't know how long that will last.'

I could hear the stress in her voice and felt sorry for her having to look after that good for nothing asshole. 'You can't watch him twenty fours a day, Maeve. If he wants to kill himself that's his choice. He's not a child. You need to try and live your own life.'

She scoffed, a little snorty huff that I knew so well. 'Huh, listen to you being all adult, that's a laugh! Well, if you must know I am getting on with my own life. . . I'm getting married in three months' time.'

That stopped me in my tracks. I definitely didn't see that coming. 'Married?'

'Yes! Married and don't sound so surprised!'

'Who to?'

'Lenny O'Brien.'

'What? You mean Lenny O'Brien from the Brewery Tap?'

'Yes, what other Lenny O'Brien is there?'

'Congratulations, he's a good guy. How long have you been going out with him?'

'Just over a year. . . and no! I'm not pregnant.'

I laughed, 'You soon will be!' She was quiet again and I could hear her thinking.

'If only mammy could be there. I contacted the Salvation Army. Apparently they can find people for you but I haven't heard anything back.' This definitely wasn't the time to tell Maeve about our new black brother and Old McDonald's cannabis farm in Chiswick. That would have to wait.

'You have to come to my wedding Emmet, you hear me? You better be there. Give me your address and I'll send you all the details.'

I had no choice but to give it to her.

Keefer caught my attention on the landing. He mimed using the phone with his thumb and little finger and then tumbled his hands over each other to indicate that I should hurry up. I said goodbye to Maeve, went to my room and lay on the bed. Lenny O'Brien was ten years older than Maeve but I could see they'd be a good match. He was well respected in the town. He was also a first cousin of Rosie Byrne. I stared up at the ceiling and tried to think how it was ever going to be possible to completely ditch the McCruddens. There were always going to be weddings, christenings, funerals. I would go home for Maeve's wedding. I owed her that much. But I was never going back to being Emmet McCrudden. Tom Joad was the guy who deserved all the credit. I liked Tom Joad, and I liked London.

A week later two letters arrived for me. One addressed to Emmet McCrudden. The other to Tom Joad. A happy 19th Birthday card from Maeve signed by the whole family. The other was from Bingo and contained an agreement for me to sign. It was an offer to write one article per week for the *Big Fret,* no less than a thousand words, and he would pay me £10 for each piece completed on the deadline. A little surge of pride ran through me. I could now officially state that I was a professional writer. £10 a week would pay my rent.

Friday night. I go to the Red Cow in Hammersmith to see a band called Ace. For the first time in my life I feel important and adequate. My name is Tom Joad and I write for *The Big Fret*. I couldn't wait to say that to someone. At first I thought Ace were American as they sounded like Little Feat. The lead singer had an amazing voice, they didn't really seem to me like a pub rock band. They had a very full sound, a keyboard, and were playing some really sophisticated riffs. I spoke to them afterwards. Their lead singer was called Paul Carrack and he came from Sheffield in the North of England.

'Hi, my name is Tom Joad and I write for *The Big Fret*.' He'd never heard of it but answered all of my questions whilst standing in the corner dripping with sweat. I wasn't far away with the Little Feat reference as Little Feat was one of their major influences. I thanked him and bought him a pint of lager.

A phone is ringing in my dream, *Durrrring durrrring. Durrring durrinnng* but turns out it's not in my dream. It's five o'clock in the morning and Keefer is above me shaking my shoulder.

'It's the blower!'

'Wha?'

'For you ya fuckin drongo some sheila that I can't understand!'

I throw on a pair of trousers and two at a time the stairs to the phone. I'm thinking it's Maeve to tell me that Drunken Daddy is dead, massive heart attack.

'Hello?' Pause on the line I can hear breathing. 'Hello who is this?'

'Hi... it's Noreen.'

'Noreen? What's wrong, are you OK?'

'Yeah, Tom Joe, I'm really fine!' I realise immediately it's not my sister Noreen, it's Eva's flatmate.

'Oh for fuck's sake! I thought you were my sister! What are you doing calling me at five o'clock in the morning?' What do you want?'

Another pause. 'You left your number on my cupboard I thought you wanted me to call you?'

'What? I didn't leave my number on your cupboard I left

it on Eva's cupboard. Why would I leave it on your cupboard?'

I can hear her sniffling. 'You were looking at me. . . I thought we had a connection! Eva is a slut!' I can hear some kind of noise in the background, maybe a door slamming? Noreen is arguing with someone. I was about to hang up when I hear Eva's voice.

'Tom Joe, it's Eva. I'm so sorry about this. I can only apologise for my bat shit crazy roommate!'

I can hear Noreen screaming! 'He left me his number you dirty Yankee bitch!'

Eva is trying to keep it together her voice is calm, but it's a fake calm. 'I'll call you tomorrow Tom Joe OK?'

'OK.'

Eva hangs up. I'm now fully awake and know there's no going back to sleep. I go to the kitchen to make tea. Keefer is sitting at the table drinking a glass of milk.

'Who the hell is calling you at five in the mornin?'

'Some crazy friend of a girl I met at the Palais. Thinks I want to go out with her.'

Keefer swirls his milk around in the glass.

'Fuckin women. . . they're not worth it mate. Unless of course they're ya mum. My dad had her sectioned, put her back in the bin again. . . I mean you should hear him! "Oh it's the best place for her she'll be safe in there." He was the one who drove her mad in the first place!' Keefer leans right back on the legs of the chair. I hate it when people do that, it always sets me on edge. 'I read your bit in that music paper ya keep casually leaving around the place. Is it true ya met ya mum at Victoria Station?'

'Yeah it's true.'

'Jeez, that's wild!'

'Yeah, my old man's a bastard as well, when's he's drinking that is, which is ninety per cent of the time. She left us two years ago. I never thought I'd see her again and then out of the blue she bumps into me in the middle of London. It's crazy. She's only living four stops away!'

'Sweet! I wish my old mum had fucked off when she had the chance.' He sighs and blows into his milk, little splashes of white on his nose. 'Nooski's been rootin with some bloke at the Casino. I guess I knew it was only a matter of toyime. I was kiddin myself that I could hold on to a fit bird like Nooski. . . Ah well fuck it! I was rapt there for a while but nothing lasts I suppose. I had a fair run. Gotta move on mate, can't linger with the piss and vinegar, eh?' Keefer downs his milk, leaves the room, then pops his head back round the door. 'That Mr Feelgood band are playing at the Greyhound Saturday night. I think that's the type of music I'm in the mood for right now. Pink fuckin Floyd are doing my head in. We should all go down there.'

'Yeah sure. I'm always up for a bit of Mr Feelgood!' A few minutes later I hear 'Roadhouse Blues' playing from his bedroom. I think this is to let me know that he's coming out from his dark cloud.

I meet Eva outside Bond Street tube station and we go to a pub called The Running Horse, her local. It's fairly quiet. We find seats by the window. She has a glass of wine, I have a Kronenbourg. The seats are leather and squeak as we move into them. I really want to stand at the bar. I don't feel relaxed enough to sit. She gives me a wry smile.

'OK, let me explain about Noreen. She's a twenty-one-year-old virgin and really screwed up about sex. Her mother calls three times a week checking up on her. I've had four dates in five months and she's scared off every single one of them. I guess she's jealous of me. Unfortunately, you did stick your number on her cupboard so she genuinely thought you wanted her to call you.'

I took a long slug of my beer. 'I thought it was your cupboard.'

Eva puts her hands over mine. 'I know you did. I feel sorry for Noreen, I really do but thank God she's gone home for the weekend so we can both cool off. But I don't think she'll change so I've asked the college to find me another apartment in the building.' She rubs my fingers. 'Your hands are so rough.'

'I lay bricks for a living.' She pushes my nose. I think about Rosie and get a little ache in my heart.

'I have cream that will help to make them soft.'

We're in bed and she's been on top of me for some time, literally riding me like a jockey, my hair gripped in both her hands. She collapses on my chest and roars something into my ear scaring the shit out of me. I want to speak, express myself in some way but I don't really know how I feel. I'm not even sure if I've enjoyed the sex or not. It's like I've been in a fight, had the crap beaten out of me but now I feel very sorry for the guy who did it. I'm confused. I think I'm still in love with Rosie. Rosie is all I can think about which pisses me off. She lies back on the bed with her arms outstretched behind her head.

'That was Russian.'

'What was?'

'The thing I shouted in your ear. I'm learning Russian.'

'What did you shout?'

Eva then says something which sounds like *Fish tortor is badeel vonya!*

'What does that mean?'

She buries her head in the pillow and laughs. 'I'll tell you later.'

I tell her my name is Tom Joad, not Tom Joe.

'Tom Joad? You mean like Tom Joad in *The Grapes of Wrath*?'

'Yeah.'

'You're shitting me?'

'No I'm not. So, you've read *The Grapes of Wrath* then?'

She laughs scornfully. 'Of course I've read it, it's an American classic.'

'When you say you've 'read it' does that mean you've 'read it'?'

'Sure I've "read it" but that was in middle school. I've forgotten most of it.'

This irritates the shit out of me. 'If you read *The Grapes of Wrath* properly you would never forget it! So I don't think you've read it!' She smiles and goes to push my nose. I grab her hand and pull it down. 'Don't do that!'

She pulls her hand away. 'Hey! What the fuck? That hurt!'

I tell her I'm sorry get out of bed and start getting dressed. 'I better be getting back. It's late and I've an article to finish for *The Big Fret*.'

She jumps out of bed and gets in my face. I notice little beads of sweat on her top lip which I think are sexy. 'Don't you ever grab me like that again.'

I get dressed quicker. 'I said I was sorry. It was in the heat of the moment, you know like the way you pull my fucking hair!'

She remains in front of my face. 'You have to tell me how you feel Tom Joad! If that really is your name? Don't be such a child! If you don't like it, I won't do it!'

I step away from her. 'OK.'

She grabs her panties and pulls them up angrily around her bum. 'Jesus. I'll walk you to the toob.'

We walk to the tube in silence. I think I'll probably never contact her again. We pause at the entrance to the station and look at each other. She has some kind of expression on her face that I can't work out and then she says, 'You have awoken something in me.'

'What?'

She turns and walks away, stops suddenly and looks back. 'That's what I shouted in Russian.'

I run it over and over in my head on the tube. *You have awoken something in me.* I'm flattered for about four stops but then start to find it a bit pretentious and ridiculous. Could I really awaken anything in anybody? I hear Rosie's voice. *Jesus, Emmet, you need to get rid of that chip off your shoulder.* OK, let's say Eva was being genuine, what was it I had awoken exactly? It didn't mean it was something good and wholesome. I make up my mind not to call her and if she calls me and wants to meet up, I will leave it until then to see how my gut feels about it.

TWELVE

WE ALL HAD a wild night at the Greyhound in Fulham Palace Road. Dr Feelgood were in superb form and the band on before them, Argus, also made an impact, maybe too many guitar solos for my liking but all great musicians. I think they were Scottish but unlike Lou I could understand most of what they said. Keefer seemed to be back to his old self. Crash Test fell over a three-foot wall outside the pub but hardly noticed. Strawbs had no luck with the girl he'd been chatting up all night and Fast Eddie drank fourteen pints of Guinness. Normal service had been resumed.

Sunday night finds Keefer and I alone in the flat. Crash Test has gone back home to Barnsley to visit his Dad in hospital. A pig had fallen on him and broken a bone in his back. Crash Test told us this like it was the most natural thing in the world. 'Fuckin big sow landed on me dad fell oft back a tray-la.'

It's Keefer's birthday. He hadn't mentioned it. 'Thurtee two mate never thought I'd get this fah.' He's reads a card signed by his mum, dad and sister Julie and suddenly he starts to cry. I'm not sure what to do or say, so I don't do or say anything. 'Look at her writing it's all over the shop.' He passes the card to me and I see what he means. I can just make out *Happy Birthday son love Mum* which looks like it's been written by a drunken daddy long legs.

Keefer tosses the card on the table. 'Sorry mate.'

'No worries.' I decide to tell Keefer about my black brother and the pot-smoking Mr McDonald. He listens intently and then makes a silent whistle at the end.

'Fuck a Duck mate, that's a lot to take on.'

'Well, she seems happier than she was, so that's something.'

'Yeah, I guess.' Keefer stands up and suddenly has a strange look on his face. 'Have ya ever tried acid Teejay?'

I really have no clue what he means. 'Acid? What do you mean?'

'LSD it's a small tab. 'You put it under your tongue, wait a while and I promise you mate, it'll take you to places in your head that's fuckin amazing. The Beatles took it. That's how they came up with Sergeant Pepper. Wanna try some?'

I tell Keefer the only acid I'd ever come into contact with was battery acid. Mickey Peach and I found a car battery in the dump and decided to take it to Mervyn Gibson the Scrap Man, but when I lifted it up, it leaked acid onto my trousers and burned a hole in my leg where I still have a scar.

Keefer laughed. 'I've tried it a couple of toyimes mate. It really frees ya mind.'

He holds out two little white tablets in the palm of his hand, then puts one under his tongue. I look at the tiny white pill and think well, it's so small what harm can it do?

I pick it up and pop it under my tongue.

Keefer grins at me. 'Just let it melt, then enjoy the trip. If you feel yourself gettin panicky just relax and remember you're in charge, you can change how ya feel just by thinking about it.'

Thirty or forty-minutes pass and I feel absolutely nothing. The floor is a bit spongy but apart from that nothing. Keefer lies down in the crucifix position. I think I will try the floor again so walk across to the window. My feet are definitely sinking into the floorboards and I'm sure I can hear piano music being played really fast. I look out of the window and Castletown Road is in black and white, cars and people moving very quickly like in a silent movie.

'Wow! Keefer, come and look at this, everything outside is in black and white. They're making a Charlie Chaplin film!'

Keefer laughs. His mouth is open but he isn't making any sound. His laughter is coming from the kitchen.

I think I'm on the tube. Keefer isn't with me. I'm not wearing any socks or shoes. I turn to a woman sitting beside me. 'Excuse me, are we on the tube?'

She smiles. 'Yes. Are you OK?'

There's a priest opposite me. His white dog collar is really sparkling and his tunic is the blackest black I've ever seen. I think it's even blacker than Kenny McDonald. This makes me laugh until I have tears streaming down my face. I begin to yawn and suddenly everything is in darkness. All I can see is the word Y A W N in white letters. It's flashing like a neon sign. I feel scared. I don't like this. The train slows down. I can see the doors opening. Thank God I'm not blind! The priest is still there. I think if I can creep inside the blackness of his tunic, if I can hide there for while in his holy dark grotto, I'll be safe. As the train moves off I get up and fall into his lap. 'I just want to climb inside you for a bit Father. In your blackness just until I feel better.'

He says something and pushes me away. 'Fuck off, Father you're a Catholic priest, I'm a Catholic I need your help. It's only for a little while!'

The priest is pushing against me he moves away to another seat I follow him. 'Come on you selfish bastard share your blackness!'

The train stops and the priest gets off. I chase him, he runs up the stairs. The stairs are really bouncy and I'm finding it hard to keep my balance. When I get to the top, the priest is gone but I'm confronted with a large poster of a pint of Guinness. The white head on it is sparkling and I think, the sneaky bastard! He's turned into a pint of Guinness. I know this is a joke and I start laughing. I sit on the floor and laugh. I can't stop.

I'm in the back seat of some vehicle or other. Someone is behind glass handing me money. 'What? What's this?' A man says, 'It's your change, mate. You alright?' I'm in a cab. 'We're here, Castletown Road.'

I get out of the cab. I don't recognise the street. I look at the numbers 26. . . 28. . . 30. I want 265 that's my house

265. My lungs feel like lead weights are attached. I'm finding it hard to breathe. I wait for a moment at a gate. I see three garden gnomes. One of them has a green hat and is fishing. The other two have red hats and are smoking pipes. They look evil and are staring at me. I don't want any trouble. I avoid eye contact and walk on. The one who's fishing throws down his rod and runs after me. The other two follow him, stand in front of me blocking my way. Green hat says, 'Who are you fucking laughing at?'

'I'm not laughing at anything, I'm just going home.'

'Just because we're small, huh? Think that's funny do you? We're gnomes, we're not fucking dwarfs!'

'I didn't say you were dwarfs.'

'We're gnomes. We're supposed to be small. We're not dwarfs!'

'OK, you're not dwarfs, that's fine, you all look great.'

'We can give people cancer, did you know that?' The two in the red hats spoke in unison in Pinky and Perky voices. 'We can give you cancer for laughing at us and calling us dwarfs!'

'I didn't laugh at you or call you dwarfs. I just want to go home, so leave me alone.'

'Come on lads, let's give this fucker cancer!' And the bastards start biting at my legs.

I know if they draw blood, I'll be dead by the morning. I pick up a rock from the garden and I smash the one with the green hat. I smash his face in. I smash all of them and run off. 265, I need to find number 265. I stumble down the street which seems to go on forever. I stop again and sit on a wall. I can't go any further and crawl under a bush.

The light wakes me, shards of sunshine on my face through the bush. I hear birds singing, the clink of milk bottles and the whine of a milk float. Jesus, I feel bad. I have very sharp pins and needles in my face and tongue. My feet are filthy and blood soaked. I sit up and immediately recognise my surroundings. I'm very relieved to be in Castletown Road. I walk slowly and painfully down the street.

There's a blue light flashing outside number 265. As I walk up to the door a policeman stops me. 'Do you live here, sir?'

'Yes, 265, that's where I live.' The policeman looks at my feet and speaks into a radio. The front door is open. I walk up the stairs. Two more policemen are in the living room with another man in a suit. The man in the suit says. 'Do you live here, sir?'

'Yes, I live here.' He looks at my feet.

'Your feet are bleeding sir do you want to sit down?' I sit on the chair. 'Are you OK, sir?'

'Yeah. I've been out walking. I must have forgot to put on my shoes.'

'Can you tell me your name, sir?'

'Emmet McCrudden.'

I knew I should have said Tom Joad. I tried to say Tom Joad but I said Emmet McCrudden.

The man in the suit sits beside me on the couch. 'Do you know a Keith Hannigan?' I can hear someone crying in the kitchen. It's the kind of crying that sounds serious. Hoarse hurts of breath that are stuck deep down inside. The man in the suit looks at me. 'Keith Hannigan. Did you know him, sir?' I hear someone screaming 'Kee-feeeeer!' I look at the man in the suit. 'What's going on?'

'There's been an accident sir.'

'What kind of accident?'

'Mr Hannigan fell from the balcony onto the railings. I'm afraid he died on the way to hospital and we're trying to find out what happened?'

Annouska appears, held up by a woman in green overalls. She looks at me and her face crumples in pain. 'Keefer's dead! He's dead!' She is about to fall, the woman in the green overalls holds on to her. 'Come on now, dear. You must try and calm down.' I feel a weakness come over me like I'm turning into water. I let the water take me away into a deep place until I'm sinking deeper and deeper into nothingness.

A few hours later, I'm sitting in Kensington Police Station. I don't know how I got there. I'm wearing a clean shirt and jeans and my new baseball boots. I obviously showered and got changed. I can smell germolene on my hands. I must have put it on my feet. I can't remember doing any of this.

The police ask me lots of questions about my movements after I left Castletown Road on Sunday night. I tell them everything but don't mention the acid. I say I was drunk. I left the house to buy some fish and chips and can't remember anything until I got back to the flat on Monday morning. They ask if I or Keefer had been taking drugs. They say they will know when they get the results of his postmortem, so I better tell them the truth. They insist I will not be charged they only want to find out what happened. I tell myself that I will not mention the acid. I look at my watch. It's still only 10am. I have a severe hot pain in the front of my head. I think I have sand in my mouth. I ask for water, there is water in front of me. I close my eyes and see Annouska's face, her voice is magnified, *'KEEFER IS DEAD!'* I have to get out of here. I ask the policeman if I can I go home. He makes me sign something. He explains what it is but I don't understand anything he says. His voice is under water. I sign the form. I stay seated at the table. He says something to me. I stare back at him. 'You're free to go.' I don't see his lips moving. I think he says it again but I can't be sure. I get up and walk out.

On the way back to the flat I see an elderly lady in her garden. I stop and watch as she picks up the smashed garden gnomes and puts them in a black bin bag. She looks at me, her eyes are red and swollen from crying. I walk on quickly. I sit in the living room with Fast Eddie and Strawbs. Crash Test has phoned to say he's on his way back down from

Barnsley. Annouska's face is blotchy and bloated. She tells us what happened.

'As I suppose you all know, I slept with my colleague at work. We were both stoned. Keefer was mad. We had the big fight. I said it meant nothing. I wanted him to forgive me. I told him I forgave him when he screwed the barmaid at the Swan pub last year. Then he calls me on Sunday evening about seven o'clock. He sounds completely out of it. Asks me to come around. I was with my mother and sister so I couldn't come. Then he called again about 12.30 that night. He sounded very bad. I said I would come. I ordered a cab which took forever to arrive. I got here about 1.45am . . . there was an ambulance outside. . . blood on the pavement. . . Oh my God.' She breaks down again.

'It's not yer fault love,' Fast Eddie says, 'it's them fuckin drugs. I keep tellin you lads to stay to fuck away from them. Sure the drink is bad enough.'

Strawbs looks at me, 'You aright Tom?'

I tell them about the acid and how it affected me. How I wished I hadn't left the house. How I couldn't remember why I left or how I was able to hail a cab to get back home. Strawbs pours a shot of whiskey into a tumbler and hands it to me. He goes to the kitchen and comes back with three glasses, pours a shot into each, hands one to Annouska and Fast Eddie, stands in the middle of the room and holds up his glass. Tears are streaming down his face. 'To Keefer!' We all stand and raise our glasses. 'To Keefer!'

Three weeks later, the coroner's report states that Keefer's death was *death by misadventure*. A curious phrase that I'd never heard before. An adventure that went wrong I suppose. A mistaken adventure. A ridiculous adventure. A high level of alcohol and Lysergic acid diethylamide was found in his system. No foul play was suspected and the deceased was alone in the house at the time of his death. Alone in the house. I can hardly bear to hear that and I keep thinking, would Keefer be alive today if I'd stayed? Why the hell did I leave the house? I knew I would probably never know the answer to that. One thing was certain. I wouldn't be taking acid again. The police investigation found cooking oil on the bottom of Keefer's feet. There was also a frying pan on the cooker containing congealed fried eggs and oil on the kitchen floor. The balcony handrail was also covered in oil. The assumption was that Keefer must have slipped on the oil and fell over the balcony. Keefer's sister Julie arrives at the flat. When I see her my heart flips over, she's the spitting image of him and that's because she's his identical twin. It has been arranged to take him back to his hometown of Townsville. Halifax Bay, in North Queensland. Julie goes through his things, most of which she's going to give to a charity shop. She asks Crash Test and I if we want anything. Crash Test says he would like some of the record collection and Keefer's Hawaiian shirt and I think I would like his brick trowel with Keef burned on the handle. This was the trowel he loaned me at lunchtime, the trowel that he taught me how to lay bricks with. The trowel that changed my life and gave me a skill that I would have for the rest of my life. Julie says that she will organise a little memorial for Keefer at St Mary's Church on Edith Road and we are all welcome to attend.

The garden centre is difficult to find. It's at the end of a mews between the allotments and a timber yard. I have never seen allotments before, little patches of land that people rent to grow vegetables in. I speak to a young guy with tufts of weird facial hair that look like they've been planted on his face in a rush. He points me in the right direction. I see three that I hope look fairly similar to the ones I smashed. All gnomes look the same to me. This was something that I felt compelled to do. I couldn't replace Keefer but I could give the old lady her gnomes back, not the same ones of course but not far off. They are cheaper than I imagined, two pounds fifty each. The one with the fishing rod is slightly more expensive and as I look down at the little fella he reminds me of Fergal and I have a sudden urge to go home and see him. They are quite heavy and awkward to carry. I'm very nervous standing outside 36 Castletown Road. But glad to see that the gnomes haven't been replaced.

The lady opens the door. The skin around her face and neck is healthy pink and looks as soft as silk. Her eyes are alert and intelligent. She is wearing an apron with the Van Gogh sunflowers on it. I can smell cooking but can't tell what it is. 'Yes?' she enquires.

'Good afternoon Madam. I live at number 265 and. . .
I'm the person who smashed your gnomes. . . I was given a
drug that made me a little crazy. I didn't know what I was
doing. I thought your gnomes were attacking me. My friend
. . . died on the same night. . . he took the drug as well. . . '
I can't stop the tears. I can't speak anymore. I try to apologise
and tell her that I've bought her some more gnomes, but
I'm in such a state I know I'm not making any sense. I open
the box and take out one of the gnomes. I can't see anything.
I have snot building in my nose and finding it hard to breathe.

'Come inside,' she says, 'come in.'

I follow her into the house. I'm still crying. I try my very
best to stop and when the tears do eventually subside, I
start sobbing like a child, great big hiccups of breath that
are being caught as they try to escape.

She removes her apron and tells me to sit on the sofa.
'Oh dear. It seems you've had those tears building for a while
young man.'

Her name is Hilda and she's eighty years old. Her
husband had bought her the gnomes for her sixtieth birthday
and she hadn't the heart to tell him that she didn't really
like gnomes. Then when she found them smashed she
realised how much she loved her husband and how she
missed him. She said she hadn't cried at his funeral, hadn't
shed a tear at all, not in five years. Nothing, until she saw
those gnomes in pieces in her garden.

'Sadness is a strange thing my dear. Grief can ambush

you when you least expect it. I think we could both do with a little nip of brandy.'

She goes to her drinks cabinet, opens it with a key and pours the brandy from a decanter. For some reason this reminds me of an Agatha Christie novel I once read, *Murder in the Gnome Garden.* I knew there was no such title, but it would do for now. I realise that Hilda hasn't the foggiest idea what a nip consists of as she pours us half a tumbler of brandy each. She disappears to the kitchen and stirs her Turtle soup. Turtle soup? It sounded like a joke. I knew I didn't recognise the smell. She asks me everything about myself and I tell her everything there is to tell. It was similar to being at confession only this was better. I wasn't sure why. Maybe it was because she also told me about herself. I thought that might be an interesting idea for the priests to adopt.

Hilda had been secretary to a British diplomat in Japan and also in India. Was addicted to opium for five years. Got shot in the leg, twice, during the Quit India Movement against the British in 1942. Won first prize for best flower arrangement at the Chelsea Flower show in 1958 and was presented with a medal from the Queen. Was married three times before she met her last husband. Had four miscarriages and eventually adopted a son who was killed in a plane crash in Canada. He was thirty-two, same age as Keefer. At the end of our conversation, she serves up the Turtle soup which is delicious. I could have eaten another bowl but I realise I'd been there almost two hours and said my goodbyes. Hilda asks me to place the three gnomes on the bare patches where the others had once stood. She smiles and says, 'Thank you Emmet. Or should I call you Tom?'

'Yeah you can call me Tom.'

'Alright, Tom, your reckless behaviour has opened up a little door that I had firmly shut. If you ever want to chat you know where I am. '

As I walk down Castletown Road I feel cleansed and also nearer to becoming Tom Joad. The talk with Hilda was like shedding skin. I imagine what Keefer would've said about me going back with the gnomes, *Ha! Yer a fuckin Larrikin, Teejay!*

St Mary's is packed, at least three hundred seated and more standing around the sides. Almost everyone from the North End Road site is here. Annouska is dressed in a black two-piece dress and veil that reminds me of Jackie Kennedy. Julie's speech is funny and very moving, about how being Keefer's identical twin had its drawbacks as they had to share a room until they were eleven. They fought all the time. Keefer had smelly feet, told stupid jokes, thought it was cool to hold her down, fart in her face and smoke his father's cigars. But there were also a lot of perks. When she was 15 years old she was trying to get rid of a boy who was two years older than her, a bit of a creep and a real sex pest. Julie had short hair at the time and sometimes wore a wraparound head scarf inspired by Twiggy. Keefer came up with the idea to wear the scarf, put on her dress and meet the boy in the playing fields after school. She said he really took the whole thing very seriously. Shaved his legs and arms, stuffed her bra with cotton wool, made Julie do his face with her make-up and practiced her voice all day long. He met the boy in the playing fields, told him he didn't want to meet him anymore and to stop being such a pain in the ass. The boy grabbed hold of Keefer and tried to kiss him. Keefer beat the shit out of him, took out his penis, waved it at the boy and shouted, 'Ya still want a fuckin root, mate?' This story gets a very big laugh. She says that Keefer had always been there for her and leaving him to the airport when he flew to London was the hardest thing she ever had to do. But going back with him now, was a thousand times worse. She thanked everyone and the applause she received was loud and long.

Crash Test wears Keefer's Hawaiian shirt and tells a story about how he and Keefer got locked in an Indian restaurant all night because they had fallen asleep behind a curtain. Keefer awoke early in the morning, made tandoori sandwiches with cold naan bread and drank all the beer in the fridge. They weren't able to leave until the cleaners arrived and on the way out Keefer said to one of the cleaners, 'Sorry cobber, my mate left a load of crumbs on the floor over there. Can't take him anywhere!'

Bingo and Lou turn up. I'm pleased to see them and a little surprised, considering they hardly knew Keefer at all. I apologise to Bingo for being late with that week's article. He waves me away and sucks his teeth. 'No pressure man at a time like this.'

Annouska tries to make a speech but keeps breaking down in the middle of it. Julie had previously asked me what song I thought might be appropriate to play at the end and I suggested 'Roadhouse Blues'. That big deep raunchy guitar, stomping piano and honking harmonica opening, plus the passion in Jim Morrison's voice, fills the church and makes my heart swell.

Annouska, Fast Eddie, Crash Test, Strawbs and myself accompany Julie to the airport with the coffin. She hugs each of us in turn and says that she's been very moved by the love which we obviously all had for Keefer. I pick a moment when I can talk with her in private and ask about her mum. I explain that I knew Keefer was upset about her. Julie tells me that her mum was out of the clinic but still heavily dependent on anti-depressants. She had moved out of the family home and was living at her place. I wish her well. On the way back we all go to the Kensington and see a band called The Winkies. I think they're good but I know I'll need to see them again if I want to write about them. I'm too drunk and sad to remember anything clearly.

THIRTEEN

KEEFER HAD BEEN IN MY HEAD all day and wouldn't stop nagging me, 'Go and see ya mum ya fuckin Dill. At least she's not in the fuckin loon bin!'

I ring the bell for the top floor flat. The door is opened by someone coming from the downstairs flat. I explain I'm looking for the people in number 5. The lady smiles, 'No problem.'

The door to number 5 is slightly open. I can hear music playing softly, some kind of African sound. Lots of percussion and xylophone. No Bab Dee-lan tonight. There is an obvious pungent smell of weed and someone snoring. I knock lightly on the living room door. 'Hello?'

I venture in and find Kenny lying on the sofa, his mouth wide open in a silent scream. One leg underneath him the other sticking out at an angle. A sandal hanging from his big toe. His yellow shirt is unbuttoned and twisted around his body. I can hear the baby sobbing and sniffling from the small room. I shake his shoulder. 'Kenny? Hello! Kenny. It's Emmet!'

It looks like Kenny is away with the fairies. I go into the room and baby Andre is standing in the cot, his nappy full of shit and almost hanging off him. To me a child's nappy isn't the worst smell in the world. Cat's shit is much worse and cat food smells like cat's shit. In fact, I think it is cat shit. I think they serve the shit right back to the cat. No wonder cats are so moody and completely untrainable. So would I be if I had to eat my own shit every day. I don't understand men who complain about changing a baby's nappy but are happy enough to clean out a cat litter tray. Andre doesn't look too happy to see me. I look around the room for nappies of some kind. I try the bathroom, search around in cupboards and eventually find some Baby Scott Pinless Diapers. Pinless? What will they think of next? I find a flannel, soak it under the tap, rub a little soap on it. I lift Andre out of the cot and lay him on the floor, his bottom lip is creeping slowly way up over his top lip, he's on the verge of tears, his face is full of fear, but he also knows he's going to get the shit-pack removed so he's biding his time. I want to hit Kenny in the face with this shitty nappy. I'm angry at my mother for getting involved with this waster. I give Andre a good wipe down with the soapy flannel and dry him off, his bum is a little red but not too bad. I let him kick his legs in the air for a bit, tickle his belly and make farting noises. He's still weighing me up but at least he's not crying. I wonder if he's hungry. In my experience children are always hungry, they were in our house that's for sure. I work out how to put on the nappy which is easy enough when I realise I have to peel the white paper off the sides and stick the sticky bits to the dry bits.

Job done. I go to the fridge and find some baby food in a jar. I read that you warm it up by boiling water and then let the jar sit in it for three minutes. I put Andre in the wooden highchair and feed him the brown gloop. The kid is ravenous, he actually grabs my hand and pulls the spoon towards his mouth. No need for, *Here comes the choo-choo train* with this boy. He eats the whole lot in a matter of minutes. I guess he's about a year old. He has one tooth at the front. There's a banana in a fruit bowl on a cupboard. I peel it for him, he wolfs it down and burps loudly, this makes him laugh. I'm shocked because his laugh isn't like a baby at all it's a very adult laugh which he follows with an *'Oooooh.'* I give him a teddy bear which is tied with string hanging on the highchair and go to see if I can resurrect old weedy McDonald. I kick his leg. 'Oy! Wake up!' I shake him much more vigorously than before. 'Hey! Ganja man! Wakey wakey!'

He opens his eyes and when he registers who I am swings his legs around, stands up and starts buttoning his shirt. 'Ah Amet. . . sorry ah fall asleep!' I have to take a pause at this point.

'You left the kid alone in there. I've changed and fed him. How long have you been asleep?'

His bloodshot eyes flicker around the room; now where have I seen this before? He looks at his watch.

'Nat too long, maybe twenty-five meanits, ah been on sheeft wok ya know eet messes with you a lat! Yoa mather wheel be back soon een half an ower. How ah you Amet? Ah deed nat know you would be comeen today. Ah wheel make tea.'

He disappears into the small room and says something to Andre. He comes back with him and hands him to me. 'Thank you Amet for doing the duties fah ma child.'

He disappears again and I can hear him clanging around in the kitchen whistling to himself. I think maybe I should give him the benefit of the doubt. But I have a nagging suspicion that he was asleep for a lot longer than twenty-five minutes and I can't see this relationship working out for my mother. But it's not my business, I just want her to be happy. I'll ask her when I get her on her own. *Are you happy mum?* I rehearse it in my head. *What are your plans with this man? Do you love him?* No. I think to myself. I'm not asking her does she love him? That's like straight out of a bad Hollywood film. *Do you love him, mom? Oh you do? Well, that's great mom! That's all that matters.*

I hear someone on the stairs. The door opens and my mother enters, weighed down with shopping bags. 'Emmet, oh my God. I wasn't expecting to see you.'

Kenny shouts from the kitchen. 'Am makin tea Mollee, ya want some?'

'Yes please Ken!'

Kenny comes in with a tray of tea and biscuits. 'Amet come up and find me sleepin. He change and feed Andre fah me. You have train heem well Mollee. Bat ah theenk he

189

is angry with me and call me ganja man!' Kenny breaks out laughing showing his crooked front teeth.

I'm taken aback by Kenny's openness and good humour. Maybe I'm wrong about him?

My mother goes into the kitchen and dumps the bags, comes back and flops on the seat beside me. Andre cries and holds his arms out to her. She takes him from me, hugs him tightly. 'Oh come here my wee stickin plaster.'

Christ! I remember when she used to say that to me. Kenny announces that he's going for a shower. I small talk with my mother about her day at the hotel kitchen. There's lots I want to ask her but I know this isn't the time. I suggest we go for a beer to the pub on the corner when she walks me to the tube.

We enter The Tabard pub beside Turnham Green tube. It's a Wednesday night so it's not too crowded. My mother wants something called a lager-top which I've never heard of. I find out it's lager with a big dash of lemonade. I tell her about Maeve's upcoming wedding to Lenny O'Brien and the fact I haven't told anyone in the family that we've met. She seems a little stunned that Maeve is getting married.

'Maeve's far too young to be getting married.'

'She's twenty two! You were seventeen when you got married.'

'I know but I had to.' She suddenly stops and stares at me. 'She's not pregnant is she?'

'Oh come on Ma, this is Maeve we're talking about. Of course she's not'

'Lenny O'Brien? I don't know him. Which O'Brien is he?'

I tell her he owns the Brewery Tap pub, he has money and prospects, and he's lucky to be getting my big sister as a wife.

'Oh the Brewery Tap, yes I remember him, big fella with blonde hair.' We sip our drinks. My mother looks far into the distance, a searching look that I imagine is full of regret, but that might just be wishful thinking on my part.

I take this moment to talk about Kenny. 'So, what's happening with Kenny?'

She looks at me and seems surprised by the question. I change tack. 'How did you meet him?'

'We met in the supermarket a few days after I arrived. He let me go in front of him because I only had a few things. We got talking and just hit it off. He made me laugh, was kind, and generous. I told him my situation and it didn't phase him at all. A month later I'd moved in with him, found a job at the hotel and then. . . Andre came along.'

Came along? She makes it sound like Andre just wandered in off the street. 'Maeve was looking for you, is, looking for you. She contacted the Salvation Army. She'd really like you to come to her wedding.'

My mother's eyes fill quickly with tears and she blows her nose on a tissue whipped from her handbag. She snaps the bag shut. 'I can't go back. How can I go back?' She wipes her eyes. 'I'm scared to go back.'

I want to say she's your eldest daughter! To hell with what people think. Go to her wedding, dress yourself up to the nines. Just roll up there like the Queen of Sheba. But I stop myself. I know I'm not qualified in the least to give advice to anyone, especially my mother.

'Kenny wants me to go to America with him. Atlanta Georgia. He has a sister there and an uncle. They run some kind of Nigerian restaurant. They want to expand and think it's safer to employ family. Kenny says that Delta Airlines who he works for at Heathrow are looking into his request for a transfer back to Atlanta. That's where they're based. Every time I talk to him about it things have moved on a little further. He's just assuming that I'm going with him. I haven't said I'm going. I don't know Emmet. I don't know what to do. . . Kenny says this country is going to the dogs, with all these strikes and God knows what. . .and it's terrible too at home. What in the hell are the IRA doing killing innocent people in London, what's that going to achieve? Jesus!'

I go to the toilet. The mirror at the sink has a wave in it which makes my forehead bulge. This is how I feel. When I come back to the table my mother is touching up her lipstick. She rolls both lips inwards and holds them for a second. I take a long slug of my pint.

'It sounds to me like you need to have a big talk with

him about America. When's he thinking of going?'

'He wants to go before Christmas, probably early November.'

'That's only three months away, Ma.'

She sips her lager top.

'I know. I know. I'll speak to him. I will.'

'I think I should tell Maeve and Noreen that I've found you.'

'Found me? You make me sound like a lost dog.'

'You know what I mean.'

'Yes, I know what you mean. I said you could tell them, so, OK, you can tell them. Give Maeve my phone number, ask her to call me.'

FOURTEEN

IT'S A SIX-INCH NAIL and it's rusty. At least three inches of it is sticking into the sole of my right foot. I'm not getting any sympathy from Fast Eddie. 'I told ye to always wear yer fuckin boots. That's what they're for ye stupid cunt! Fuckin running shoes? This is what happens if ye don't wear the right gear! It's a building site for fuck's sake not a fuckin discotheque! Ye could lose yer foot!'

Shit! Now he's scaring the crap out of me. Blood is everywhere and the pain feels dangerous. Fast Eddie and Crash Test help me into the works van and break the speed limit all the way to St Stephen's Hospital where they dump me at A & E reception. Crash Test wants to stay but Fast Eddie's having none of it. 'He's not having a fuckin baby. Yer not his husband. Back to work ye lazy bastard! Any fuckin excuse!'

I'm seen by a female doctor. She tells me her name is Sally. She sounds American. I'm put into a wheelchair by someone who looks very like Bingo. His name tag tells me he's called William. William pushes me down a few corridors. I feel sick and that's what I do. The vomit shoots out of me like water from a hose pipe. William makes no sound, he swerves around the vomit and carries on. Rips a paper towel from somewhere and hands it to me. I wipe my face. I'm wheeled into a room where Doctor Sally is waiting for me. I have sick on my trousers. William hands me more paper towels and a wet wipe. I clean myself down.

'OK let's take a look at this. Wow! You really got skewered. OK we've got to get that out of there. Give you a tetanus jab, clean that up and put you on a course of antibiotics. OK?'

I don't know why she's asking me is it OK, I'm hardly likely to start disagreeing with her. 'I guess we'll also give you an Xray just to make sure nothing's broken. William will take you down to Xray and then we'll take the nail out.'

A hour later Doctor Sally looks at the black and white plastic prints of my Xray. I can see the nail and it really is a long way in. She flaps the X-rays back and forth like she's swatting flies. 'No bones broken so that's good.' She informs me that I'm going to be injected, then immediately injects me in the space between my big toe. This is to numb the area so the nail can be removed and the wound cleaned. After a few minutes she prods me with a needle. 'Can you feel that Mr Joad?'

I can't feel anything. I lie back, look away and have a vague sensation of the nail coming out of my foot. I breathe a sigh of relief and say louder than I need to, 'Wow that's better. I didn't feel a thing doctor.'

Doctor Sally smiles, 'I haven't done anything yet. Just relax.' I try and relax but feel my face burning with embarrassment. 'There we go.' She holds up the bloody nail for everyone to see, looking pleased with herself. 'Do you want to keep it?'

'No,' I say, 'you can have it.' This statement makes me blush even more and I wish I could keep my mouth shut.

She opens a bin with her foot and drops it in. 'Think I'll pass on that.'

I'm on crutches. Crutches are much harder to use than I thought. William adjusts them, moves the legs down a few more inches. 'Try and relax, don't hold the handles so tightly and don't swing out too far as you go along, small steps until you get the hang of it.' I thank him. 'Make sure you drop them back when you're finished. A lot of assholes are too lazy to bother.'

I work on a building site and I hear swearing all the time but for some reason I find William's use of the word assholes shocking and out of place.

I call the site-office from a phone box across from the hospital. I don't fancy crutching it on a bus or a tube. It rings on and on like it's in the bowels of a monastery or a lost room in Buckingham palace. I can visualise the small site office. I know how big it is, twelve-foot by twelve at the most. There's only two people in there, Bridgid and Malcolm. So why aren't they answering?

Eventually I hear Bridgid's voice 'Heloooo M-Jayyy Gleesooons' She has one of those annoying Irish accents that accentuates every word.

'Hi Bridgid, it's Tom Joad here. Can you ask Fast Eddie

to come and pick me up from the hospital'. I hear a noise which sounds like she's put the phone on the table. . . 'Hello. . .Bridgid?' Nothing. I can hear the squeaky office door opening and closing. Bridgid is talking to someone else, laughing at something. 'Hallo. . . Bridgid?' She's left me hanging. I'm shoving ten pence pieces into the phone like an angry loser at a one-armed bandit. More laughter and jokes about Malcolm's bald spot. 'HALLO BRIDGID!'

She answers as if nothing has happened. 'There's nooo neeed to shout like. I'll pass on your message to Eddie but we're nooot a taxi servissss you know.'

I'm just about to say something I'll regret but thankfully she hangs up. Fast Eddie arrives an hour later and drops me home to Castletown Road. He is silent the whole way. I figure he's pissed off with me. I say nothing. Before I get out of the van he says, 'I'll organise a whip round for you on Friday. You're gonna be out for six fuckin weeks at least.'

I try to thank him and he tells me to fuck off and polish my boots.

Crash Test introduces me to our new flat mate. Her name is Sam and she's from New Zealand. Sam looks like an out-doorsy type, sandy haired, very energetic, smiley and freckly, probably in her early twenties. She's like one of those tomboys in Bunty or Judy, the comics for girls that my sisters used to read. Sometimes I would read them and fantasise about having sex with one of the Four Marys. I think Mary

Radleigh was my favourite. I remember she was blonde, good at hockey and putting up tents. Sam tells me she's starting a new job as a researcher at a clinic for something or other, my foot is throbbing so I'm not really listening to her. She smiles and says something else. I nod and she bounds out of the room like she's on springs.

Crash Test and I had considered that one of us could move into Keefer's room as it was the biggest but in the end we decided against it. Even though it had been stripped clean of his things, his presence was still very much there, hanging around in the corners. Crash Test has met someone and is meeting her at a place called Trader Vics. I have to ask what that is. He doesn't know. He looks nervous and keeps changing his shirt and combing his hair in different styles. At one point he has a parting in the middle and I laugh so much my foot gets hot and starts to sting. He tells me to fuck off. Sam comes back into the room and asks if I want some *fush and chups?*

I think fish and chips is a great idea as I realise I haven't eaten all day. 'Yes please, Sam, thank you.'

Sam is back in no time with the food and she doesn't want any money. I hobble into the kitchen to get plates. I open the cupboard and see two packets of Tasty Toobs unopened. It's like I've been punched in the stomach. I wonder does Sam like them? New Zealand is only a kick in the arse from Australia. Sam has never heard of Tasty Toobs. Turns out she's good company, funny and intelligent. I don't think she's aware of it but when she moves around on the sofa her dress rides up her legs and I can see her knickers which are bright blue. I'm finding it hard to concentrate on my fish and chips. Her legs are strong and muscular but also very feminine, she has a butterfly tattoo on the inside of her right thigh. She leans back to put the salt on the table and I get a full view into the great blue yonder. I have a sudden fantasy about having sex with her on the sofa and feeding her chips. I have to stop myself from laughing out loud and my foot starts to throb again. I hope this isn't a feature of things to come in my idle days off work.

I remember I have an article to write for *The Big Fret* and promise myself I'll start tomorrow. I also remind myself I have to tell Maeve about Ma and our new addition to the family which I'm not looking forward to. Sam gets up and makes us tea. I tell her where everything is by shouting from the armchair. When she's back on the sofa she tells me how she's nervous about her new research job but also excited. I am sure this woman has no idea that when she sits down in the dress she is wearing, it moves almost magically up her thighs. She drinks her tea and suddenly her legs just fall wide open. I can now see everything. The butterfly is a Red Admiral. The front of her blue knickers has twisted up inside her. Her pubic hair is light blonde. I spill my tea. She jumps up and is back with a kitchen towel wiping it up. I hope when she sits down again her dress will behave itself. Thankfully she tucks her legs underneath her. This is how

Rosie sits on a couch. I wonder if Rosie is seeing anyone. I hate thinking about this. It makes me anxious and angry. I know the only reason I've been looking forward to Maeve's wedding is the hope that Rosie will be there. I'm also half hoping that Rosie is engaged to some fat farmer and I will be put out of my misery. Maybe she won't be at the wedding – it would be better if she wasn't. I feel downhearted and do this breathing thing through my nose that I've started doing recently. She's a first cousin of Lenny O'Brien, of course she'll be there. I immediately start to feel better. Sam has been saying something to me.

I stare blankly at her. 'What?'

'I was just saying, Trevor says you write for a music mag.'

I had to think for a second who Trevor was.

'Oh yeah that's right. It's called *The Big Fret*, it's more of a fanzine really. It's not in the shops or anything. Just gets sold at gigs.'

Sam shrugs, 'It's still a music mag, thit's pritty cool. I'd like to go to a gig one night if thit's alright? Just tag along. When your foot is bitter thit is!'

'Yeah of course, no problem.'

The phone rings from the landing interrupting our chat. No one answers as usual. Sam jumps up from the couch. 'I'll git it.' She bounces out of the room like Zebedee from The Magic Roundabout. I hear some muffled conversation. Sam is suddenly back in the room. 'Do you know anyone called Eeemit?'

'Ah yeah, I can take that.' I hobble to the door on my crutches and hop the rest of the way down the stairs using the bannister for support. My mothers's voice is strangled and clogged with tears.

'He's gone Emmet!. . . The bastard is gone. . . Jesus! He left Andre with the woman downstairs and just. . . he's gone to America!. . . Can you come round?'

I get a taxi to Turnham Green. I have no idea how people can afford taxis all the time. It's a bit of a luxury riding in a cab and I'm enjoying it. I ring the top bell at 135 Abinger Road and straight away I hear a baby crying. This is crying above and beyond the call of duty. My mother opens the door. She's a jumping bag of nerves and her hair looks like it's been electrocuted. Andre is squirming in her arms, his face a screaming ball that's leaking snot from everywhere. A man appears in the hallway wearing a vest and shorts, half of his face covered in shaving cream. 'Oy! Can't you keep that fucking brat quiet? He's been yapping since six o'clock this morning.' This sets Andre off into gold-medal-Olympic-screeching. I tell the half-shaved man to fuck off! Unless he wants a fucking crutch wrapped around his face. He grunts something and disappears, slamming a door. When we get to the living room Andre is beginning to wind down a notch. I try and distract him with funny faces. My mother lowers him into the highchair and gives him a green lollipop. This seems to do the trick.

'I hate to give him sweets when he cries because then he

just cries when he wants sweets.' She sits on the edge of the couch and blows her nose on a hankie. 'What happened your foot?'

'I stood on a nail at work. It's not serious.' She shoves the hankie quickly up her sleeve like a bad magician.

'We had a big row about Atlanta. I found a letter he got from his sister it said, "She's a white girl, Kenny, are you sure about her? It's not like you're married to her or have children." He obviously hadn't told them about Andre. He wasn't going to tell them until I arrived. It was then that I made up my mind not to go. He said I shouldn't have been snooping in his private letters. Can you believe that? Private letters? He never said anything for two or three days and all that time he was planning to leave. I got home from work on Friday and found out that Liz who lives in number 3 had been looking after Andre all day. There was a note from Ken saying that by the time I read it he would be on his way to Atlanta. He's paid the rent for the next month but I don't know what I'm going to do Emmet. I can't work and look after Andre, and I can't afford a childminder!

I hear myself saying, 'I can look after him if you want? For the next few weeks anyway. I'm not working, so I can stay here while you go to work.' My sensible head is thinking, *What the hell are you talking about? That's a mental idea.* My mother's jaw actually drops open. 'No Emmet, I can't let you do that, you're on crutches for God's sake. Liz is out of work at the moment so maybe she can look after him until I sort something out?' I'm praying to God Liz says yes.

'Well the offer is there if you want it.' I don't know why I always feel the need to play the hero. I absolutely don't want to live here with my mother and look after Andre all day. That's the sole reason I came to London in the first place, to get away from this sort of crap. I promise myself there and then that I'll never say this kind of thing again. From now on I'm going to be honest with myself and everyone else.

My mother gets up from the edge of the couch. 'I'll go and speak to Liz now and explain the situation.'

Andre licks his green lollipop. I notice his face still has snot on it. I wipe it with a tissue. He doesn't want his face wiped and starts to cry again. I keep wiping and blow a big raspberry. He gives a hint of a smile through his tears. I look at Andre. Look at him properly for the first time. He reminds me of someone but I can't figure out who – and then it dawns on me, he looks a bit like Muhammad Ali. The more I look at him the more I can see it. This makes me laugh. I start to shadow box around him hopping on one leg. 'Are you the greatest, Andre, are you? Huh? What's my name? Huh, what's my name? My name's Tom Joad, you hear me? What's my name? Float like a butterfly sting like a bee. I'm gonna whup yo nigger ass!'

I can hear my mother on the stairs. She comes in smiling. 'That woman is a saint. She said she can look after him for a month.'

'Thank God. I mean. . . that's great Ma.'

'I told her I would pay her a hundred quid. I don't know why I said that Emmet, it just came out of my mouth. I do this kind of thing all the time.' Now I know where I get it from. 'I'm so stupid, Emmet. I don't have a hundred quid.'

'I have a hundred quid ma. I'll pay her for you.' This time I do mean what I say. My mother hugs me and starts to cry again. She looks into my face.

'I don't suppose you've called Maeve yet?'

'No, not yet.'

'That's OK, I was thinking you could call her from here.' My gut feeling is, this isn't a good idea. I suggest that I write to her first. I explain it will be awkward for her to hear this news at the Pattersons. Mandy is very nosey and always wants to know what's going on. My mother knows Mandy Patterson very well and agrees that I should write first and arrange a time for Maeve to ring.

'OK, Monday or a Wednesday evening around eight o'clock would be best.'

FIFTEEN

SAM HAS CLEANED THE FLAT within an inch of its life. Hoovered and scrubbed and dusted everything in sight. It smells like a fresh summer meadow. She's wearing some kind of overalls and a mask. When she sees me hobbling into the room she switches off the hoover and pulls the mask down.

'Oh hi. I'm allergic to dust mites. Just thought I'd give the place the once over, hope you don't mind?'

I realise that neither myself or Keefer or Crash Test had ever cleaned the flat. The most we did was the washing up. I didn't even know there was a hoover so there must have been at least two years of dirt, we just didn't see it. But it's amazing what Sam has done. The place looks like new, especially the kitchen.

'No, I don't mind,' I say. 'You've done a great job. We're dirty bastards. We'll try and keep it cleaner in future.'

She grins and her freckles bunch up on her nose.

'How's your foot?'

'It still stings a bit but I need to go back tomorrow and get the dressing changed.'

'Nah! No need for the hospital. I'm a first aider. I can change it for you. Just need to git a few things from the kumist, proper bandage peds, surgical tape, a tube of antiseptic ointment. I'll have it done in a jiff.'

I'm a bit stumped. I can't figure out if she's really trying to be helpful or if it's something else. Maybe a slight hint of desperation to be liked? She's only known me for two days and already she's offering to change a stinky bloody bandage on my foot. I want to say yes, OK, go ahead, but I've promised myself I won't do this anymore. I have to be honest.

'No, that's OK, Sam. I think I need to go in and let them have a proper look, you know, make sure it's not infected.'

She goes up and down on her tiptoes. 'OK, yeah, you might be right. Listen do you like Thai food?'

'Thai. . . em I've never had it, so I don't know.'

'Do you want to give it a go? I'm going round the corner to get some. Prad Priew Wan is nice, that's just sweet and sour chucken or fush.' I have no idea what sweet and sour chicken is. It sounds disgusting so I say, 'Yeah, why not. Let's go for it!'

'Great! I'll be bick in a jiff.' I don't really want Thai food. I'm going to have to work on this saying no business.

Sam comes back with sweet and sour chicken for her and sweet and sour shrimps and jasmine rice for me. It's the most beautiful exotic food I've ever tasted in my life. My God, I'm drooling as I eat it. 'Sam, this is really amazing!'

She laughs loudly. 'It's only bloody Thai!' Her laugh starts with a little scream and then an accordion of giggles in and out. Her laugh cracks me up, the two of us are in stitches and don't hear Fast Eddie and Crash Test come in.

Crash Test looks around the room. 'Bloody hell fiah! Who cleaned the place?'

'I did, Crash Test. Did it all this morning on one leg.'

Sam's glowers at me. 'He bloody didn't!'

Crash Test bows in front of Sam. 'Thank thee, Sam. Looks like ya found owar flat unda durt!'

Fast Eddie picks up one of my crutches studies the extendable leg like he's never seen one before. 'How's the foot?'

'It's starting to itch so I think it's getting better. I should be back in a couple of weeks.'

He grunts and throws me a brown envelope. 'Huh! That's from the lads. Ya don't fuckin deserve it. I'll let meself out.' Fast Eddie disappears.

Crash Test sniffs the air. 'Listen, it's nowt paysonal, but it bloody stinks in eer. So I'm off out to get mesen fish n chips.'

'You don't know what you're missing Crash Test, it's delicious.'

He's halfway down the stairs. 'Aye tell us tha when your ont toy-let!'

Sam suddenly looks puzzled. 'Why do you call him Crash Test?'

'It's his nickname. He keeps getting run over by cars and bicycles but it never seems to do him any harm. He's indestructible.'

'The other man seems a bit grumpy.'

'Fast Eddie? Nah, that's just a front. He's a great guy really.' I'm pleased Sam is wearing jeans. I wouldn't have wanted to be distracted eating this wonderful food.

'Oh!' She says, remembering something, goes to the table and takes a card from her handbag. 'I found this under the bead. It's a birthday cad, must belong to whoever hid the room before me.' She hands me Keefer's 32nd birthday card. A surfer riding the waves. Signed by Julie, his dad and the scrawly hand of his mum. I hear Keefer crying, *Look at her writing, it's all over the shop.* I stare at the card and suddenly think maybe I should look for another place. There is just too much of Keefer in this flat. Sad memories that keep ambushing me like a slap in the face.

'You OK, Tom?'

'Yeah sure. . . it's eh. . . yeah it's the guy who had the room before you. . . Keefer. . . his name was Keefer. It's his.' Sam has a mouthful of food she waits until she's swallowed it.

'If you have a forwarding address, I can send it on.'

'No don't worry about it. . . I can do that. . . '

The hospital are very pleased with the progress of my foot. The hole has closed over and there's no sign of infection. I get the tube back home. People get up to let me sit down. English people are mostly friendly and polite. Even with the IRA bombs going off. I haven't had any shit from anyone. Fast Eddie says this is because English people are stupid and think I'm Scottish. He reckons they can't tell the difference between the Scottish and Northern Irish accent. I tell him that the Hammersmith police know the difference. He says he gets plenty of stick from the general public which isn't fair as it's us Nordy bastards who are causing all the problems.

When I'm back in the flat I count the money in the brown envelope – £220. I'm really shocked, I wasn't expecting this much. I check my post office book. I have £585.45. I hear Madge McGuckian's advice, *Saving is sensible son. There's always going to be plenty of rainy days. You'll always need savings. It's something you should always do.* How right she was. Good old Madge. I go to my bedroom, get my best pen and notepaper and write to Maeve.

Dear Maeve

It's not long now until Lenny O'Brien will make a dacent woman of you. I have your last letter here which says you tighten the noose on his neck on the 25th of November, so that's only weeks away.
I have some good news, and there's some weird news. The good news is I bumped into Ma on the street a few weeks ago. It was her who recognised me from my walk. I think, it was meant to be, as they say. Whatever that means? Anyway, she's living in Chiswick which isn't far from where I live in West Kensington and she would like you to call her. Next Monday or Wednesday night at 8 o'clock would be good. She doesn't want you to tell Da yet, just Noreen, nobody else for now.

She will tell you the weird news herself. It will better coming from her. Her number is 01 994 6635.
Can you let me know if you've seen Rosie Byrne around? Is she still at Queens?
Talk to you soon. See you on the 25th.
Emmet. oxox

Dear Emmet
Oh my God! Meeting Ma in the middle of London? That's incredible. How is she? Is she alright? Did she look OK? What the hell is the weird news? I wish you'd just tell me. I can't sleep now with all this and I've enough on my plate. I will call on Monday with Noreen. I will ring from the Brewery Tap. The phone is inside a booth there, so it's more private. I won't tell anyone else. I wouldn't have anyway until I know the lie of the land.
I haven't seen Rosie Byrne. Why don't you write to her? You're such a coward always running away from your feelings. Anyway talk to you on Monday. I'm so glad Ma is safe and well.
Talk to you and Ma on Monday.
Maeve oxoxo

I'm walking without the crutches. I have to walk slowly. I suppose this is how old people have to walk all the time. It's incredibly tedious. It takes me forty minutes to shuffle to the shops for a pint of milk. Twenty minutes each way. When my foot was pain free I could do it in three minutes. As I pass by Hilda's house I stop and have a look at the gnomes, they seem to be smiling at me. I feel a real affinity with these little men. I smile back and give them the thumbs up. 'Alright lads?' I considered going in to see her but decide against it. I'm not really in the mood. As I'm climbing the stairs the phone rings and I answer it.

'Hello.' A pause on the line.

'Hi, is that Tom?' It's the unmistakable voice of Eva. I'm surprised when my heart flutters a bit.

'Yeah, is that Eva?'

'Of course, it's Eva. How many other American girls do you know Mr Joad?'

'You're the one and only Eva.'

She huffs. 'Yeah, right. Listen, do you want to meet up. Have a drink or something?' I'm in two minds about this. I have to be true to my FEELINGS! I try and stop my mind from whizzing around. Should I say no. I think I'll say no.

'Tom?'

'Yeah. . . I was just thinking . . . you'll have to come here because I'm injured. Stood on a nail at work.'

'Oh, that's gross. Yeah, I can come to you. How about tonight? Say 7.30?'

'Yeah that sounds good.' I give her the address.

'Oh Castle-town Road Ken-sing-ton!' She draws out the words with fake impressed sarcasm. 'That's posh huh?'

'Absolutely, the Queen is always walking up and down our road, all the time. . .'

'Oh how exciting. I'll bring my autograph book. See you at 7.30, bye.' Well, it didn't take me long to change my mind on that. Either I'm a weak-willed fool, or I'm becoming more assertive.

When Crash Test gets in from work, I tell him I have a girl coming over. He says, 'Is she frum one o those prossie callin cads out phone box?' I tell him to fuck off. We tell each other to fuck off quite a lot, Crash Test and me.

He shakes his head in mock despair. 'Awright, ave no choice then but to go down t pub!' I ask him about his date at Later Dates or whatever it was called? 'Trada Vics!' He says with venom. 'It's only top a fucking Ilton otel. A cocktail ba! Cost me bloody faw-tune and then the silly cow kisses ma cheek, gets a cab om and leaves us right in middle a street! Ya live and learn mate.'

I laugh loudly. 'I'm trying to imagine you in a cocktail bar, Jesus!'

He laughs along with me. 'A telt thee Tum there wey a mirror in the bloody toy-lets where ya piss like, so you cud see ye sen pissing. Ah mean who wants to see them sen pissing? Fuckin Lundeners mate. I can't mick em out me. A need a showar!' He disappears up the stairs.

Our doorbell rings. It never fails to startle me it's so frigging loud, like a school yard bell. Eva is forty minutes early. I haven't shaved or brushed my teeth. I plod my way down the stairs, one step at a time. It's Sam. 'Oh sorry, Tom, I forgot my key. At least I hope I forgot it and not lost it.'

Sam runs up the stairs like an antelope. I follow slowly in her wake. I'm actually out of breath when I get to the top.

I can't understand how walking slowly can be more tiring than moving fast? Sam is all smiles, shaking a bunch of keys at me. 'Found thim on the bead! Hey do you fancy a little Thai tonight?'

I really do want some Thai. My mouth is instantly watering at the thought, but should I tell Sam I have someone coming over? No why should I? I'm having dinner with my flatmate. Eva will have to put up with that. 'That would be great Sam. It's my turn to pay this time.'

She gives a big, exaggerated nod of her head. 'Yeah, it bloody well is.' I like the way Sam is getting into the swing of how we behave in this flat, she's fitting in very well.

Sam and I are halfway through the Thai, I think I'll move to Thailand if the food is this good. Sam tells me about a guy at her work who keeps touching her ass as he goes past. 'He kinda just brushes his hend across my butt when talking to me or explaining something, like it's a casual thing, you know like it's on my shoulder or something. He's my minager so I hiven't sid anything yet.'

I tell her I have an idea. She moves in closer. 'Oh yeah what's thit?'

'Ask him if he knows who the IRA are? He'll know who they are. And then you feign surprise and say, "Oh my God, really? I had no idea that's what they were. It's just that my boyfriend's from Ireland and he told me he was a member. He was drunk at the time, so I suppose he's just kidding." And then just walk away and leave it hanging. I bet you a hundred quid he doesn't touch your ass again.'

Sam almost chokes on her Thai. 'Oh my God, Tom. I can't. . .' she laughs and spits food everywhere. 'I can't say I'm going out with a terroreest.'

'He won't really believe you have a boyfriend in the IRA but he'll get the message, unless he's a complete Dick.'

Sam shakes her head and wipes her face with a tissue. 'OK, if I'm disperate I'll give it a go! But I'm blaming you if I get sicked.'

The doorbell clangs like a fire engine. Sam jumps up, 'I'll git it!'

Before I can tell her it's Eva, she's already halfway to the door. Footfall on the stairs. I can't hear any chat. Sam comes in. 'It's someone called Eva for you.' Sam flops down on the sofa and continues eating, then gives me a secret glance and whispers, 'She's a bit of a looker.'

Eva appears at the door with a bottle of wine in her hand. She's wearing white sneakers and bobby socks, a red polka dot skirt, white blouse with small red flowers on it. Her jet-black hair is falling over her shoulders, the lipstick on her lips is bright red and glistening in places. She really is stunningly beautiful. I have no idea how I can possibly be going out with her. If that's what I am doing? I think of Keefer again, can hear his voice. *I was kiddin myself that I could hold on to a fit bird like Nooski.* I notice I have a piece of cooked onion on my shirt and suddenly feel like a crippled homeless tramp.

Eva looks around. 'Nice room. 'Really big and airy. I love it.'

I get to my feet. 'Sam this is Eva, Eva, Sam.'

They exchange smiles. 'Something smells good.'

'Yeah,' Sam says. 'We're just funishing off a Thai. I would have ordered you something if I'd known you were coming.' I think I detect a hint of blame towards me in Sam's voice.

Eva smiles 'Oh, that's OK, I've already eaten.' She waves the wine bottle. 'Anyone like a glass of Chianti?'

Sam rises quickly from the couch, picks up our empty takeaway boxes. 'Not for me thanks.' Sam turns to me. 'Think I'll pop down to the pub and keep Trevor company. Nice to meet you Eva.'

Eva raises those eyebrows. I go to the kitchen and get two glasses. I haven't used these since we toasted Keefer, more memories. Eva points at the top of the wine bottle. 'Corkscrew?' I go back to the kitchen and rummage for a corkscrew. I find something that could be one.

When I come back into the living room I casually hand it to Eva but she gives me the bottle. This corkscrew thing has what looks like two arms that go up and down and a screw in the middle of a round open cap type thing with a sort of bottle opener at the top. I fiddle with it, turn it upside down. The screw bit drops down. I move the arms up and down but I'm not sure what I'm doing. My face is reddening. I go to the kitchen so as I can cool down. Eva grabs my arm. 'Give it to me. ' She moves the arms up, inserts the corkscrew carefully into the centre of the cork and gently twists the bottle opener top which inserts the corkscrew into the cork. As this is happening the little arms of the thing are coming up like a skinny woman exercising. When the corkscrew is fully in, Eva pushes the arms down which slowly pulls the cork out of the bottle with a little pop! She grins at me. 'It's called a lever opener. Now you know how to use it.'

I shrug, 'We don't drink a lot of wine'.

I pour two glasses and we get comfortable on the sofa. Eva gives me one of her knowing smiles. 'She likes you.'

'Who?

'Oh come on you know who, Sam.'

I laugh like a bad actor in a bad film. 'Nah she doesn't. She hardly knows me, she just moved in.'

Eva shrugs. 'OK, if you say so, but I know when someone likes someone, and she was pissed that you didn't tell her I was coming.'

I start thinking about Sam's butterfly. Was it fluttering innocently or did she let it go on purpose? I think about how to change the subject. 'Have you moved into a new apartment yet?'

'Yes I have! I'm now free of the crazy Noreen. I see her sometimes in the refectory and she just glares at me like Baby Jane.'

I try and work out should I just smile and nod as if I know who Baby Jane is – No. I'm not doing this anymore – 'Who's Baby Jane?'

'It's a character in a movie played by Bette Davis. It's a great movie, we should go see it. Sometimes they show old movies at the BFI.' Before I can ask Eva says, 'The British Film Institute.'

Sometimes I wish I had a custard pie so as I could shove it in Eva's face. I wish I hadn't thought of this because now I want to laugh and have to fight it. I'm not doing a very good job of it. Eva is all over me, 'What's funny?'

I'm sniggering like a ten-year-old. 'Oh. . . for some reason I was just thinking about Crash Test, my flatmate. He went to a cocktail bar at the Hilton Hotel and there was a mirror in the toilets.'

Eva screws up her face. 'What's funny about that?'

'The mirror was on the urinals you could see yourself when you were. . . you know, having a pee.'

Eva sips at her wine. 'That's what you were thinking about in the middle of our conversation?' She sighs. 'You know something Tom. Sometimes you're so full of shit.'

I consider whether I'm feeling angry about this or not, or if I have a sneaking admiration for her being able to see through me but before I can come to any conclusion she says, 'Let's go to bed, you wanna go to bed?'

I stand up, my foot is suddenly throbbing. 'Yeah. . . sure, let's go.'

The iron frame of my bedstead has two big brass rods on each side with six or seven smaller ones in the middle. Each of the big rods has a copper ball on the top. One of them is loose and every time Eva and I move together on the bed it spins around making a dinging sound like the bell on a hotel reception. *Ding Ding Ding!* This has never happened when I've been in the bed alone. My head has been between Eva's legs for what seems like a long time. She has hold of my ears. I've never done this before. I don't know what I'm doing. It's as if I'm eating some kind of fruit that has no end to it and I don't have a choice when to stop and take a breather. Every now and then Eva goes into a kind of spasm, arches herself into my face and pulls my head hard towards her groin. She's in total control of my face, moving it up and down and sometimes sideways depending on which position is the most satisfying to her. The only reason my tongue is going in and out is because I think I'm trying to yell. She's the driver of this speeding sex bus and I feel like an innocent passenger who can't get off. *Ding Ding Ding!* Eva is making all kinds of noises and little screeches through her teeth which sound as if they're gritted. Finally she almost rips my ears off and shouts, 'FUCCCCCK!' at the top of her lungs. Jesus Christ! I come up for air. I'm literally gasping and roll on to my side like a drowning man saved. Eva cuddles me and kisses the back of my neck. We lie like this for a long time. I can feel her heartbeat against my back. My own heart galloping. Gradually her breathing becomes shallow, soon I can barely hear it at all and realise she has fallen asleep. I have to pee and as quietly as I can, disentangle myself from her. Slip on my underpants and creep upstairs to the bathroom. I catch sight of my reflection in the mirror. I look like I've been slapped hard around the face with a wet flannel and my ears have been painted bright red. Once again, I don't know how I feel. When Eva wakes up I'm going to have proper sex with her. Sex where I'll be involved in what's going on and when it's over, I will ask myself how I feel. This never happened with Rosie. I always knew how I felt with Rosie. It was never an issue.

I ease myself quietly into bed beside her. She puts her arm on my shoulder and gently pulls me around to face her. She kisses me. It's a tender deep kiss. I feel her legs opening beneath me and we're making love, she is very wet from all the kissing. Her eyes are open, she's looking at me. It's a questioning look, a look I don't understand. We kiss again more urgently. She brings her legs up and holds her ankles, never taking her eyes off me. It's like she's saying, *Is this the way you want it?* Everything becomes a little frantic like a race to the finish. Our breathing is rapid and together and finally I collapse on top of her. She takes my face in her hands and stares at me. 'What?' I say to her. She doesn't answer. I roll off her and lie on my back. I've never noticed the ceiling rose before. There is also a brown damp patch in the far corner under the window. She gets out of bed and puts on her black knickers and bra. I'm aware of a change of atmosphere. I get out of bed and take her hand. She pulls it away. 'Hey. . . are you OK?'

She steps into her polka dot skirt. 'I don't know Tom.

It's just. . . I think you're not really present with me. Look, I know you're in love with someone else. I'm right aren't I?' She pulls a little zip across on the side of her skirt. 'You're in love with someone tell the truth!'

'YES!' I shout, 'yes I am. Her name is Rosie. She was my first love. I think about her all the time. I've stopped writing to her. She's at university in Belfast. I don't know if she's with anyone else. I'm hoping she isn't. I'm going home for my sister's wedding and I'm hoping she'll be there. I don't know what good that will do because as soon as the wedding's over I'm coming back to London. I had to leave home because I couldn't stand living in the same house as my father. My mother left him as well and came to London, she moved in with a Nigerian guy and got herself pregnant and now she has a child and he's fucked off to America and left her alone to fend for herself. So yeah! I am in love!' I'm totally annoyed and surprised at myself. I didn't want to say any of these things.

Eva's eyebrows go up and stay up. She sits on the bed beside me. 'Jesus Christ Tom. You've been holding all that in? Is it any wonder you're uptight.'

This assumption really pisses me off. 'I haven't been holding it in. It's private stuff. What would you like me to do? Go around spouting my feelings all over the place like some ponce? I'm fine. And I'm not uptight! And I'm surprised that you think I'm not present, because it feels to me like you're only concerned about yourself when we're having sex! I don't feel included at all!'

She backs away from me. 'Wow! You have a lot of anger inside you.'

'Oh don't give me all that bollocks! Everybody has anger inside them. What about you Eva? What are you angry about?'

She looks shocked. Her face goes into lockdown. She puts on her white blouse and carefully does up the buttons, and without looking drags a lipstick quickly and expertly across her lips, ties her hair back and speaks to me in a hoarse angry whisper. 'C'mon let's go to the bar around the corner. I need a beer and I have to tell you something.'

I suggest we go to the Old Oak. I know that Sam and Crash Test will probably be in the Clarence. It's a slow walk for me but my foot seems a little better. I remember I'm still on antibiotics so I order an orange juice for me and a beer for Eva. We sit in the corner. It's right next to a dart board so I'm hoping no one starts playing. My orange juice is warm. Eva opens her bag, takes out a tissue and cleans the lipstick from her lips. I wonder why she's doing this, she's only just put it on. Maybe she needs sensible unsexy lips to tell me whatever she's going to tell me. One of her eyebrows arches and then comes back down slowly.

'A year and a half ago I was sexually attacked. His name was Rick. He was three years older than me. Worked as a mechanic in town and rode a motorcycle. I thought he was cute and kind of real, you know, not like the boys I knew at college. I'd been flirting with him for a while. Made it more than obvious I was interested. So one day we hook up. He drives me out of town on his bike, we take a walk into the woods and all of a sudden he just. . . drags me into the bushes, pulls my skirt down, throws me on my back and rapes me, and then, jumps on his bike and takes off. . . I had to walk three miles back home.'

I realise I've drunk all of my orange juice which I don't remember doing. I'm not sure what to say. But I know I have to say something. 'So what happened to him?'

She shrugs. 'Nothing.'

'Nothing? Didn't you go to the police?'

She shakes her head slowly. 'No. This is the first time I've spoken about it to anyone.'

I go to drink my orange juice but remember I've none left. 'When I arrived in London I tried to get back to normal. So I started dating again. But every single one of them was just too keen to get inside my pants. It was obvious that's all they wanted. I blamed Noreen for scaring them off, but if I'm honest, I guess I wasn't ready. And then you came along. All that trouble you went through to find me. Climbing on rooftops, almost getting arrested. What girl wouldn't be flattered? But when we kissed for the first time. . . there was so much love and affection in that kiss, I just knew you had to be kissing someone else. Turns out I was right, and for some reason, that made me feel safe. But it also made me a little jealous. I suppose I thought if you're in love with the person you imagine you're kissing then, you wouldn't ever hurt me physically. I don't know why I behaved the way I did. The hair pulling, all of that. I guess that's what I meant when I said you had awoken something in me. You made me feel I could do that to you, be in control. It was like you had liberated me. Oh Christ. . . I don't know if I'm making any sense?' Eva starts to cry. She takes a bunch of tissues out of her handbag and holds them to her face like she's stemming a blood flow.

I want to hug her but we're in a pub so I say, 'I'm just amazed that you could get all that from a kiss.'

She nods and smiles. It's a rueful smile. 'Well, maybe getting raped has heightened my sensitivity.'

I look into my empty orange juice glass. 'I need something stronger than a warm orange juice. Do you want another beer?' She shakes her head and blows her nose. I return with a pint of lager.

Eva is staring into her Heineken. She looks up at me. 'Do you know the song 'It's in His Kiss?' by Betty Everett.'

'I'm not sure. I don't think so.'

'I used to love that song. I still do.' Eva starts to sing softly under her breath. It's a strange change of mood as she still has tears in her eyes. When she finishes, she sips her beer.

I give a gentle applause. 'I have heard that song before. My mother used to sing it around the house.'

'Yeah, it was a big hit in the sixties. What's the baby's name?'

'His name is Andre.'

'Andre. That's nice.' We sit in silence for some time.

I can hear a song coming from somewhere, maybe from a car radio stopped at the traffic lights or from an open window of one of the high-rise flats on the other side of North End Road. It's a new song from David Bowie, 'Rock n Roll Suicide'. I'm not sure what I think of Bowie. His music is hard to pin down, but I think I like this one. I've heard it played a lot on the radio. The way he sings 'you're not alone' sounds like he really means it, a real cry from the heart. But then he is a showman.

I walk slowly with Eva back to the tube station. She suddenly looks vulnerable. Not like she looked when she swanned into the living room two hours ago. I don't know if I should hug her or not, or ask to see her again. I don't really know what to say or do. I feel stupid. She's the one to break the silence. 'We don't have to make any arrangements yet, OK?'

'Sure.'

'When are you going home for the wedding?'

'In a couple of weeks.'

'OK, let's leave it until you get back.' She gives me a peck on the cheek and disappears into West Ken tube.

SIXTEEN

MY MOTHER AND I sit around staring at her phone. Andre has been fed and is out for the count. This boxing analogy reminds me he looks like Muhammad Ali and makes me smile. My mother tells me that the half-shaved man came up and apologised, brought flowers and a bottle of wine. Said he'd lost his job and was sorry he took it out on the kid. We are drinking his wine. I'm no connoisseur but it tastes like petrol. The flowers look OK, though. The phone rings making us both jump. My mother stares at it, lets it ring. 'Do you want me to answer it?'

'No.' She picks up the receiver. 'Hello. Maeve?' I can hear the far away tinny voice of my sister she's talking quickly. From here on in I'm hearing a one-sided conversation which is always annoying, even if you don't care who the people are or what they're saying.

'Yes yes I'm fine I'm. . . OK. . . I know, it was a million to one chance. . . I knew it was him right away with that walk of his. . . I just had to get away Maeve. . . I was going mad . . . I know you do but I just had to leave. . . It wasn't easy love, believe me. . . I couldn't tell anybody, I didn't want to think too much about it. . . otherwise I couldn't have done

it. . . how is he?. . . I know but how many times has he said
that?. . . Yes I am. . . in a hotel in Victoria I work in the
kitchens. . . I don't know darlin. . . I know you do. . . but
look. . . Maeve, I've something to tell you. . . It's. . . I met
this man when I was here, and we moved in together and I
. . . I got pregnant. . . I know it is. . . Maeve listen. . . listen to
me. . . Jesus Maeve. . . I know that. . . but it's happened now
and I have to deal with it. . . A boy. . . Andre, he's thirteen
months. . . Kenny. . . he was from. . . Nigeria. . . Yes Nigeria
. . . yes of course he's black. . . Well he's half and half . . . well
I don't care about that. . . I'd love to come to your wedding
darlin you know I would. . . but. . . it's going to take the
focus away from you if I turn up with Andre in my arms and
that's not fair on you on your big day. . . well, that's the
thing – Kenny has left me. . . I know. . . I know. . . but that's
the situation. . . I do have someone looking after him when
I'm at work, yes, I could but. . . Maeve darlin even without
Andre people are still going to be asking me questions. . .
and I want the day to be about you. . .'

I get up and go into the kitchen. My foot is so much
better. I'm almost up to my old speed. I make myself a coffee
to hopefully get rid of the taste of the Esso petrol. It sounds
like Maeve has taken the baby news well and from what I
can gather still wants Ma to come to the wedding. I can now
hear Ma talking to Noreen. The conversation doesn't seem
as strained. She talks for another twenty minutes or so. I
hear the bye byes and the receiver clicking back on the cradle.

I go back out with my coffee. My mother gives a long deep sigh.

'Well, that went alright, I think. . . much better than I thought. She wants me to go to her wedding of course, but I don't know Emmet, you know what that town is like for gossip and people bad-mouthing. I'll have to think about it. I don't want to spoil her day and who knows how your father will react when he's had a few?'

'Ma, she obviously wants you to go and sure Da is Da, there's no knowing what he'll do. But that's always been the case with Da. If he wants to find an excuse to go off his head then he will. If not at you then at somebody else. It's not like it'll be a surprise for anybody. The whole town knows what he's like. And if he starts anything, I'm fit for him now. I won't let him away with it.'

She lies back on the sofa. 'That's all we need, you and your father going at it at Maeve's wedding.'

'I'm sure he'll be fine. He stayed sober for granda's funeral.'

The landings and hallway of Castletown Road flat are being painted. There are step ladders and white sheets draped all down the bannisters. It's like walking into a sailing ship. There's something about the smell of fresh paint. It's always positive. A new start. I'm speaking to Bingo on the phone but it's hard to hear every word with the work that's going on. Painters always have radios blaring. Brickies never listen to radios. Bingo is saying he liked the article on Ace and would like me to write another this weekend. 'Befah ya go to Island.'

I like the way he makes Ireland sound like Island which it is of course. 'I want you to go see Kilburn and the High Roads. They're playing Dingwalls in Camden try to get a few words with the lead singer, Ian Dury. He's quite a character and has polio. I've already spoken to their manager he says it's cool.'

I'd seen Kilburn and the High Roads before at the Kensington but had only caught the the last two songs of their set. I remember liking the lead singer a lot. Sam had asked me on the first day we'd met if she could come to a gig, so I thought the High Roads at Camden would be a good introduction.

Dingwalls at Camden Lock was a bit of a barn. It had quite a long bar so we didn't have to wait long to be served. Sam had dressed up, even though I told her she didn't need to. She looked a little out of place in her green low-cut dress, big sparkly earrings and high heeled boots. I never imagined she had clothes like that. Then someone bumps into her and spills beer down the front of her dress. They apologise 'Oh sorry sorry sorry, so sorry.' Sam makes a face at me. 'No worries mate someone told me I shouldn't a dressed up.'

The room wasn't completely full but I could sense the band had accumulated a few more fans since I first saw them at the Kensington. There was an air of excitement. Finally, twenty-five minutes late, they took to the stage. It was hard to describe the music. They were quite a ragged bunch and had a varied repertoire with songs like 'The Naughty Lady of Shady Lane'. And novelty songs such as 'Fuck off Noddy'. Dury's left leg and arm were almost useless but he was one of the most animated performers I'd ever seen, throwing himself around the stage and he sang the way he spoke, with a thick cockney accent. The piano player was amazing – he really stood out. They also did a beautiful country ballad called 'Crippled with Nerves' where he showed that he could actually sing a bit. The evening was a mixture of a piece of theatre and a music gig. When I finally got to speak to him he looked exhausted. I asked him about the inspiration for his lyrics.

'Well, it's a mix mate. Bit of Max Wall. Bit of Jazz. Everyfing just comes out of me, fuck knows where from? I gotta very eclectic taste mate. Gene Vincent, John Coltrane, the Mississippi Chain Gang stuff, bit of Skiffle and then there's me gran. She could knock out a tune.' His laugh is smoky and infectious. 'I love it mate, love it all, I love words and poetry and I like to shake em up, rattle and fuckin roll em. I'm not scared of juxtaposition, love a bit of that. If it's not the norm then it must be OK, that's what I believe. People say I'm an eccentric. I don't think I am, and I suppose if you think you're an eccentric then you're definitely not. We're working on a new album at the moment, 'Handsome'. That's the name of the album mate. I'm not referring to you!' And he's

Tom Joad and Me

off again with that laugh. 'It'll be released soon, make sure you mention it.' He was very giving and we spoke for another twenty minutes until he said, 'Sorry, gotta go now, mate. I'm cream crackered.'

I definitely had enough for a thousand words. I would have to go to the library and look up who Max Wall is and what 'juxtaposition' means.

It was interesting to hear Sam's take on the evening. She enjoyed Kilburn and the High Roads but felt they were very much a live band and she couldn't see herself listening to them on an LP. She said she couldn't understand half of what he was singing about but really liked the ballad. The front of her dress had a stain on it which she pointed out was in the shape of New Zealand. She put her finger at the bottom of her left breast and said, 'I live there. Christchurch. South Island.' And then she started prodding them all over. 'Auckland is up here. North Island, and then across here is the Bay of Plenty and right down here again is Dunedin and Invercargill.'

I said I wished all my geography lessons in school had been this much fun. This made her laugh and I started thinking about what Eva had said. 'She really likes you.' I had never thought of Sam in that way, but I had to admit she was looking very attractive tonight.

As we entered the flat she took off her high-heeled boots. 'God, I hate the smell of paint!'

'I love it Sam. That was my first job in London.'

'Yukk, not for me.' She hoisted up her dress and ran up the stairs on tiptoes. It seemed Sam could never go anywhere slowly. When we were in the flat she opened a new packet of coffee. 'Should we try this? Is this yours?'

'Yeah.'

Sam sticks her nose into it. 'Smells great. Turk Khavasi. Where'd you git this? I've never seen you drinking coffee.'

'Eva made it for me first night I met her and I really liked it, so I thought I'd buy some. I've never opened it. I can't be bothered to learn how to use the coffee maker.'

'Jeez, you're a lazy bugger. It's easy, come here and I'll show you. You unscrew this steel filter basket and you can see the pump tube and spring inside. Yeah? Then full it with about three bug mugs of water. Then fold the paper filter like so and cut a small hole like thus in the bottom and place it over the hole in the plunger there, and full it with four tablespoons of coffee keeping your finger over the hole like thit. Are you listening?'

I laughed. 'No Sam, I've lost the will to live. I can tell you now, I'll never do this. I don't need coffee this badly!'

'Oh come on, Tom. Every time you drink thus coffee it'll remind you of the beautiful Eva, the starlet of your heart!'

It was only when Sam said this did I realise she was actually a little drunk. I decided to tease her. 'Well Sam, I do believe you're jealous.'

She laughed and the laugh seemed genuine. 'Bloody right I am. I'm jealous of all skinny beautiful size eight beetches!' She stops and looks into my eyes. I'm not sure if she's messing with me. 'Yes Tom I'm especially jealous when they also get to go to bed with the bloke I fancy.' I look back into her eyes. So Eva was right. I lean in to kiss her and she pushes me away gently. 'Oh no no. Thit's not hippening. I don't snog blokes who are already spoken for and those blokes shouldn't be trying to SNOG me! Lit me know when you're single, Tom, and maybe then I'll lit you snog me. I might even give you a proper tour of New Zealand.' She shakes her breasts at me and laughs. 'Go on! Go and sit down and I'll bring you your coffee.'

I sit down on the sofa feeling like a bit of a knob. I had misjudged the situation, but if that wasn't a come-on I don't know what was?

Sam brings over the coffees and sits beside me on the couch. It's as if nothing has happened and nothing has I suppose. I ask her about her bum-toucher at work. 'So what about your butt-stroker, any more trouble from him?'

'Oh yes him. Well, he did it the other day and I just said quite calmly "Don't put your hend there, Jonathin, I don't like it and it's not professional." He actually blushed and tried to make out he didn't realise he was doing it. He did apologise. So hopefully that's the end of it. I really did want to tell him about the IRA thing. That would've been a scream, but then he might have thought I wasn't being serious.'

'If it happens again. I'll go down to your work, catch him before he jumps in his car, pretend to be your IRA boyfriend and scare the shit out of him.' Sam laughs. I love her laugh, that little scream followed by the accordion of giggles in and out. I like Sam. I feel comfortable with her.

I'm back at work. The office block I was on before I got injured is almost finished, so we've started a new unit. Fast Eddie arranges a meeting with us in the canteen. The unions are pressing MJ Gleeson to put everyone 'on the cards' meaning they want us to go legit and start paying tax and insurance. There's a purge on and the tax people are trying to plug this loophole. Eddie reckons this will cut our wages by about twenty-five pounds a week. He has an idea to start up his own company, says he has enough contacts in the business to go it alone. He explains he will get a 714 tax certificate where he will be liable for all the tax but it's easily fiddled by not declaring all the income. So we won't be any the worse off. He wants to start with eight brickies, four hod carriers and three plasterers and anybody who wants in, can put their name in the hat. He's already been offered a contract to build a warehouse in North London and a synagogue in South Ealing.

Crash Test, Strawbs and me are on the list for Eddie's new company. Eddie tells me that I'll have to start laying bricks much quicker. 'Yer too fussy like, especially on the twelve-inch Jack walls. They're goin to be plastered so you don't have to fuck about with them so much. At the moment yer laying five hundred bricks a day. I need you to do at least seven, eight hundred. When you're workin for me it'll be all about piecework. So you'll have to get your finger out. I can't afford to carry any passengers.'

One thing about Fast Eddie, you always knew where you stood. He had thrown down the challenge. I was going to have my work cut out to lay eight hundred bricks a day but if that's what I had to do then I was up for it.

Maeve has invited Auntie Fiona and Patti to her wedding and Auntie Fiona has asked Ma and I over to her flat in Dalling Road to discuss the details. This sounds to me like a very boring evening so I try and get out of it. I say to Ma. 'You go, I'll look after Andre. No need for me to be there.' But Ma says she needs me for something called emotional support. Liz is called upon to look after Andre and off we go to Fulham.

When I get to Auntie Fiona's I realise it's only seven weeks until Christmas. She has already put up a Christmas tree and has twinkly lights all along the hallway. Holly over the fireplace. It's a new gas fire which has artificial logs blazing in it. I've never seen artificial logs before. I don't like the look of them. The uniformed flames all exactly the same size flickering around two logs which don't look like logs to me. Artificial logs must take the joy out of lighting a real fire. I used to like cleaning out all the old ash from the fireplace in my grandparents' bedroom. I loved the smell of it. Placing tightly wrapped newspaper in the grate with small twigs on the top. Then progressing on to the slightly bigger sticks and finally to the logs and, if it wasn't catching, I'd kneel down and blow into it, setting the paper alight and off it would go again. It was a whole joyful satisfying process. I missed the hissing of the sap and crackling of the flames, the smell of the smoke. I also like to poke a fire. You need to be able to poke a fire. There's something primal and basic about poking a fire. And spitting in it. My granda would always spit into the fire. You couldn't spit into this stupid fire. Auntie Fiona has laid on something which she calls a finger buffet. Food you don't need a knife and fork for. There are small pieces of cooked crumbed chicken cut into squares, triangles that look like apple turnovers but are very spicy. Crisps, the smallest sandwiches on the planet and some other little pie things that Patti calls *Voloo Vants*. Everything tastes the same to me. Patti pours wine into my glass. It's pink and has bubbles in it. I drink it. It tastes like chewing gum.

Patti flashes her teeth at me. 'You are looking good, Emnet. I think you have grown a lot, you look more like a man now. And imagine running into your mother. There is eight million people in this city. It is a miracle from God that you two should find each other again and become reunited and now Maureen you are going to your daughter's wedding, what a great story this is.'

I wish Patti would shut up. The sweat is lashing off me. The gas logs are sucking the oxygen out of the room along with the hot air coming out of Patti's big piano gob. Auntie

Fiona tells us her plan. We will all fly together on the same plane from Heathrow the day before the wedding. She has an old school friend in Carricktown where she and Patti can stay. She will book all the flights and we can pay her at the airport. They talk about wedding presents and what would Maeve like and who is Lenny O'Brien and what about my father, why does he drink so much? He is such a good man when he's not drinking and it's the demon drink and blah blah blah. We've been here an hour and ten minutes and I am going out of my mind with boredom. I need to somehow escape from this but I don't know how. I think about feigning illness, but that's all a bit too dramatic. Nothing for it but to sit it out. 'Oh!,' I say suddenly, surprising myself. 'Oh my God!'

Ma looks concerned. 'What Emmet. What is it?'

'I've just remembered I'm supposed to meet the guy who runs the music paper I write for. He. . . eh. . . he needs to see me about the article I wrote, eh. . . he owes me money and. . . wants to have a chat about cutting some of it. . . and I don't want him to cut it, so we have to. . . chat about that.'

Patti laughs 'You write for a music paper? What music paper? I think you are fibbing again Emnet!'

'It's called *The Big Fret*, Patti. You don't listen to music, so I don't think you would've heard of it.'

Patti sucks her teeth. 'Huh, I listen to Sam Cooke and Smiley Lewis. That's real music, not like the rubbish you young people listen to.'

'Yeah, well, I'm sorry but I have to go. You might as well come with me on the tube, Ma, it's on the way.' Ma knows what I'm up to and so does everyone else but I don't care. I have to get out of this house. I get up slowly and do a big fake yawny stretchy sound. I don't know why I'm doing this.

Auntie Fiona says, '*The Big Fret,* well, I'm going to have to buy a copy from WH Smiths. How much is it?' Patti and Auntie Fiona burst out laughing. I try not to rise to it.

'It's only a fan magazine. But I'll give you one at the airport. It'll be something for you to read on the plane.'

Auntie Fiona gets our coats. I notice the empty parrot cage in the corner surrounded with Christmas lights and what's that? Jesus! It's a photo of the parrot. She has glued a cardboard cut-out photo of the parrot onto the perch and the heat from the fire has warped its head which is falling backwards and looks like the parrot is laughing its head off. Auntie Fiona sees me looking at it.

'A dirty fox dug up Oscar!'

This almost makes me laugh. I'm pleased at how restrained I am. Patti chips in, 'Was either a fox or a dog.'

Auntie Fiona nods in agreement. 'I didn't bury him deep enough.'

I'm thinking, yeah, I could've told you that. I should've said something at the time.

Auntie Fiona shakes her head sadly. 'I went outside to water the clematis and found the hole all dug up and just the empty box and one feather, which I've kept.' She goes to a drawer and takes out a blue feather. 'Poor Oscar. We should maybe have taken him to the pet cemetery. I'm thinking of getting a Macaw. There was one for sale on the hospital notice board.'

I'm so pleased I'm getting away from these two. Ma and I go to the pub and have good laugh about it. It's good to see her laughing. She seems to be getting some of her fight back. She's going to need it.

SEVENTEEN

I RESENTED PAYING Auntie Fiona the full fare for the flights home, but I knew we couldn't rely on getting a stand-by. People were already going home for Christmas and it was still three weeks away. I gave Auntie Fiona and Patti a copy each of *The Big Fret*. My article on the Kilburns had pride of place on the inside page. HIGH ROADS TAKE THE LOW LIFE TO ANOTHER LEVEL describing the band as a *Ragbag bunch of unique musicians with a very original lyrically gifted front man*. Of course they didn't believe I wrote it as the name on the bottom was Tom Joad which I'd stupidly forgotten about. I told them that was my pen name. Patti laughed and said, 'You fib all the time Emnet and live in a dream world.'

Maeve is waiting for us outside Johnson's taxi rank in Carricktown High Street. She has a confidence about her that makes me feel safe and relaxed. The way she stands with her back straight, greeting everyone. She doesn't make a fuss about Ma and hugs her with the same affection as she hugs Auntie Fiona and even Patti. She punches me on the arm and says, 'What are you looking at?'

This is my sister and I know her better than anyone. The punch on the arm is a signal that she has something

239

important to tell me in private. We have a shorthand Maeve and I, perfected over many years of fighting the devil. 'Come over to the Tap and meet Lenny. Noreen is there as well.'

Lenny has prepared a meal in the back function room. He hugs my mother like she was his mother. 'Mrs McCrudden. I'm so glad you're here. There's food comin everyone, I hope yez are all hungry.'

We are hungry. First time I've ever tasted pheasant pie. Lenny jokes that he shot it himself this morning. Maeve laughs and says, 'Shot it himself? Hah! Jesus if a squib went off he'd be jumping into my arms.' Lenny laughs gives a little jump and squeals.

I try to read my mother's expression and I'm sure she looks relaxed. As does everyone else. Noreen is busy looking at bridesmaids' dresses in a magazine. Auntie Fiona does most of the talking, reminiscing about old friends and the sexual high-jinks she used to get up to with the local boys. This was obviously in her pre-lesbian days. Patti shifts uncomfortably and looks like she's hearing these revelations for the first time.

After the meal, when the others are drinking coffee and winding down, Maeve gives me the nod and we sidle off into another room. She folds and unfolds her arms. 'We have moved out of Tullybern and into a new four bedroomed council house in Burren View Park.' I suddenly feel weak, my blood drains away to some other place beyond where I'm standing.

'Where's Burren View Park?'

Maeve smiles hopefully at me. 'It's a new housing estate. You can see Burren Fort from the front window. The house is great, Emmet. Has gas fired central heating. A big brand new Rayburn range. A bathroom and toilet upstairs and a toilet downstairs. A garden at the front and back with a big shed, and would you believe, there's a birch tree at the side.'

I don't know why I ask the next question. I know it's stupid. 'What's going to happen to Tullybern?'

Maeve puts her hands on my shoulder. 'It's being sold Emmet. I think some developer has bought it.'

I have to sit down. Why did I care? Why was I feeling so sick to my stomach about this? I tell myself Tullybern ceased to be yours the day your family moved into it. Tullybern was the place you've been trying to escape from since the age of nine. So what is the matter with you? Bring your blood back Tom Joad, it's not McCrudden blood anymore. That was the plan wasn't it? So pull yourself together. Maeve sits down beside me.

'I know how you feel about Tullybern, Emmet, but to be honest I'm glad we're out of it. The younger ones will have a decent house to live in. I'll be moving in with Lenny after we're married. Noreen is getting promotion at Anderson's and will be getting a rise in wages so between the two of us we'll be able to get some decent furniture and beds. It's for the best, and sure you can chip in now that you're the big man in London.'

She pats me on the head. My mouth is dry. I run my tongue around the front of my teeth before I speak. 'I know. It's for the best. That's right. What does Da think about it?'

'Oh you know what's he's like.' Maeve does an impression of Da. ' "It's bloody long overdue. I'm not dancing in the friggin streets just because them Orange bastards have given us a house we should've had ten years ago!" ' I smile. It's a good impression. Maeve gets up and goes to the door, stops. 'Oh, and by the way, Rosie Byrne and her family will be at the wedding. Just thought you'd like to know.' Maeve gives me one of her knowing smiles, a smile that no one else could ever give me, a smile that says *I know you Emmet McCrudden. I know your every move.* She goes out and closes the door gently behind her and I'm so glad that Tom Joad has a sister like Maeve McCrudden.

The last time I was in this church I was spilling my guilty guts to Father Hurson. I made him a promise that I had no intention of keeping. That was a private promise which is easier to break. A wedding is a public promise, a little harder to escape from. I stood alongside Fergal. He looked very grown up in his three-piece suit, he was still only ten but already up to my shoulder. Aisling, Sean, Robert and Connor had also all grown taller. I felt I didn't really know them that well and I suppose I didn't.

The bride was late, everyone smiled and said this was customary but I'm thinking Maeve is late because she's probably trying to extract Drunken Daddy from a hedge or find him a new pair of trousers that didn't smell of shit.

A frisson of excitement ripples through the church as the organist plays 'Here comes the Bride'. I turn around and scan the church for Rosie. See her straight away. She stands out like a beautiful stain on all this ordinariness. Dressed in a scarlet bell-bottomed trouser-suit, black floppy hat and a big white carnation in her breast. But what? Jesus who the hell is he? She's arm in arm with someone. He has his hand over hers and he's not a fat farmer, who is he?. . . Tall guy, athletic looking, reddish blonde hair, blue suit. I feel everything withdrawing from within me. It's like all my pride and hopes and dreams and self-esteem are ashamed to remain. They've had enough and are all scattering like rats from this sinking ship. *We can't stay here, they scream! You're a loser pal! Look at her, she's beautiful and you had the gall to not even write to her, to abandon her. Serves you right. Who do you think you are?* Maeve's wedding was taking place but I couldn't see any of it, couldn't hear Father Hurson, asking them to make their vows, didn't hear her say yes I do and I will and I promise and. . . I didn't hear any of it. I needed to get out of here, needed to escape.

I'm outside with everyone having my photo taken and being told to smile and say cheese. Someone says to me, 'I think all brides are like newborn babies, they transcend criticism.' I don't know what they're talking about. The sun is shining but a sudden flurry of small dots of snow appear whirling in the air. I hear Patti's voice shouting, 'Oh look confetti from Heaven' and everyone laughs.

Rosie is standing in front of me, smiling like nothing has happened. 'Emmet this is Gregory.' Gregory? What kind of a name is that? I stare at Gregory, he has my hand and is shaking it. I don't remember giving him my hand to shake.

'Hi Emmet. Good to meet you.' His accent is refined, educated. He has a small gap between his front teeth and something glittering in there that looks like gold. Yes it's a gold tooth bottom right hand side. It almost matches his hair. Rosie is asking me about London. I'm saying something but I don't know what. She tells me Gregory is studying to be a vet. Yeah of course he is. I bet her parents both came at the same time when they heard that piece of wonderful news. I make an excuse and walk away.

I go and talk to Fergal I tell him he looks great in his new suit. He whispers that he hates it, says it's like wearing a straitjacket. Asks me how long I'm home for. I tell him not long. He shrugs like he knew that would be the answer. I wish he was ten years older.

The wedding reception is in full tilt. The speeches are over. My father remarked in his speech that he was glad *all* of the family had managed to attend the wedding and every head turned towards my mother who took a drink to hide whatever expression was on her face. I'm mingling but staying away from Rosie and Vet Man. Everyone tells me the same thing. I had made the right choice to leave and go to London, there was nothing in this town for anyone. The country was in the shit and weren't we the laughingstock of the world, killing each other over religion. My father had managed to stay sober long enough to walk Maeve up the aisle, but now the leash was off he was limbering up. I knew all the signs. He was talking out of the side of his mouth to Lenny who I could see was waiting his chance to be rescued by someone. His voice getting louder, his face more animated, that fake laugh. He tugs at his tie like it's a noose around his neck, his shirt is beginning to hang out a little from the front of his trousers. It was only a matter of time.

He hadn't spoken to me yet so I decide to have a word. I come up behind him. 'Hey Da, c'mere a minute, I'd like a word.' Lenny gets up and moves away gratefully. My father shoots me a look that says *fuck off* but follows me behind a pillar. 'I just want to say well done for staying sober long enough to walk Maeve up the aisle.' He pulls his tie off and shoves it in his pocket, some of it is still hanging out.

'I don't fuckin need you to patronise me. I'd never make a show of my daughter on her wedding day and to hell with you for suggesting that I would.'

'OK great, but the day isn't over and I'm watching you firing those whiskies down your throat. You've just had a heart attack and Ma is back, you have a new house and if you really want her to stay like you said you did, then don't get any drunker! The children need their mother, so make an effort.' I go to walk away and he grabs my arm.

'What's this all about Emmet?'

I pull away from his grip. 'I just told you what it's about Da!'

His face turns into a snarly smile. 'Are ye sure this isn't about a vet!'

'Fuck off.'

He laughs his chesty laugh as I walk away into the crowd. The band are playing 'Sweet Caroline'. I catch sight of Rosie dancing with Golden Gregory. I keep walking through the dancing throng, pick up a bottle of something from a table and I'm out the back door and into the icy cold late-evening air. I take a slug from the bottle. . . holy shit! I look at the label, it's Bacardi Rum.

The car park is full of cars. I sit on the wall and sip the Bacardi, it's got a sweet kick to it. Just what I need. A British army helicopter hovers into sight, its searchlight sweeping the area like the start of a Twentieth Century Fox movie. I immediately think of Mickey Peach. The searchlight locks itself into the car park like a giant full moon. I wave my bottle of Bacardi at them. The helicopter tilts to the side and banks away over the rooftops *chugga chugga chugga chugga*. This sound is replaced by the *waoh waoh waoh* of an ambulance, more than one it seems like. Something is happening somewhere. I realise the *Mid Ulster Mail* office backs on to the Brewery Tap car park and I remember vividly pushing Mickey's bony arse through that toilet window which I now notice has three bars across it. I wonder how Mickey is. Should I drop in and see him before I go? We probably don't have much to say to each other anymore so I decide against it.

I hear people behind me. The clickety scrape of women's high heels on the concrete. Echoey laughter, car headlights spill across the car park and I realise how dark it's getting. More talking and 'Oh it's a shame you have to go Greggy'. Greggy? I look across and see Mr and Mrs Byrne and Rosie bidding goodbye to Doctor fucking Dolittle himself. He's laughing *Har Har* and saying stuff like *Duty calls!* He reverses the car, some kind of low to the ground red sports job, and there he goes out of the gate *vroom vroom*. I tell myself I'm behaving like a crybaby but that does no good. I take another slug of the Bacardi and say to my sensible self, *Piss off and leave me alone with my misery*. My teeth start to chatter and my body is shaking with cold. Alcohol and a freezing temperature do not mix.

I go back inside. I'm looking for Rosie although I tell myself I'm not. I see my father dancing with a pint in his hand, it splashes on his trousers. I know I need to get away from here. I find Rosie talking to Imelda Ryan of all people. I find out she broke up with Mickey two months ago, but they're still friends. Imelda makes her excuses and leaves, saying she's drunk too much and needs to go home before she tries to shag the groom, but I think it may be the desperate pleading look on my face for her to leave me alone with Rosie. I find two glasses and pour us two shots of Bacardi. Rosie says she needs coke in it. I find some Pepsi and we sit in the corner. She swirls the rum around in her glass. 'You couldn't wait to get away from Gregory, did you have to make it so obvious?'

'Where did he go?'

'His uncle has a farm, they have cow trouble.'

This is the first time I've felt happy in a long time, sitting here with the woman I know I love and I'm going to tell her exactly that. 'I love you, Rosie. I miss you. I feel like I've had a limb removed. I'm sure Gregory is a lovely nice, wonderful Vetty Man, but I hate him.'

Rosie laughs, Oh my sweet Christ! That crazy beautiful donkey laugh. 'Vetty Man? Are you pissed?'

'How long have you been going out with him?'

She does a very posh English accent. 'Six months and who are you going out with, dear?'

'I was seeing an American girl for a while but I'm not going out with her as such.'

Rosie smiles. 'As such. What the hell does that mean?'

'Means she's not my girlfriend and I'm not in love with her and don't tell me you're in love with Golden Greggy because I know you're not!'

Rosie pokes her cheek with her finger and makes a stupid lovesick face. 'I might be verwee much in love wifth heem.'

This makes me laugh loudly. I can't remember the last time I laughed like this. My laugh is cut short when I suddenly see my father pulling my mother onto the dance floor, she's trying to get away from him. I can hear her over the music.

'Frank please, I don't want to.'

He's gurning at her 'What's the matter, are ye ashamed of me? Come on have a fuckin dance with yer husband! I'm not goin to bite ye.' He has her by the shoulders.

'Frank! No!'

I'm across the dance floor and have him by the scruff of the neck, buttons fly off his shirt. 'She doesn't want to dance!'

He takes a swing at me. I feel the wind of it sail past my nose. I hit him hard under the ribcage and follow up with a vicious wild punch to the middle of his face. It couldn't have connected any better. He somehow grabs me as he falls backwards and the two of us crash onto a table of wedding guests some of whom start to scream. I can hear my mother shouting 'No! Emmet no!' My father is trying to get up, his shirt is ripped and hanging off him, blood everywhere. I punch him twice on both sides of the head and bring my knee up into his face.

I hear Maeve's voice it's an angry screech, 'Stop it, stop it!'

Lenny O'Brien has me in a bear-hug and is trailing me away. His strength is vice-like and I know it's pointless to struggle. He drags me into a storeroom and locks the door. 'Alright, calm down, Emmet. Fuck's sake! Look, I know yer Da. I know what he's like but ye can't go hitting him, he's yer Da after all and he's my father-in-law now.' A smile breaks across Lenny's face. 'How dare you hit my father-in-law.' I start to laugh and Lenny cracks up as well. 'Shoosh, Maeve will have my bollocks if she hears me laughing. Just stay in here for a while and I'll sort things out. Maybe get yer Da a taxi home. Now stay in here Emmet please.' Lenny goes out and I sit on a cardboard box full of Tayto crisps, hear them crunching underneath my weight.

The band are playing 'Crazy Love' by Van Morrison. I try to hear what's going on outside the door, it's just a babble of noise. The door opens. Lenny is standing there. Maeve is behind him, her face white and rigid. 'I'm too angry to talk to you now. Just keep out of my sight for the rest of the night!' Lenny nods at me as if to say do as she says. I can see my father sitting at a table, he is wearing his jacket but his chest is bare. My mother is nowhere to be seen. Noreen is cleaning his face with a white napkin streaked with blood. He looks like a boxer waiting to get up for the next round.

Rosie is at my side holding the bottle of Bacardi. 'Do you want to get out of here, go for a walk?'

The High Street is full of Army and RUC, two helicopters circling. A young soldier, both his cheeks streaked with black lines approaches us. 'There's been an incident. Dungannon Road and Omagh Road are blocked off for the moment. We've been instructed to tell people to stay off the street until we get the all clear. Unless you're going home.'

Rosie answers before I can say anything. 'We're on our way home.'

The soldier nods, 'OK.'

Then Rosie says. 'Oh by the way, your mascara is running.'

He smiles. 'Yeah, right. Thanks Love.'

We walk aimlessly up the street. She asks where we're going. I tell her we'll be there in twenty minutes. It's not long until we're passing by the Pattersons. A light burns dimly in their living room. Up ahead I can see Tullybern Cottage in silhouette. It looks much bigger than it is. The side gable seems to swell and fuse into the darkness around it. The chimneys have crows perched on them. They look like sentinels keeping guard on the old place.

'I thought you had all moved out?'

I open the creaky gate. 'I just want to have one last look.'

The front door is locked. I break a wooden panel on the back door, lift the latch and we're in. The place is freezing, even colder than it is outside. I trip over the tin bath in the scullery. Rosie snorts and hee haws.

'Jesus, it's freezing Emmet and it's a bit spooky.'

'Don't worry, I'm going to light a fire.'

Rosie snorts again. 'Are you going to burn it to the ground?'

'In the fireplace you big eejit.'

I switch on the light. The living room has been stripped of almost everything apart from a wonky chair and two wooden crates full of old newspapers and magazines. I climb the stairs, Rosie holds on to the back of my jacket. I go into the front bedroom, my grandparents' old room. Switch on the light. The room is bare. A patch on the wall where Jesus used to hang, his heart on fire. I tell Rosie to wait.'

I go downstairs and come back up with the wooden crates and the wonky chair. Shit, I don't have matches. Rosie sups the Bacardi and shivers.

'Oh, let's go Emmet. It's too friggin cold to stay here.'

'I'll be back in a few minutes?'

'Where are you going?'

I'm running down the hill to the Patterson's. I knock on the front door. Jem answers, his eyes are swimming and he looks pleased to see me.

'Hey man, you back from your travels?'

'Yeah, for a bit. Listen Jem, do you have any matches?'

'Sure, yeah, think so.' He disappears and comes back with a big box of Swan Vestas rattles them at me.

'Here you go!'

'Thanks Jem.

'No worries, good to see you, man. Mandy will be sorry to have missed you she's soaking in a blackcurrant bath.'

I run back to the cottage thinking I'm glad it was Jem who answered the door. Mandy would've given me the third degree.

The fire is soon roaring in the grate. The chair is made of pine and burns well, the two crates will be next and anything else I can find. It's ironic that my last night in Tullybern involves burning the furniture. Rosie spreads her big black coat in front of the fire.

'Switch out the light.'

I switch it off. We snuggle up together. Our shadow looks

like a fat man with two heads. I take Rosie's face in my hands and kiss her. Holy Jesus! This is where my lips were always supposed to be. Rosie pulls my head towards her. It's like we're fending off time. This kiss feels desperate, it's like we're sucking the very air out of the room. The wood spits in the heat. We are naked from the waist down but I don't remember us taking our clothes off.

We make love like we are being chased at gunpoint. Rosie wraps her legs around my waist, her long dark hair smells of woodsmoke. We roll on to our side and lie there, waiting for the firing squad. I love her so much. I don't want to think about it, but a voice in my head is asking, *What are you going to do?*

The fire is dying. I break up the crates and get it going again. We sit and stare into the flames. Rosie says quietly as if to herself, 'The control of fire was a turning point in the technological evolution of human beings. It provided warmth, protection from predators, a method for cooking. Light in the darkness. It was the beginning of everything.' She smiles at me. 'I wish this was the beginning of something, Emmet, but it's not, is it?'

I cup her face gently in my hands. 'It could be. You could come to London once you finish university.' She sighs and looks away. 'I can't stay in Carricktown Rosie. You saw what happened tonight with me and my da.'

Rosie scrabbles around and finds her panties, puts them on, pulls on her red bell bottoms. Sits close to me. I put my arm around her. 'My dad has already got me a job at the Irish Independent. He says he didn't have to pull strings to get me the job, he had to pull ropes.'

'Rosie, I had to leave here to do my own thing. Nobody was going to get me a job. I didn't have a choice.'

She sighs. 'Don't let's talk about this now because we'll just end up arguing. Is there any Bacardi left?' I shake what's left in the bottle. We finish it off, wrap our arms around each other and fall asleep.

When I awake Rosie's hair is in my mouth which makes me gag. I try to disentangle myself from her, my left leg is numb. She groans softly and does not want me to move, she mumbles sleepily. 'Naaa Em-met ess cole.'

The aftermath of Bacardi rum has an unfamiliar horrible taste like everything in my mouth has been stuck together with a rotten smelling glue. I shake Rosie. 'C'mon Rosie, we gotta go. . . Rosie!' She stirs underneath her black coat and eventually sits up, she has an imprint of a button on her cheek, she tries to focus, her eyes looking in different directions, checks her watch.

'Half eight? Oh shit Emmet. I'm in so much trouble… why did we come here?'

I stamp my leg into life. 'I'm glad we came here Rosie.'

I help her up. She suddenly looks very young, like a lost toddler. 'Come on.'

I take her hand and we go downstairs. The sky is dark grey and hammock heavy. The morning air unforgiving with the promise of a far bitter cold to come. I look back at Tullybern and think for a second that maybe I should've burned it to the ground. But I know that Tullybern is in my head which makes it fireproof. Our footsteps are the only sound as we pass the Patterson's. A flock of pigeons flap out of nowhere into the sky like an applause. Our breath steams from our mouths in short puffs. Rosie checks her watch again.

'What am I going to say when they ask me where I've been all night?' For some reason I feel myself becoming annoyed.

'Jesus Rosie, you're twenty years old.'

She pulls her hand away from me. 'You have no fucking idea Emmet! It's disrespectful just to clear off from a wedding reception and not come home all night. They'll be worried! And they've just got back together. They nearly separated. I don't want to be the one to set things off again'

I backtrack quickly. 'Yeah, OK, sorry. Look, just say you stayed with Imelda. You had a few drinks and fell asleep on her sofa.'

I can see Rosie weighing up this idea. She suddenly stops, dusts herself down, takes a hairbrush and a small mirror from her handbag. 'Oh my God what's that?'

'It's just an imprint of the button on your coat.'

She rubs it. 'Shit!'

She flings her hair forward and brushes it vigorously with stiff downward strokes. Throws her head back and it all falls miraculously into place. A tube of lipstick and a little tin of brown make-up appear and within a few minutes she is, if not exactly transformed, a little more presentable. She turns to me.

'How do I look?'

I want to kiss her, but I know I can't smudge her lipstick. 'You look like a fillum star!'

She smiles. 'Yeah, one who's been out all night drinking raw rum and shagging on a wooden floor.'

When we get to Gort Hill crossroads Rosie decides she will go and see Imelda and call her parents from there. We stand at the crossroads and this isn't lost on us. Rosie's eyes look up and down the four roads, she shrugs and her eyes fill with tears. We hug, it's a hug that gets tighter by the second until there is no more hug left. A helicopter hovers low over the football field, the grass waving underneath like a green sea. Rosie steps away from me.

'I don't know what's going to happen Emmet, so don't ask. I don't know if I love Gregory, but he's a good person. It was great being with you last night. I don't regret it, but I feel like shit about it.'

I take her hands in mine. 'I feel great about it.'

She squeezes my hands then lets them go. 'I can't promise you anything.'

She turns and walks away. The helicopter lands on the football pitch. Four soldiers emerge from it, running in a crouch, their rifles poised for something, somebody.

EIGHTEEN

SOME OF THE HOUSES on Burren View Park are still under construction. The road is steaming from being tarmacked. I love the smell of fresh asphalt, the heat of it, how the roller compacts and cooks it into a brand-new surface. Sweating men with hot black faces, pulling everything into shape with their long-handled rakes clagged with tar. A new road, hopefully leading to somewhere. I hear a car horn behind me but take no notice, it becomes more insistent Beep beep beep beep! I turn to see Harry Lagan's bread van. He leans out of the window, 'Emmet! can I have a wee word?'

Lagan is the last person I want to talk to. I'm in no mood to fuck around with him, so I'll tell him straight. I'm not interested in saving Ireland. I walk around the tarmackers. Harry is out of the van and waiting for me. He's wringing his hands together, his breathing out of control. He grabs my shoulders. His face is strained and his eyes dart around like a frightened child.

'I wanted to tell ye before ye hear the names on the news . . . it's a fuckin tragedy. . . Jesus Christ Emmet.' He takes out a hankie and wipes his face.

'What tragedy, Harry? What's going on?'

He shakes his head from side to side. 'The car bomb last

night. . . three of our volunteers lost their lives. . . It went aff prematurely. . . Paddy Larkin, Tony Mulgrew and. . . Mickey . . . Mickey Peach, all killed. . . I'm sorry Emmet, I know you and Mickey were tight from when ye were wee boys.' Lagan has hold of my shoulders. 'Mickey's a hero Emmet, a fuckin martyr! One of the best! He'll never be forgotten.'

I push Lagan hard in the chest and walk away. It's a half-run almost a stumble. He's shouting something but I can't hear, don't want to hear. I start running. I run like I'm demented until I get to the Burren Fort. I sit on the clump of grass that Mickey and I used to sit on. I'm panting hard and it seems to be coming from someone else. I can see the whole of Carricktown, and hear the distant cry of seagulls swooping on the town dump. I try and make sense of what I've just been told. Harry Lagan's voice plays over and over in my head.*It went aff prematurely. . . and Mickey. . . Mickey Peach, all killed. . .* and each time I hear it I'm more shocked than before. I feel as if some unseen thing is shaking the life out of me. I grip the grass mound in both hands to keep myself from falling.

It's almost dark when I reach the new house. Noreen and Aisling are at the window putting up Venetian blinds. Fergal peeks through the slits and is chased away by Noreen. The grass in the lawn still has bald patches here and there, a birch tree leans in towards the gable. It's a young tree, unclimbable at present. The front door opens. Noreen greets me with, 'I hope you're not here for another fighting match?

Da's in bed.' The living room is big, the Rayburn range taking pride of place. There is a new carpet smell and I'm told by Aisling to take off my shoes. The carpet is red with black wriggly shapes, they come alive and dance before my eyes. I feel I'm going to pass out. I hold on to the door and take a deep breath.

Fergal wants to show me the bathroom, he takes my hand and leads me there. 'I had a bath last night Emmy, it was class and I kept me head under for ages.' Fergal throws toilet paper into the bowl and flushes it.

Noreen shouts at him from the living room. 'Fergal if you flush that toilet one more time I'll stick your bloody head down it!'

Fergal grins at me. 'There was a big car bomb on the Omagh Road last night.' He makes a noise like a bomb going off. 'Boooofffffh! We heard about it on the news.' Fergal gives me one of his searching looks. I swear this kid can see into my soul.

Noreen calls him. 'Fergal come here and stop bothering Emmet.'

Fergal mimics Noreen under his breath, 'Fergi cum her and stap batherin Emmet.' He curls his lip, 'Ya gotta stay cool,' then runs off. I think it's good advice.

Tommy Forbes suddenly appears coming down the stairs. 'Oh how are ye Emmet. I didn't know you were here atall. I was just having a word there with yer Da. He's up in his bed, a bit fragile from yesterday.'

Tommy steps back into the hall and beckons me towards him mouthing the word 'C'mere.' I go into the hall. 'Listen Emmet I think yer Da might be ready you know.' Tommy makes an O shape with his mouth.

'Ready? Ready for what Tommy?'

'I have to go Emmet I've said too much. Don't mention any of this to yer father.' Tommy opens the door, bows his head to me and is gone. I hadn't a clue what the old bollocks was on about. But I knew I didn't really care about any of it. My instinct to leave this place had been proved correct. I only wished I'd been able to persuade Mickey to do the same. I wondered about Tony Mulgrew, Rosie had never mentioned him, so I doubt there was anything between them. I would ask Maeve if I could sleep in the pub tonight and I'd be on my way tomorrow. I'd left this miserable place too many times already, this would be the last.

It was as if I could see and hear it everywhere, from a workman's radio. . . *car bomb carrying*. . . from the open door of a house. . . *the three men were on their way to*. . . A glimpse of a newspaper headline as I walked past a cafe.

IRA MEN DIE IN CAR BOMB.

I watched the full report on Scene Around Six on the Brewery Tap's new television. The polite Ulster accent of newsreader Barry Cowan, the way he pronounced Mickey's full name, Michael Kieron Peach, made it sound like he was talking about someone else. The public bar was silent. People either staring into their pints or shaking their heads, and afterwards I was stunned at how many people, some of whom I hardly knew, approached me to say how sorry they were, like I was a relative. Maeve never mentioned the fight with Da, she said Ma was staying with Uncle Brendan and was going back with Auntie Fiona and I could stay in the loft room of the pub for as long as I needed to, then she squeezed my arm and whispered, 'Poor Mickey. God rest his soul.' I really wished I could believe that. I thought I should go and see Mickey's mother before I left. I would go tonight and get it over with.

The small front room of the terraced house on Gort Hill was packed. A framed photo of Mickey rested on the mantlepiece surrounded by burning candles. The smell of candles always depressed me. There was nothing joyous about candles, the light they gave was never enough and it wasn't supposed to be enough, that was the whole point. They signified death, and a gloomy death at that. They were lit for lost souls or dead children screaming in limbo and when they were blown out the acrid smoke was like a warning drifting into the air. When Mickey's mother saw me she exhaled loudly and threw her arms around me. She kept patting and rubbing my back like the way mothers do when they want to wind a baby.

'Oh God son, I'm glad ye came. Mickey was always talking about ye and he was heartsore when ye went away to London. He would always talk about ye when he had drink taken. I miss my pal he would say. He called ye a few names as well you know.' She smiled through her tears. Her face was a grey colour and exhausted with grief. 'But you were his best pal. The trouble the pair of ye used to get up to! Youse had my heart scalded. God bless ye son, ye'll come to the funeral won't ye? Mickey would have wanted that.' She looked into my eyes. I didn't want to go to the funeral. I wanted to get on the first flight out of here in the morning.

'Of course I will Mrs Peach. I'll be there.'

I was handed a drink and it was then I saw Rosie and Imelda in the kitchen. Imelda was sitting on a chair staring into nowhere. Rosie was kneeling beside her trying to get her to drink something. I hung back for a bit and spoke with Mickey's father Sean and two of his brothers. Mostly small talk, there was no other talk to be had.

I could see that Imelda was now drinking whatever Rosie had been trying to give her. I made my way to the kitchen, shaking hands with people I knew and some I didn't know. When Rosie saw me she took my hand in hers, kissed my cheek and whispered, 'Jesus Emmet, this is so awful.'

I took a drink of the whiskey which burned my throat. I hate whiskey. 'I was going to go back tomorrow but I'll go after the funeral.'

She nodded then pulled me to one side. 'I went to the pictures once with Tony Mulgrew, we had a drink afterwards and that was it. He wasn't the sharpest, but I think he was very shy. I always felt sorry for him.' I nodded. 'I can't see you again, Emmet. I want to but it's not fair on Gregory. I wouldn't like it if he did that to me.' Her face was trying its best to be sincere, but I didn't believe any of it.

'Sure, I understand.'

It took three days for the bodies to be officially released. Mickey was identified by his dental records and a silver Celtic Claddagh ring given to him by Imelda Ryan with both their names inscribed on the inside. This was on his left hand which had been found nearby. The funerals were to take place in the Old Graveyard of St Augustine's Church. This was the traditional graveyard for Irish Republicans. The New Graveyard had a different policy. Some conservative Catholics didn't want to be associated with Nationalism.

Mickey's funeral was at 9.30 in the morning. I had stayed away from Rosie, even though every fibre of my being wanted to be with her, but I knew it was pointless and selfish. She would be here today. I would say my goodbyes and that would be the end of it. A light rain began to fall. I wasn't sure if I was cold because of the occasion or the weather. There was hardly any wind, the air was like the inside of a fridge. I waited at the top end of the graveyard where I had a good view of the main road, any minute now I would see the hearse followed by the walking mourners. I had decided not to go to the funeral mass. I couldn't bear all that waffly religious shite. The endless kneeling and sitting and kneeling and sitting then being judged for not taking communion. The hearse nosed its way into view and Jesus, walking behind it was a hundred, two hundred, three hundred people. They just kept coming. The RUC and British Army were there but kept a respectable distance. I made my way down to the freshly dug grave surrounded by hundreds of wreaths.

Mickey's coffin, draped in the Irish flag, was carried by his four brothers and sister and his father Sean. The grave-yard filled quickly with people, some had to stand outside the gates. A helicopter circled overhead. All the usual suspects from Sinn Fein were there. The priest took out his bible and began to read. His voice carried across the graveyard and above the sound of the helicopter determined to drown him out. 'Our brother Michael has gone to his rest in the peace of Christ. May the Lord welcome him to the table of God's children.' I mean who the hell writes this stuff? How can they sleep at night? I zoned out until the end passage. 'Eternal rest grant unto him oh Lord and let perpetual light shine upon him may he rest in peace. . . ashes to ashes. . . '

Mrs Peach was being held at each side by relatives, her legs were giving way but she managed to remain upright, her voice breaking with a wail of hurt and I'm sure I could hear anger in there as well. Suddenly three men appeared out of the crowd dressed in camouflage jackets, black berets and balaclavas. They shouted *Ordú Lámhach!* (Command to shoot), fired twelve shots over the coffin and disappeared back into the mourners who cheered and applauded. The flag was removed and the coffin lowered into the grave. The crowd dispersed, leaving only close family to comfort each other and read the cards on the wreaths. I waited for the right moment and shook hands with Mrs Peach, told her how sorry I was. I was genuinely sorry and heartsick. So I knew it wouldn't come across as lip service. She thanked me for coming, her face imprisoned behind a black veil. I couldn't see Rosie anywhere which was probably a good thing. As I approached the gate, Harry Lagan came from behind a car.

'Emmet!' He shook my hand and gripped me by the shoulder. 'It's a sad day and we have a long hard road ahead of us, but we won't give up until this Island is free from British rule, and listen, the offer still stands if you'd like to write a wee article for *An Phoblact*. Maybe something about Mickey?' Harry wasn't going to let this go, he was challenging me, his eyes full of threat, his big breadman hand crushing my fingers. 'I'm going back today Harry but maybe I'll send you something in the post?' Like a fucking bullet you old cunt!

'OK Emmet. I'll look forward to receiving that.'

He let my hand go and slapped me just a little too hard on the back.

When I got to the new house Fergal was throwing darts at a blackboard hung on the shed door. This was perfect as I didn't want to say goodbye to anybody else.

'Hey little fella, I'm away. Don't know when I'll see you again. But keep it lit OK? I'll write to you and you can keep me up to date with all the girls you're going out with.'

Fergal flung a dart and missed the board completely. 'I'm shite at darts. . . did you go to the funeral Emmy?'

'Yes I did.' He threw another dart at the dartboard, it hit the wire and spun away.

'I remember Mickey gave me two quid one time. I didn't ask him for it he just give to me.'

I can't speak for a bit, have to compose myself.

'Yeah, well Mickey was a good lad. C'mere give us a hug. I won't tell anyone.'

Fergal hugged me around the waist then give me one of his looks. 'I'm gonna practice hittin the bull.'

'Yeah you do that. I'll see you Fergal.'

I walked away through the new estate with the sound of Fergal's darts thudding into the shed door which may as well have been my heart.

Back at the Brewery Tap some of the mourners were having a drink in the function room. I went straight to the loft room and began packing my holdall. I could still feel the ghost of Harry Lagan's grip on my hand. I hoped I'd be able to get a stand-by flight. I'd sleep in the airport tonight if I had to. I found Maeve in the office and told her I was leaving. She hugged me.

'It was great to see you and I was delighted that Ma was able to come. As Irish weddings go it turned out alright. Look after yourself Emmet and don't be a stranger you hear me?'

It was funny but that's exactly what I'd always felt like in this town, a stranger.

'Oh, by the way. I found your medical card and birth certificate when I was packing. You might need them so I'll send them on to you, and. . . Rosie left this for you.' Maeve handed me a small envelope and gave me one of her looks. 'Hmmm.'

I stood at Johnson's taxi rank and read the note.

> I decided not to go the the funeral, it was just too depressing. I'm at my aunt's place looking after her cats. She's back at 2pm. I'm leaving for university around 4pm. Maybe we could share a taxi, drop you at the airport? Not a problem if you've made other plans. Otherwise have a safe journey. R x

When I arrived at Rosie's aunt's house, we didn't speak a word to each other. I followed her into a small bedroom and we undressed. This time it felt like I was making love to Rosie for the first time. Discovering her all over again. It also lasted longer than normal and we kissed a lot. I think we must have kissed every inch of each other, even continuing as we were getting dressed. We were watched throughout by Pope Paul the V1, John F Kennedy, Eamon de Valera and somebody called Mario Lanza, all staring at us from around the room. I waited outside until her aunt came home and then pretended I'd just arrived to share the taxi.

We held hands for the duration of the journey. We both knew there wasn't anything left to say. At the airport the RUC checkpoint waved us through. The taxi pulled up at departures. We untwined our clasped fingers.

I say to Rosie. 'I love you Rosie.'

She smiles. 'I love you too Emmet.'

I grab my bag, get out and don't look back.

PART THREE

BOTTOM OF THE BLOODY WORLD

NINETEEN

I'M TOLD THERE ARE NO MORE stand-by flights. The next one I can get my name down for is 8.30am the following morning. There is absolutely nothing at Aldergrove airport. I buy the Irish Times and try and do the crossword, give up after half an hour, who am I kidding? I try not to think about Rosie. The cafe closes at 9pm. I walk around and read every sign twice. I could get drunk, but I'm scared I might do something stupid like turn up at Rosie's house threatening to kill Gregory. I watch the Guinness clock hands join at midnight and eventually fall sleep across two slippery plastic seats. In the morning I have a greasy sausage roll and a cup of warm tea. At 11am my name is finally called and I board the flight to Heathrow. I sail through departures and security checks without any incident, no questions from sarky Special Branch bastards.

But it's a different story when I reach Heathrow. I'm stopped not by two, but three plain clothes detectives. They all look exactly the same. The three Wise men *Caspar, Melchior,* and *Balthazar* who I've never forgotten from my Catechism, and here we go again with the same fake politeness.

'Could we please just have a word with you, sir, if that's alright?'

I'm taken into a room the size of a broom cupboard. It's just about big enough for four people. We go through the same rigmarole.

'Could we see some ID sir?'

'I'm sorry I don't have any ID at the moment. I have a medical card and birth certificate and when my sister finds them she'll send them on to me.'

'What's your name?'

Emmet McCrudden. They search my bag and find a wage slip with Tom Joad written on it.

'Tom Joad? Who's Tom Joad sir?'

'He's. . . just a friend of mine. I picked up his wages for him. He owed me money.'

They take turns firing questions at me, they're suddenly not polite anymore. 'We don't believe a word you say sir! No indeed not a fucking word! Emmet McCrudden? Tom Joad? You could be Tom fucking Jones for all we know? Who are you? Englebert Humperdinck? What were you doing in Northern Ireland? At a wedding? What wedding? Your sister? What was the name of the church? Who did she get married to? Who was the best man? Where was the reception held? What song did the bride and groom dance to?' On and on it went like this for at least two hours. I finally stopped answering their questions.

'You better start telling us who you really are and what

you know Mr McCrudden Joad.'

'I've told you everything. I would like a drink of water and if you're going to charge me with something then I'd like a solicitor.' They think this is hilarious and fall about the place laughing.

'Oh, no, no, no, we won't be doing that. You see we're a bit like Spiderman and Superman. That's right! We've got special powers.'

I knew they were referring to the prevention of terrorism act which was strengthened lately to give them special powers to hold suspected terrorists for a month or longer, depending on how serious they thought the threat was.

They suddenly leave me alone for half an hour and only one of them returns. Let's call him Caspar. Caspar has a green folder under his arm. He produces a can of coke from his pocket and a packet of cheese and onion crisps.

'This is all I could muster. The water here is not safe to drink.' He taps the folder with his index finger. 'So, what were you really doing in Northern Ireland? Think carefully before you answer.'

I can't imagine what he's got in the folder. It's obviously a bluff. 'I told you. I was at my sister's wedding.'

He opens the folder and produces two black and white photos of me shaking hands with Harry Lagan at the gates of The Old Graveyard. It's grainy but clear enough to show that it's definitely me. I'm still wearing the same clothes. My suit jacket with the three buttons, white shirt, black tie.

Fountain pen in the pocket of my shirt. He smiles at me, takes a pen from his inside pocket.

'I like a fountain pen myself, very reliable. Have you heard of Paddington Green station?' I hadn't. 'It's a police station, well actually it's a concrete bunker with 16 cells all underground, specially built for the interrogation of cunts.' He pauses for effect. 'It's not a very pleasant place. We can keep you there for weeks on end. No solicitors, no visitors, no doctors, no fuck all. Do you understand? We've broken some hard men in there and you, my son, don't strike me as a hard man. My two colleagues aren't as patient as me and I can assure you they're itching to get you down there. Now, all you have to do is tell me what you were doing at an IRA funeral and give me a few names. Mr Handshaker here.'

He points at Harry. 'We know he's an IRA member. We're fairly sure he's a unit commander. We need to know his name and what he does for a living?'

I had to think quickly. If the police already knew who Harry was and I tell them he's somebody else, they'd know I was protecting him and I'd never get out of here. I couldn't really say I didn't know him, they wouldn't believe that either. I reckoned if they knew he was in the Provos, it was highly likely they already knew his name. I would have to take my chances. Balthazar and Melchior suddenly appear with hot tea and sandwiches. I pop open the coke and take a sip. Caspar says, 'He's just about to tell us what he knows. Isn't that right Paddy? I'm going to call him Paddy until we know

what his real name is.' He leans in towards me and cups his
ear with his hand.

'My name is Emmet McCrudden. I've nothing to do with
the IRA. I was at the funeral because the person that was
being buried was my best friend. Mickey Peach. I'd known
him all my life. The man in the photo is Harry Lagan. I don't
know what he does for a living. I hardly know him. He drank
in the pub I used to go into.'

Balthazar bites into his sandwich and talks with his mouth
full. 'Why is he shaking your hand like that? That looks like
a serious fucking handshake to me.'

'He knew Mickey was my best pal and he was saying he
was sorry. That's what people do at Irish funerals. I shook
about a hundred people's hands that day.'

Caspar gets up quickly and angrily from his chair, picks
up the photo and shakes it in my face. 'That doesn't fucking
look like an *I'm sorry* handshake to me! Look at it. Look at
the expression on that face. That's intense! Do you really
expect us to believe that you didn't know, that this man who's
shaking your hand like that was in the IRA?'

'I'm telling you the truth. Look, one thing I do know
about the IRA is that if you're in it, you don't go around
publicising it.'

Balthazar empties two sachets of sugar into his hot tea.
'You're just a bit too cocky for my liking. You should be
shitting yourself, but you're not. Looks to me like you've
been in this position before, it's almost like you've been

trained for it. I'm right aren't I?'

'No, you're not. The only thing I've been trained for is to lay bricks and that's what I've been doing for the last two years.'

Melchior leans back on his chair. Which I hate. I think of Keefer who used to do it all the time. 'Why didn't you tell us you were at the funeral, why lie about it?'

'I didn't lie. I just didn't mention it. I was at my sister's wedding. I've told you she married a guy called Lenny O'Brien and he owns a pub called the Brewery Tap. That's easy for you to check. That's why I went home. The car bomb happened later that night. I went to see Mickey's mother and she asked me would I come to the funeral and I said yes! I didn't plan to go but I'm glad I did.'

Caspar puts the photos back in the folder. 'How many best friends do you have in the IRA Paddy?'

'I had one. I don't have any now.'

They all huddle in the corner and speak in hushed tones which is ridiculous as the room is so small I can hear everything. They want to take my fingerprints. I decide to let them. I just want out of here. Caspar turns to me. 'We're going to take your prints and a mug shot.'

They bring out all the paraphernalia from a little cupboard. Roll my fingers and thumbs on the black ink-brick and roll them again onto a white piece of official paper. I'm told to sit up straight, they take my photo from the front and sides with a polaroid camera and staple them to the paper.

'There we go Emmet McCrudden. You're in the file Paddy boy.' He takes a notebook from his pocket, pulls the top off his fountain pen. 'Write down the name of your handshaker. Print it, along with your address in London.'

I write Harry's name, then, 136 Abinger Road which doesn't exist. I wasn't about to give them everything. Caspar picks it up and looks at it. 'Right, we need to check all this out so we're taking you down to Paddington Green. You'll stay there for the night. If it's all kosher then you can be on your way. If not, then your fucked Paddy boy. Stand up, hands behind your back.'

I stand up and Balthazar clicks a pair of steel handcuffs on my wrists which bite into my skin. Caspar and Melchior parade me through the airport everyone gawking at the prisoner. We go down a series of escalators and out into a car park. Casper puts me into the back seat of an unmarked car. As he does so he covers the top of my head with the palm of his hand in case I bump it. I'd only ever seen this on TV cop shows and I could never understand it. When has anyone ever bumped their their head getting into a car? It's not a helicopter. Caspar gets into the driving seat. Melchior jumps into the back with me. Caspar drives like a lunatic with the blue light wailing. He goes through every red light and at one point screeches up on the pavement to get past a van that was indicating to go left. We arrive at Paddington Green police station in twenty-five minutes. I wasn't sure if the high-speed car journey was supposed to intimidate me or if they were just amusing themselves? Either way it was beginning to dawn on me that I could be in a lot of deep shit.

They weren't exaggerating about Paddington Green Police Station. It looked like an ugly misshapen block of flats. The front entrance was built from heavy dark blue engineering bricks. I'd only ever seen these bricks used to build sewer manholes. The processing area stank of dettol and stale smoke. The walls were a lovely vomity beige colour, the hard rubber floors scuffed with heel marks. The cuffs were removed. My details were taken again by a uniformed policeman. He held out a clear plastic bag and ordered me to put all my possessions into it including my belt and shoe laces. When all this was completed, Caspar took me to a windowless cell in the basement. It had a brown vinyl floor and cream coloured tiles. There was a narrow bed with a foam mattress, a grey blanket and pillow and in the corner was some sort of chemical toilet minus the chemical. It stank of shit. Caspar winked at me.

'If you think of anything else, Paddy, just shout good and loud.'

He disappeared and the door slammed behind him, the sound of two locks ratcheting into place. I guessed it must be about three-thirty in the afternoon. I was thirsty and starving with hunger. Surely they weren't going to leave me here all day and night? I sat on the edge of the bed and tried to remember what I had told them. The only real lie was my address. It's not a terrorist offence to give a wrong address. What the hell was I thinking? Hundreds of people were interned at home for nothing. No jury, no evidence, no nothing. Trailed from their beds at dawn and thrown in prison. Every drop of saliva in my mouth began to evaporate and my heart had decided to go AWOL and gallop about all over the place. Why was this happening to me? It seemed every time I tried to escape I kept being drawn back in again. Deep down I knew that was my own fault. I hadn't made a clean break and this was going to keep happening until I did. I lay on the bed and closed my eyes. I tried to think about Rosie's lips, but all I could hear was *Ordú lámhach!* Followed by gunshots over Mickey's coffin and feel Harry Lagans's insane handshake. That bastard, why did he have to come near me? He probably did it on purpose. He would have known they were taking pictures.

I tried to breathe and not let my negative imagination run riot. I closed my eyes and took long slow deep breaths. I went through all the thirty-two counties in Ireland and fifty states of America. When I got bored with that I started on the south American countries. When that was exhausted, I sang the lyrics of every song I could think of. I eventually fell into some kind of anxious sleep state. I had a nightmare about Tullybern Cottage being on fire with Rosie trapped inside. She was screaming my name but I couldn't get to her. The sound of the door unlocking woke me up. I leapt up from the bed drenched in sweat. A fat policeman in a light blue shirt and navy blue trousers with keys and a torch and other crap hanging from him handed me a tray with two tin-foil containers on it, a plastic mug of hot tea and a plastic knife and fork. I asked him the time he told me it was a quarter past nine. I'd been asleep for quite a while. Inside one of the containers was a pie and the other was half full of creamy mashed potatoes and peas.

The mashed potato tasted like baby food and some of the meat in the pie was cold, but I didn't care and wolfed down the lot in a matter of minutes. Sometime later the door opened and my tray was taken away.

'Excuse me sir, how long am I going to be kept in here? Hey!'

The fat bastard ignored me, slammed the door and locked it. I took off my jacket and did some press ups. This is what prisoners did in the films. I got to seven and stopped when the cell was plunged into darkness. It was the blackest dark I had ever experienced. I literally couldn't see anything. I was almost about to panic, start screaming and kicking the door. Instead, I lay on the bed and thought about Master McKenna slapping me around the face when I'd tried to tuck my thumbs in to keep them from being caned. *Don't try and be clever, wee sonny.* I remembered how determined I was not to cry. This was the resolve I needed now. I had to remember that pain, that indignity, that rage. I mustn't lose that. I needed it now more than ever.

Being consumed in this total darkness I began to play a

game. I held my arms out straight with my palms up and measured the length in steps from the bed to the door. Six steps. I walk back to the bed. From the side of the bed to the wall on the left, seven steps. From the side of the bed to the wall on the right, seven steps. I knocked my shin on the chemical toilet. I needed to piss. I felt for the lid, lifted it up. I tried my best to piss into it but my aim wasn't great and I knew I was pissing everywhere apart from in the bowl. I lay on the bed and began to build a wall in my head. This was going to be the best wall I'd ever built in my life. I would build it in English garden wall bond. The bricks were red rubbers the nicest brick to work with. It was a sunny day and I was building the wall around the garden of my house. Rosie was washing up but watching me from the kitchen window. I had my shirt off. Every time I looked up she was there, watching, smiling at me. Maybe I slept. I don't know.

I'm not sure if I finished the wall. Fast Eddie wouldn't be happy with me. *Seven hundred bricks a day. I can't carry any passengers.* He would be wondering where the hell I was. The light suddenly came back on. The long fluorescent tube buzzed and blinked and struggled until the room was brightly lit. I hid under the blanket closed my eyes tightly. The locks clanked open, the blanket was ripped from me, Caspar and the fat policeman were standing in the doorway.

'Woaaggh, it fucking stinks in here.' Caspar looked at the pool of piss on the floor. 'Fuck me, didn't they teach you how to piss straight in whatever slum you crawled out of? Come on. Rise and shine, Paddy boy!'

I followed him up four flights of stairs. The fat policeman was close behind me, he was breathless. I could almost hear him wobbling. Red blobs jumped around in front of my eyes. I couldn't focus properly. I walked into a door.

'Watch where you're going, you fucking idiot.'

I was taken into a room with Interview Room written on it. There's a well-worn wooden table with three tin ashtrays full of dog-ends. Four mis-matched chairs. One of them had a slit down the back with the stuffing hanging out of it. The walls were dark green and the carpet felt sticky under my feet. Melchior is busy looking at my file. Caspar tells me to sit. Melchior continues to look through my file then produces three photographs and pushes then towards me.

'Take a good look at these and tell me if you know who they are?' I recognised Jackie Westwood straight away. I thought one of the others may have been Willy Coulton's son Dermott, but I wasn't sure. I didn't know the other one. I look at them for a reasonable amount of time.

'No. I don't know who they are.'

'You sure?'

'Yes. I'm sure.'

'Well, that's funny because we're fairly certain they're all from Carricktown. The population of Carricktown is no more than eight thousand. These photos were taken at the funeral you attended but you're telling me you've never seen any of these people before?'

'That's right. I don't know everyone in Carricktown. I've been away for nearly three years.'

'We can keep you here for another four weeks,' Caspar says, 'and there's fuck all you can do about it. So just give us the names of these three and you'll be free to go, simple as that.'

I suddenly hear myself shouting. 'My name is Emmet McCrudden but I hate that name! I hate it because it's been dragged through the shit by my useless drunken father. I was stopped last year at Aldergrove. I give them all my information. You can check it out. I want to get as far away as possible from the McCruddens of Northern Ireland. I'm not involved with any organisation. You can put me back in the cell for a month if you want but it won't do any good because I don't know anything!'

Melchior snaps the folder shut. 'Spoken like a true fucking IRA man.' Caspar pulls me up from the chair and marches me back to the cell effing and blinding behind my back calling me every name under the sun. The cell door is opened and I'm flung into it. I shout at him as he slams the door in my face.

'I don't fucking know anything!'

I rest my forehead against the cold steel blue door. I'd heard tales about how people just sign or say anything to get out of situations like this. I didn't know how long I could hold out for? I'd been here less than twenty-four hours and I couldn't imagine how I would survive for four weeks. I lie on the bed and watch a fly head-butting the fluorescent tube. It just keeps flying straight into the light. *Buzz buzz buzz bang! Buzz buzz buzz bang!* It never lets up. After a while the fly starts to make me laugh. *Buzz buzz buzz bang!* I can't stop laughing. I'm out of control. Roaring my head off, almost hysterical. *Buzz buzz buzz bang!* The door ker-clunked and burst open. Caspar grabbed my jacket and pulled it over my head punched me several times around the kidneys. These were vicious and wicked punches. He meant business. He whirled me around the cell kicking my legs. I caught glimpses of his black shoes and flashes of white sock. It was like he was dancing. I could smell his cheap aftershave. He punched me several times in the mouth through my jacket which was still over my head, white lights exploded behind my eyes and I could feel the immediate flow of warm blood. He continued to swing me around in a circle using my jacket as purchase, began kicking me in the ribs and head. Next thing I'm on the floor and he's sliding my face up and down the pool of piss. He slams my face into the floor, grabs my hair and washes the floor with my face. He whispers in my ear. 'You're not laughing now are you? You Paddy cunt! You'll be sucking my cock to get out of here. You hear me! Fucking scumbag!' I hear the door slamming and the locks turning.

It's pitch dark again when I awake. Snapshots flicker into my consciousness. Black shoes, white socks. The taste of piss. I have no idea of time. I'm not sure if what happened to me just happened minutes ago or hours ago. As I raise my head slowly from the floor there is a soft squelching sound. The side of my face is sticky and wet and I can only open one eye. My nose feels as if it's been stuffed with paper. I try to breathe but the pain in my chest is excruciating. I'm not sure I can move, or if it's a good idea? I begin to shake with cold. I start to tremble uncontrollably. I decide I need to get up. I make a huge effort and raise myself on one elbow. I try to find the bed, slithering slowly on my hands and knees an inch at a time. I feel the edge of the bed and howl with pain as I drag myself up and lie half across it. The pain is too bad on my front so I roll slowly on to my back pushing the ground with my heels. Eventually nearly all of me is on the bed. I can only breathe through my mouth.

I feel myself fading away. I have a dream about shooting The Three Wise men. It's a moonlit night in the desert. The sky is full of uncountable stars. The Wise Men are on horses. They are wrapped in flowing red and purple robes and turbans, looking at the sky and following one big star in particular. They don't see me as I step from behind an olive tree and gun them down. The sound of the gunfire is deafening as the bullets rip into them. They fall from their horses in slow motion. Their presents for the baby Jesus fall in the sand. Colourful boxes. I open them and they are full of hissing wriggling snakes. I got there just in time.

The light comes on. I cover my eyes with both hands. I'm being helped up. I don't want to move. The pain is too severe. The voices are far away. I am walking slowly out of the cell. I know I'm on my way to be executed. Someone will write a song about this. Maybe Dr Feelgood. I'm sitting in a room, a white room. I smell TCP, someone is washing my face, there is blood in the water. My sleeve is rolled up and I'm injected. A little plaster is put over it. How kind. After a few minutes my head begins to clear a little. Out of my good eye I can see Caspar. He is talking to someone. Voices are raised. My pain is subsiding. I'm helped up by someone and given a clear plastic bag and my holdall. Then I'm going through a back door and down an iron staircase. The staircase leads through another door on to the street. The air is freezing cold and takes my breath away. It's so good to feel this cold. I can breathe again. My pain has gone. The streets are quiet. Two black taxis idle with their yellow lights on. I shuffle across the road. One of my shoes comes off. They don't have laces. I get into the back of the cab.

'265 Cassatown Road. Wess Kissington.'

'West Ken did you say. Castletown Road?'

'Yeah.'

'You OK, Squire?'

'Yeah, yeah, fine.'

The taxi pulls off and I start to cry. My tears feel hotter than normal, stinging through the slit in my closed eye.

I'm not in any fit state to find my key to 265 Castletown Road. I ring the bell. It feels like dawn. I can hear birds. Everyone will be pissed off I've woken them up. That bell would waken the dead. I stand at the door shivering. I'm not sure how long ago it was that I rang the bell. I think it was a minute ago, but maybe it was twenty minutes ago? I ring the bell again. Sam opens the door, both hands go across her mouth to stifle a scream.

'Holy shit Tom, whit hippened? Oh my God. I bitter ring for an ambulance.'

'Nah. . . Sim. . . dunt do that. . . am aright.' She takes my arm and carefully steers me up the stairs.

'Jesus, whit hippened to you?'

'A got beaten up. . . ess okay. . . I'll be OK.'

Crash Test is in the living room dressed only in a pair of weird star-spangled banner underpants, his hair sticking up like Stan Laurel.

'Fuck me Tum wha the hell happuned?'

'A got mugged, ess Ok they didn't get any-thing. I'm fine.'

'Ya dunt look fine me old mate. Looks like you had argument wey a fuckin bus! Anyway Fast Eddie's bin afta ya. We've started wurk on synagogue. I'll tell um wha happuned. He'll probably come round ta see ya.'

'Yeah thunks mit.' I wander into my bedroom and crawl under the blankets. I need to sleep. Sam comes in and arranges the blankets around me.

'I'm here if you need me, Tom.'

TWENTY

It's dark when I awake. I feel like I've had the shit kicked out of me and then remember that's exactly what happened. I can hear a TV or radio coming from the living room. Every part of me aches. I'm still wearing my suit and can smell my own stale sweat and urine. I get out of bed as carefully as I can and switch on my bedside light, it hurts my good eye so I switch it off. My other eye is still badly swollen. I walk slowly to the window and pull open the curtains. The light from the street is enough to see my way around the room. The alarm clock tells me it's 7.30. Every breath I take is a struggle. I go into the living room. Sam jumps up from the sofa.

'Oh sorry, Tom. Did I wake you with the TV? Is it too loud?'

'Nuh Sim, ut's fine, am goin fur a shah.'

Sam is staring with concern at my face. 'If you feel like eating. I've some chucken soup I can heat up.'

'Thunks Sim. . . at would be gray. Um stavin.'

This is easily the best shower I've ever had in my entire life. I want to stay here under this soft warm water which is wrapping its liquid self around every part of me. Washing away all the terror. I try to piece together what happened,

288

why did they let me go? I come to the conclusion that Caspar must have snapped, my laughing had really got to him and he lost control. I'd always heard from those in the know, those that had been through it, that the plan at any interrogation centre was patience, a waiting game to break you down slowly, sleep deprivation, lack of food, piping in loud music to your cell day and night. Showing you photos of your family and threatening to arrest them as well. It was never to kick the crap out of you on the first day. I was no good to them after that, so that's probably why I was let go and given a pain-killing injection. Or maybe they followed my taxi, knew where I lived and were watching me? It was easy to become paranoid. I mustn't let that happen. But I knew whatever happened I wasn't out of the woods. I brace myself to look in the mirror. My lips are bigger than Mick Jagger's, a bluey brown bruise has spread across half my face which is lopsided and swollen. My left eye looks like a closed oyster. The worst injury is my ribcage. I can't see myself back at work anytime soon. I won't be surprised if Fast Eddie gets rid of me.

Sam's chicken soup is out of this world. I can't really eat properly. I'm not sure where my mouth or lips are. It feels similar to when I've been to the dentist and had my gum injected. But hunger has no dignity and I manage to slurp three bowls of the soup and suck four crusty white rolls. Some of the soup is on my T-shirt. I fall asleep in front of the TV watching Porridge. Ronnie Barker is a funny man. I wished all prisons were like that. Sam wakes me. Tells me it's 11.30pm. She's in her nightdress.

'I'm off to bead Tom. I think you should go as well.'

'Surry Sim I can't slip with you tonut, um not fit.' She laughs her weird laugh and pats me gently on the knee.

'Here, these are painkillers. If you need them, they're pretty strong, so don't take more than two.'

'Yuh my Fluren Nutingale Sim.'

'Yeah. I know. G'night Tom.'

The following evening Fast Eddie arrives at the flat.

'Fuckin hell Tom. Crash Test wasn't exaggerating. You do look like a bag of shite. He says ye were mugged?'

I was tempted to tell Eddie the truth. I hated lying about this, but I thought it was for the best.

'I was. Two lads jumped me, tried to steal my holdall. Give me a bit of a kicking but they didn't get anything.'

'Jaysus. Did you go to the cops?'

'No, there's no point. I didn't really get a good look at them.'

'Black fellas were they, yeah?'

'No, they were both white.'

Eddie looks disappointed. 'Ah well, listen. We've started on the warehouse in north London. I didn't hear from ya like so I had to start another fella. Joe Eagan, you know Joe?'

'Yeah I know Joe, good brickie.'

'Yeah, well lookit I'll see what the craic is when I get the other synagogue contract confirmed in Ealing, but at the minute I've nothing for you Tom, but yer not in any fuckin shape to be laying bricks anyway wha?'

'No I'm not. It'll be a few weeks at least before I'm fit to work.'

'Alright so, take it easy now. I'll be in touch.'

I got the feeling this was Fast Eddie's way of letting me down easy. Joe Eagan was a top brickie, twice as fast as me. I sighed deeply and instantly regretted it as the pain raked across my chest. I needed a plan. A proper plan this time. I'd read about an organisation called deed-poll where I could change my name legally. As soon as Maeve sends me my medical card and birth certificate I'd look into that. It seemed that every time anyone called me Emmet, or McCrudden, something bad happened. It was like the name was jinxed.

I'm a fast healer. It's taken me just over two weeks to get to a painless fitness. Eighteen days to be precise. There is still some slight bruising on my face but it's fading. It would have taken a lot longer if it hadn't been for Sam. She's been brilliant, feeding me, shopping for me, making me do exercises. I have feelings for Sam but they're complicated. I respect her too much to start anything serious. I'd be scared that it wouldn't work out, or if by some miracle Rosie turned up. If that happened I know I'd drop Sam like a stone. She hasn't said anything or made any moves since the night she had a few drinks and told me she fancied me. So maybe it was just the booze talking?

I haven't heard anything from Fast Eddie and I haven't been to see my mother yet. The phone rang a few times last week but I let it ring, so that could've been her trying to get in touch. The doorbell clangs! Clang Clang! I go downstairs. It's the postman with a package for me to sign. I almost sign Tom Joad which I think is a good thing. I stand on the landing and open it, it's my medical card and birth certificate. The phone rings making me jump again. It's probably my mother.

'Emmet, it's Maeve. I just wanted to check that you got your medical card and birth certificate?'

'Yes, right this minute. I just signed for it. Thanks.'

'How are you keeping?'

'I'm fine working away everything's good.'

'I spoke to Ma last night, she says you haven't been over to see her for ages.'She's been trying to get hold of you.'

'I, eh, I've been busy. I'll go next week.'

The line goes silent. This is Maeve telling me I'm a bullshitter. She's the only person who can read my mind and give me a telling off without saying anything.

'Listen Emmet, something has happened to Da.' I'm hoping it's another heart attack.

Maeve clears her throat, 'He's found Jesus!'

This makes me laugh out loud.

'Honestly, Emmet. That headcase Tommy Forbes has been round at the new house with three or four others having Bible classes. Noreen says Fergal attacked them the other day with his rifle and cap gun. It's all happening here I can tell you. But look, as long as he's not drinking I couldn't care less what he does. . . and I have other news. . . I'm pregnant.' I feel genuinely pleased for her.

'Congratulations Maeve. that's great.'

'I know. We're very excited. Lenny is being all stupid and saying I've to put me feet up and all that nonsense.'

'I would if I were you, take advantage of it. He won't be saying that when the child arrives and is bawling in the middle of the night.'

Maeve laughs. 'Oh Emmet, you make it all sound so wonderful! Look promise me you'll go and see Ma. I'm worried about her on her own in London with a baby.'

'I will I promise.'

'And I was thinking I'm going to tell Da about Andre. If he really has found religion, then this will be a good test of his newfound Christianity.'

'Are you sure Maeve? It could put him back on the drink again.'

'Emmet, he has to know at some point. I've made up my mind. I'm going to tell him. I spoke to Ma about it and she thinks I should.'

'OK, I'm just sorry I can't be there to see the look on his face.' This sets the both of us off into hysterical laughter.

'Oh Jesus, Emmet, I know. But he has to be told.'

'OK, let me know how that goes.'

'I will. Listen what are you doing for Christmas? You should come home.'

'I can't Maeve. I've lost so much time at work with my foot and everything, so I need to stay here. We only have three days off.' Another silence.

'Well, make sure you go and see Ma. I might try and persuade her to come home.' I want to say that's a great idea, but that might seem like I'm trying to get rid of her, which would be true.

'I'll go and see her on Monday Maeve, I promise.'

'Alright, I have to go. Oh Emmet, I nearly forgot to tell you that Harry Lagan, was lifted last night, they have him in Castlreagh barracks. I can't believe that old eejit's in the IRA but then you never know who's in it. I've got go. It'll be a summer baby. You'll come to the christening! Bye see you soon bye.' Maeve hangs up.

Harry fucking Lagan! That man was becoming a millstone around my neck. All I could hope for was that his arrest wasn't a bad smell drifting towards me? I call Bingo, explain that I've been in Ireland and been injured at work but I'm ready to go back out and see some bands.

'Ah Tom. Listen man I was meaning to call you. . . um. . . me and Lou are not a ting anymore. We've gan our separate ways.' I really wasn't expecting to hear this.

'Ah Bingo, I'm really sorry to hear that.'

'Yeah man and right now I've decided to go back to Antigua and see my mother. She's not very well. Listen man,

it's a shame but I'll be wrappin up *The Big Fret*. Maybe someone else will take it on and if so I'll tell them to get in touch
with you. I'm sorry Tom, it's been great workin with you
and I tink you have a flair for writing, so keep it up. You
should try Melody Maker or NME. I tink you're good enough,
man, I really do.'

'Thanks Bingo, I appreciate that and thanks for giving
me a chance to work on *The Big Fret*. I enjoyed every minute
of it.'

'Yeah, OK man, you keep well, and I'll be touch in a
while when I get back.'

'Yeah, have a safe trip bye.' I felt things were slipping
away from me. First Fast Eddie and now Bingo. I needed
some kind of change. Maybe I should get out of Castletown
Road? It really felt like the right time to move on. I thought
if I changed my name legally that would be a start. Lift the
hex, be born again! Everybody else was doing it. Hallelujah!

North Kensington Library was a proper old fashioned
redbrick library, all wood paneling and big oak doors. Signs
that actually said SILENCE. There is a difference between
the smell of old books and new books. I trust old books
more, new books are just too unopened, and it's like they
don't know anything yet. The lady at the reception desk
looked like she really belonged there. She wore a red
cardigan over a dark pink polo neck sweater, a pleated kilt
and black stockings. Her hair was wire-wool grey, most of it
sat on top of her head in a big bun and had a brown pencil

sticking out of it. She looked at me over her glasses, which were attached to a gold chain around her neck.

'Can I help you, dear?'

'I'm looking for a book on how to change my name by deed poll.'

She took her glasses off and let them drop down her front. 'Och, you don't need a book for that. All you need to do is go to a solicitor, bring a witness with you, but not a member of your family or anyone who lives with you. You'll also need some identification of your current name and address and, Bob's your uncle, they can do it right away. You may have to wait two weeks or so to have it confirmed, but it's a simple procedure, dear. I think it costs about six or seven pounds. I can recommend a firm in Sloane Square.' She puts her glasses back on, pulls a sheet of paper from somewhere and writes on it. 'Richards and Fenton. They're very good.' She hands me the address.

'Oh, OK, thanks for that.'

'Not a problem, dear.'

When I got back to the flat Crash Test came out of the kitchen eating a ham sandwich. There was a large bump on his forehead.

'Eh-up Tum! Fast Eddie says he's got a start fur ya at synagogue in Ealing. I have the address here.' Crash Test produces a grubby piece of paper with an address on it. 'Wants you there for 7.30 sharp tamarra!'

'What happened your head?

'I walked into glass door. In pub. It's a brand-new door, They coudda fuckin told us like, or put warning on it or summit. I walked right inta bastard! I wooden a minded like but a spilled ma pint! Fast Eddie sent us ome cos a wuz seeing two of everything.'

Crash Test chuckles and devours the rest of his sandwich in one bite. I was pleased that Fast Eddie still had faith in me. I should never have doubted him.

It's eight thirty in the evening and I haven't seen Sam. I knock gently on her door, no response. I call her name. 'Sam? Are you in?' Nothing. I go back and continue watching TV. It's a show with Bruce Forsyth and people who have to guess stuff that's on a conveyor belt. I can't believe the shit they put on TV these days. I wanted to ask Sam if she fancied a Thai but I make myself a sandwich instead, eat the rest of Crash Test's ham. I've guessed almost everything on the conveyor belt and I'm shouting at the idiots who can only remember four things.' *Toaster, golf clubs, typewriter, dartboard, guitar, tea set, lawnmower, come on you gobshites!* I didn't hear Sam come in.

'Oh, Generation Game, I love thit show.' Following behind Sam is somebody in a suit and moustache.

'Tom this is Mark, Mark this is my flatmate Tom.'

Mark holds out his hand. I shake it. He smiles broadly and says, 'Very pleased to meet you.' He sounds Indian although Mark isn't a very Indian sounding name.

'I've just come in to get changed. Mark and I are going

for a drink, you can join us if you like?'

I was jealous. I couldn't believe I was jealous. What the hell is wrong with me. Why am I jealous? 'No that's OK I have an early start in the morning.' Sam gets all excited.

'Oh you're bick working, thit's great Tom.'

'Yeah, I'll be glad to get into the swing of things again.'

Sam touches Mark on the arm, sort of squeezes it gently. It's not a touch you would give a friend or colleague, it's a girlfriend touch. She smiles at him. 'I'll just be five munits.' He smiles back. 'That's OK, take your time.' Mark looks around for somewhere to sit. I tell him to sit on the armchair. He smiles at me again.

'What is it you do for a living Tom?'

'I lay bricks.' He smiles again and this time both ends of his moustache smile with him.

'Oh, that's like a proper man's job. I just move paper around all day, look into microscopes and read textbooks. I work in the same lab as Sam.' I'm thinking, are you the wanker who keeps touching her ass? But I know it can't be him. Bruce Forsyth has apparently said something funny and the audience are howling.

I couldn't resist saying what I say next. 'Have you been going out with Sam for long?'

Mark looks puzzled. 'Going out? You mean like *going out* going out?'

I nod. 'Yeah, as in *going out* you know.' I raise my eyebrows, something I never do. I'm wondering why I'm behaving like a dickhead. Mark shakes his head.

'Oh, no, no. We are not "going out" in that sense. We are just having a drink tonight so I can pick her brains about her experience on collecting and analysing biological data and the relationships between organisms and their environment.'

Well, that shut me up. I felt like a prize prick. 'Oh right, well, that all sounds exciting.'

I wished I could keep quiet. Mark smiles at me and strokes his moustache with his finger and thumb. He can see straight through me. I start to blush. I haven't blushed in years. Sam arrives in the room, she has put on lipstick and a new blouse. I think she's lost a little weight. Maybe she fancies this guy.

'See ya later, Tom.' Mark gets up and it's a big grin he gives me this time.

'Good to meet you, Tom.'

'Yeah, have fun.' As they clatter down the stairs the phone rings on the landing. I can hear Sam answering it.

'Tom, it's for you!' I go downstairs. Sam looks at me before she goes out the door and whispers. 'It's your starlet!'

'Hi Tom, it's Eva just thought I'd catch up and see how things are. How was the wedding?'

'Wedding was great. Irish wedding you know, lots of alcohol and talking and alcohol followed by a lot more talking. How are you Eva?'

'Honestly. I'm feeling pretty shit. I have to redo two of

my papers and I cut my finger really badly. I was trying to slice chicken. I can't write, so I'm way behind with everything. I need cheering up. You wanna come over tomorrow night?' I hesitate, the pause gets longer. I'm making hurry-up faces at myself. 'Jesus Tom, just say no if you don't want to!'

'No, I do want to, it's just that I've been off work for a while with my foot and one thing and another and I just can't do weekdays anymore. What about Friday?'

'OK, Friday would work.'

'Great. Eva, there's something I'd like you to do for me, a favour.'

'A favour huh, well depends what it is.'

'I'd like you to come and be a witness for something official I need to do at a solicitor's office.'

'Something official, like what?'

'I'll explain when I see you, could you meet me at Sloane Square tube station at 6.30 on Friday night? Then we could head back into town, still plenty of time for a drink.' Now it's her turn to be silent.

'Hmmm, I'm intrigued. Did you say Sloane Square? OK I guess I can manage that.'

'Thanks Eva, I appreciate you doing this.'

TWENTY-ONE

IT WAS GREAT to get back to work. I was eager to impress Fast Eddie but he got in first.

'This job's about gettin it right. I had a look at the plans and it's not fuckin straight forward atall. There'll be lots of piers and corbelling, double bullnose walls everywhere and at least four bullseye windows, and there's a diamond feature on the two main gables with different coloured bricks. So yer in luck, it's not a job for a speed merchant but that doesn't mean you can relax like.'

I was going to have my work cut out. I'd never attempted corbelling before. Corbelling is where the bricks are stepped out from the wall to form a weight bearing arch or buttress. Done right it can look great. But I'd seen it done wrong and it's an embarrassing pain in the ass to put right. Fast Eddie could see I was nervous about it.

'Joe Eagan's coming down from North London to keep an eye on things, so if you get stuck just give him a shout. But listen, don't fuckin mention we're building a synagogue.'

'Why not?'

'He has a thing about Jews.'

The woman at North Kensington Library was absolutely right. Changing my name was one of the most straight-forward things I've ever had to do. I couldn't believe how easy it was. I showed the solicitor my birth certificate, filled in a deed poll form which was signed and witnessed by Eva. I signed the form twice and that was it. I was now officially Tom Joad. The solicitor asked me if I wanted to enrol the name for safe keeping at the Royal Courts of Justice, but that was another eight pounds, so I declined the offer. I didn't fancy the idea of my name being anywhere near the Royal Courts of Justice. Confirmation and a copy of the form would be sent to me in ten days. This form allowed me to get a driving licence or passport in the name of Tom Joad. The whole thing took fifteen minutes and cost £6.99. Bob was indeed my uncle. Eva moaned at me when I said I had to drop off the crutches to St Stephen's hospital.

'Oh Mr Joad, can this night get any more exciting?'

I put them in a little bay that said CRUTCHES. William was in an office surrounded by glass, he saw me, smiled and gave me the thumbs up. Eva and I ended up in the Running Horse in Bond Street.

An old guy who was bald on top but with long hair to his shoulders was in the corner playing guitar and murdering 'Streets of London'. We sat well away from him. Eva was looking stunning as usual. She had a white bandage around her finger with a spot of blood at the tip. She said it probably needed stitching, but she couldn't stand the idea of having her finger darned like a sock. We chatted about music and films and books. She said I had to see Electra Glide in Blue as it was the best movie she'd seen in a long time. The director James Guerico was also the music producer for the rock band Chicago. I never thought of Chicago as a rock band, if it was rock then it was fairly soft rock. She drank quickly and I noticed she was blinking her eyes a lot. She was eager to show me her new flat and suggested we go back there.

Her flat was identical to the one she had shared with Noreen and the Chinese girls. It was a single apartment so just smaller. Eva opened a bottle of wine and poured two large glasses. I didn't know a lot about wine but it didn't seem right that it should be in a glass full to the brim. We got comfortable on the small couch. I sipped my wine careful not to spill it then spilled some on my shirt. Eva didn't notice.

'I knew you were shitting me when you told me your name was Tom Joad. But Emmet McCrudden! I can fully understand why you wanted shot of that moniker! Emmet McCrudden? Sounds like a hillbilly pig farmer.'

'Ha! You can talk, Evangapenis Alibaba Membrain Copperbollocks!'

Eva choked laughing and spat out her wine. 'Oh my God! That's a much better name than mine!'

When we had almost finished the wine she made some cheese and crackers and something called salami, which I wasn't keen on, but I ate it anyway. She gave me a thoughtful look as she ate her crackers.

'You can't change who you are by changing your name.'

My gut instinct was to disagree with that. 'Yeah, but you

can change the way other people think about who you are.'

She shakes her head softly. 'Maybe, but blood is blood. When I look at the photo of my grandmother it gives me chills down my spine. I couldn't be anybody else even if I wanted to.'

That statement made me jealous. I wished I could feel like that. But I knew my situation was different. It was almost midnight, so it looked like I was staying over. Eva stroked my face and kissed me hungrily sucking my lips and rolling her tongue around the inside of my mouth. She stood up. 'Come on.' I followed her to the bedroom.

There was a poster of the New York Subway on the wall and above the bed Lou Reed and the Velvet Underground. We undressed quickly. Eva kept on her red bra and knickers. Things started calmly enough. I took off her bra, kissed her gently on the back of her neck. We lay down on the bed. I kissed her breasts, then slowly took off her knickers. For a moment it felt like she wanted me to be in control, but I could soon sense her urgency and impatience. Eva wasn't really into foreplay she took hold of my penis and inserted it into her. Inserted is the right word, it felt very inserted, like a bolt sliding into a door, or a plug into a socket. We are making love, I am getting into a rhythm, Eva is thrusting her hips up to meet me, it's all getting very frantic I know it's going to be over quickly unless she slows down, but she doesn't slow down, she grabs my hair, not too tightly at first but then suddenly wrenches it, 'YES!' She shouts in my ear.

'FUCKING YES!' Then slaps me around the face, What the fuck? She starts spitting at me and hitting me with both hands, pulling my hair. 'YOU BASTARD!' She's screaming at me. 'YOU FUCKING BASTARD!' I am still inside her going hell for leather. She hits me again. 'Jesus Christ Eva, what the fuck is wrong with you?' 'SHUT UP AND FUCK ME!' She drags her nails hard down the sides of my arm and slaps me across my ear. I try and get away from her but she has both thighs wrapped tightly around my waist. She's spitting and screaming. 'FUCK ME YOU BASTARD!' I slap her hard across the face and fall back off the bed onto the floor.

She's covered in blood, it's on the wall, splattered over Lou Reeds face, the sheets are sprinkled with red dots. It's coming from her finger, the bandage is stuck to the headboard. The wound has opened and is pouring blood. I can see the beginnings of my handprint on the side of her face. She curls up and starts to sob.

'I'm sorry Tom. . . I'm sorry. . . I don't know what's wrong with me?'

I stand back against the wall naked and shaking. Her blood is on my chest and stomach and hair. I grab some tissues from a box on the bedside table and try and stem the blood from her finger. The tissues redden and are immediately soaked. The bedroom resembles a murder scene.

'Ohhhh Tom. . . what is wrong with me?'

'Come on, let's get you to the bathroom.' I guide her to

the bathroom, switch on the shower, she pushes her hair back and streaks her face in blood. We both stand under the water. I watch the swirls of red going down the plughole. She puts her bleeding finger in her mouth, holds on to me, her body is trembling she goes to speak and blood flows from her lips. I switch off the shower, grab a small white towel and wrap it tightly around her finger, tell her to keep pressure on it. I find another larger towel and dry her off.

She puts on a bathrobe that's hanging on the door. I ask does she have band aids? She nods and I follow her into the kitchen. She opens a cupboard and takes down a tin box with a green cross on it. Inside is everything I need. The cut in her finger is a deep slice. I squeeze the skin together and wrap it tightly with tape, place a white pad over it and wrap more tape around it. The red hand of Ulster is imprinted across her cheek.

'I'm sorry I hit you, Eva. I just didn't know what else to do.'

'That's OK. I deserved it.'

My teeth are chattering with cold. 'I need to put some clothes on.'

I go into the bedroom and get dressed, there is blood everywhere. It's amazing how much blood can come out of a cut finger. I go back to the living room. Eva is on the couch, our glasses of wine are still half full. I sit beside her, she pulls a green tartan blanket from the back of the couch and puts it around our knees. My instinct is to get away. I look at the clock. It's 1.30 in the morning. I would stay until it was light and get the first tube home.

'I need help Tom. I've known it all along, but. . . I've just ignored it. . . can you forgive me?'

I'm still angry but I also feel sorry for her. 'I've been in far worse scrapes than this I can tell you. So don't worry about it. But, you probably do need to talk to someone, a doctor or. . .'

'A shrink?' I'd never heard the expression before, but I guessed it was some sort of head doctor. I smile at her and take a large gulp of wine. She sighs and tears appear quickly in her eyes.

'When I'm having sex. . . it's like revenge. I want revenge on that bastard who raped me. It's like I'm back there in those bushes, but this time, I'm winning. . . does that makes any sense to you?'

It didn't, but I said yes. I told her I understood. I'm suddenly exhausted. Eva lays her head on my shoulder, we cuddle up as best we can on the couch Her eyes are closed. I'm glad the conversation is over. I have nothing left to say. I let my legs hang over the the end of the couch and listen to her breathing.

The early morning, before the traffic starts, is the only time you can hear the birds in London. They are on the tree outside. A blackbird I think, or maybe a song thrush. I always think everything is OK when I hear birds singing. My back is aching. Eva is asleep with her mouth open. My handmark has disappeared from her face. I get up and pour myself a glass of water. Each individual streetlight has its own dull yellow halo of mist. From the small kitchen window I can see the sky is a blank canvas of dark grey with darker smokier clouds scattered below, almost touching the rooftops of High Holborn. Eva wakes and looks at me. She staggers from the couch and hugs me.

'I'm so sorry Tom.'

I kiss her on the cheek. 'Stop apologising. There's none of us right in the head. I've got to go.'

'Oh Tom stay for breakfast.' She squints at the clock. 'It's only 6.45.'

'I need to get going Eva. I might have to work today.'

She hugs me again. 'Can I call you?'

'Yeah, of course you can.' I grab my coat from the back of the chair. 'I'll see you soon.'

She looks like she's going to cry again. I know I need to get out of here.

'Thanks for helping me change my name.'

She smiles sadly and says something in Russian which sounded like *Ya duma, shtow yet ta baya blue. Tom Joad.*

Strawbs had apparently let slip to Joe Eagan that we were building a synagogue. Eagan never shut up about it all morning. I thought he was a nice guy until all this started. He was beginning to get on my nerves. Laying the footings was tricky. There were tree roots everywhere and the soil was very loose. I spent the morning cutting the roots with a saw whilst having to listen to his ranting. I stopped him in mid-flow.

'Listen Joe, I don't care how you feel about the Jews. I don't want to hear about it.'

He stood up from the trench, his face flustered. He was way ahead of all of us and had already built six course of bricks.

'I'll speak my fucking mind and no cunt will stop me! Every fucking Jewish firm I've ever worked for has done me out of money. They're a penny-pinching parcel of bastards. They cause trouble wherever they go. They've done it throughout history. Nobody wants them. Why do you think they've had to go to Israel? And they fucking stole that from the Arabs.... And here I am building their fucking house of prayer? House of prayer my bollocks. Them cunts aren't interested in prayer, that's all a front. Money is their God! Hah! I know what I'm fucking talking about.'

He was around six-foot-three, weighed about seventeen stone and he was right in my face. I wasn't about to get into a fight with him about this, so I buttoned my lip. Lunchtime came around. Strawbs, Crash Test and me had brought a packed lunch. Thankfully Eagan went to the pub which give us all a bit of peace for an hour. Eagan had really got to me. Being a Northern Irish Catholic I knew what it was like to be discriminated against and even killed for your race or religion. It wasn't nearly on the same scale as the Jews but I could identify with it. I'd always remembered the poem about the holocaust by Martin Niemoller, that Miss Flannigan had me learn and read out in class. *First they came for the socialists and I did not speak out because I was not a socialist.*. It went through a list of people who he did not speak out for because he was not one of those people and it ended with the line *and then they came for me.* That poem had a powerful effect on me, and I never forgot it.

Eagan was late coming back from lunch. He turned up carrying a large plastic bag. At first I thought he'd brought back a carry-out of beer but, it wasn't beer, it was pork pies. Six packets of pork pies, which he then proceeded to build into the wall, dropping them down the cavity. I couldn't believe my eyes. He saw me gawping at him and turned on me.

'What the fuck are you looking at?'

'You can't do that Joe that's not right!' He started laughing. 'Who's going to know? Are you going to tell them are ya? What the fuck is it to you?' He turned his back and continued building the pork pies into the wall. A few of the other brickies thought it was hilarious and started laughing. Crash Test grabs hold of me and pulls me back.

'Jus leave it Tum. We'll have wurd with Eddie tonight.'

My mother kept cleaning the table in her small kitchen. The table was already spotless. I could see she wasn't thinking about what she was doing. The kettle had boiled but she turned it on again. Andre is rubbing his face with a half a peach then lobs it onto the table. My mother starts the table cleaning process all over again.

'Ma please, just sit down and talk this through.'

She makes two cups of coffee.

'I spoke to Maeve last night and she wants me to come home. She told your father about Andre and apparently he said, honest to God Emmet, I can't believe this, but apparently he said, "All children are God's children and he wants his wife back at his side." '

My mother stares at me with a look of astonishment and then we both crack up laughing. Andre joins in clapping his hands.

'Jesus Emmet, can you believe that? What the hell is he up to?'

'I don't know Ma, but the question is do you want to go back?'

'Of course I want to go back. I feel guilty every day. I miss my children and I really want to be there when my first grandchild is born. I want to be with Maeve for that. But I don't trust that man. I don't know how I'm going to survive here. I can't afford the rent of this place on my wages, and I definitely can't afford a childminder.'

I blow on my coffee. 'Then take the chance and go back. If it doesn't work out you can always find a place in Carricktown to live. At least you have our family there to help you.'

She leans her head against the wall and stares at the ceiling. 'Would you travel back with me, Emmet?'

'Christ Ma, I can't take any more time off work.'

'We could go on Saturday and sure you could come back on Sunday, that way you wouldn't miss any work. It's just the thought of arriving in Carricktown on my own, with Andre.'

'Ma, people are going to have to get used to Andre. They'll either accept him or they won't.'

'I know that Emmet I'm just asking you to travel with me, that's all, for a bit of company.'

I really don't want to go back to Carricktown. I promised myself I'd be stronger when it came to this.

'OK, if that's what you want. I'll come with you.'

Sam is hoovering the hallway, her face covered in a mask. Wispy smoke drifts from two thin sticks of something which are giving off quite a pungent smell. She pulls her mask off.

'I'm just funishing. You wanna go round the corner and grab us both a Thai? I'll have shrimp.'

'What's that smell?'

'Joss sticks.'

I'm none the wiser. I feel like kissing Sam. It's an almost overwhelming urge. She gives me a strange look. 'Whit's up?'

'Nothing. I'll just go and get the food.'

We sit at the table in the kitchen. Sam has warmed the plates and we are eating with knives and forks. 'Thought we could be a little civilised tonight.'

We both eat in silence and this is fine as Sam is as much a lover of Thai as I am. We understand that the food shouldn't be interrupted with talk. Crash Test comes in and makes a 'Phaaoorgh!' Sound.

'This bloody flat's beginning to smell like Chinese whore ouse!'

Sam is straight back at him. 'You pay me ten dollar Engrish man I love you long time.'

He laughs. 'OK, that's a deal I'll see ya later. Listen, I'm going for showhar anyone want to use the bog speak now, or forever hold ya piss!'

After we have eaten and I have been told to wash up. Sam tells me she has a bone to pick. We sit on the sofa.

'I hear you asked Mark if he was going out with me?'

I start to blush. She smiles.

'Tom Joad. Why is your face turning into a tomato? Tom?'

'Yes, I did ask him. I was just curious.'

And then she does something that really stuns me. She pushes my nose with her finger. What the hell is it with my friggin nose? 'Pinocchio.' she says.

I don't get this. 'Pinocchio, what do you mean?'

'Oh come on Tom you know the story of Pinocchio when he lied his nose grew bigger.'

'Oh, I see.'

'Mark said he thought you sounded a little bit jealous. Were you jealous, Tom?'

My face is still red hot. I don't know what to say. I feel about ten years old.

'Tom?'

'OK I was jealous.'

She grins from ear to ear. 'Why are you jealous? You have a lovely starlet.'

The next thing I say I haven't thought about until now but I know it's true. 'I'm not seeing Eva anymore.'

Sam looks genuinely surprised. 'Oh, whit hippened?'

'I think she has some stuff going on. She's a complicated person. We weren't right for each other.'

Sam says, 'Hmm.' It has an unconvincing ring to it. 'Have you told her?'

I start blushing again. 'No, not yet, but I will.'

Sam pushes my nose again. 'You sure?'

'Yeah, I'm positive.'

Sam looks at me. It's an intense look. I feel like I have to do something or my face will burst and all my blush will fly out all over the place. I lean in and kiss her. She puts her hands softly on my face and kisses me back. It's the gentlest unhurried kiss I have ever experienced. Her hands are in my hair. She stops and looks at me, takes my hand and we go to her bedroom. She unbuttons my shirt. I unbutton her blouse. We are smiling at each other and are soon naked. She likes to kiss and so do I. When we eventually make love it feels like we've been together for a long time. We are both noisy at the end which makes us roar with laughter. It's the first time I've ever laughed after sex and as I lay in her arms, I realise I haven't thought about Rosie or Eva or anything. All I can see is Sam.

TWENTY-TWO

I fill in an application form for a passport. I'm applying for a British passport as it seems less complicated. One of the questions on the form asks, Do you have a criminal record? Emmet McCrudden had his prints taken under duress, so no, I don't have a criminal record. I take the form to Father Curran, the local parish priest at St Mary's church. He signs it for me and I drop a fiver in the poor box. Irish priests are all gangsters. I check my post office book I'm down to £237.80 I need to start saving again. I book two flights, one to Belfast leaving on Saturday at 11.30am – we don't work on Saturday as it's the Jewish Sabbath and a return to Heathrow coming back on the 11.30am on Sunday. Andre travels free.

Maeve has arranged for a Johnson taxi to pick us up at Aldergrove. We go through departures. My pulse is racing as we pass the two suits standing behind the security desk. I give them a quick glance but I don't recognise them. I have Andre in my arms and walk past as casually as I can waiting all the time for the *Excuse me, sir*. But it doesn't come. I breathe a sigh of relief and hope it's the same at the other end. The flight is quite bumpy and Andre cries all the way. A man behind us keeps huffing and kicking the back of my seat saying 'Jesus Christ' under his breath. When the plane lands I stare him out, and then suddenly think why do I always have to react to everything? But I still stare at him until he grunts and looks away first. There is no problem at Aldergrove. No inquisition. I decide I must travel with a woman and a baby all the time.

Having spent so long in London, Carricktown now seems like everything's in slow motion. Two women with a pram and a young boy with a lampshade on his head are crossing the main road. It takes them forever, if this was London they'd be dead, splattered all over the place. The taxi man is so patient. He whistles to himself until the road is clear. He drops us off at the taxi rank in the High Street and that's when I hear my father's booming voice. I look across and there he is, standing on two green crates. I recognise the crates, Cantrell and Cochrane! His arms are spread wide, one hand gripping the bible.

'But in your hearts revere Christ as Lord. Always be prepared to give an answer to everyone who asks you to give the reasons. Saint Peter said, repent and be baptised, every one of you in the name of Jesus Christ. I was a sinner but I could not hide from Christ, he found me under the stone of secrecy. He turned over that stone and I crawled out to him! I was deep in the dark dry well of despair but Jesus dropped the water of life on my head and I was born again!'

I had to admit he really looked and sounded the part. It was as if he'd been preaching all of his life. He was putting his 'actor's' voice to good use at last. My mother's face is a shock of disbelief.

'Oh my God, Emmet, what have I come back to?' She hands Andre to me. My father sees us, his eyes look wild with, well I can't tell what it is. I've never seen it before. Zeal, religious fervour, madness?

'Maur-eeeen!' He shouts my mother's name and runs towards her. 'Maur-eeeen!' He flings his arms around her and lifts her up. 'Oh my God, thank you Lord!'

'Frank, please, not in the middle of the street! Please!' My father's head whips around and he looks at Andre. 'Oh suffer the little children to come onto me.' Fucking hell he really has lost it. He is on the verge of tears. He holds out his arms. 'Can I hold him? Let me hold him.'

I hand the kid over. Andre's face is red and straining he makes that noise 'Nnnnfff' that kids make when they've shit their nappy. Great timing, Andre lad. My father looks at him. 'I'm going to love you like all the rest little man, have no fear about that.' The smell of nappy coming from Andre is top drawer. My father doesn't seem to notice, his smile is wide-eyed and glazed. 'Come on! Let's go home everyone. Let's go home.'

The taxi takes my parents and Andre on to the promised land. Well, to Burren Park View at least. I don't go with them. I've done my part and need a drink. I go across the road to the Brewery Tap. Maeve and Lenny and half the pub have witnessed the homecoming. Lenny smiles at me and shakes my hand.

'Good man, Emmet, fair play to you. Jaysus yer Da's in good form! I think he'll save us all by the time he's finished.'

Maeve gives Lenny a dunt with her elbow. 'It's no laughing matter Len.' But I see she's smiling.

There is a murmuring across the bar from some of the locals, 'Sure there's no harm in him.'

'Not at all.'

'Jaysus, I'd rather see him bible mad than drunk mad.'

'Ah that's right sure, God love him.'

I spend most of the evening in the Brewery Tap. Maeve says I can stay in the loft room.

I go to the toilets at the back of the pub and when I come out something is put over my head, I'm dragged out to the car park and into the back of a van. The van drives off. There's two men at least maybe three and one driving. Nobody has said anything yet including me. One man is kneeling on my back and pushing my face into the floor. I can smell sheep shit and hay. I'm in this position for at least half an hour. The van then hits a rugged part of the road, or it's probably a lane and we rumble down that for five minutes until we finally stop. The doors open and I'm dragged out. I feel grass under my feet and then gravel. We go through a door and I'm pushed down onto a chair. I can hear a lot of heavy breathing. Whoever these guys are they're not fit.

A voice I don't recognise says. 'There's a gun on ye, so don't take aff yer hood. We jist want tay ask ye a few questions.'

I hear him drag up a chair and feel he's pretty close to me. 'We know ye were pulled in and taken to Paddington Green station and we know what ye told them. I jist want ye to tell me the truth. It'll be easier on ye if ye do. So how long have ye been working for them?'

I clear my throat and hope my voice doesn't betray the fact I'm shitting myself. 'I'm not working for anybody. They showed me some photos of Harry Lagan shaking my hand at Mickey Peach's funeral. They asked me who he was and I said I didn't know.' There is a long pause.

'Stop fuckin lyin and taking us for cunts. Harry Lagan was lifted so we know yer a fuckin tout travellin back and forth to England so cut the shite and just tell us what else you told them.' I feel something hard poke into my temple. 'Just own up tell the truth otherwise this isn't gonna end well for ye.'

'I swear to God I told them I didn't know him. I'd seen him around the town but I didn't know who he was. They didn't believe me, they asked why was he shaking my hand and I said because he knew Mickey was my mate and he was saying how sorry he was. Later on they showed me three more photos. I knew Jackie Westwood. I didn't know the other two, but I told them nothing. I said I didn't know any of them.' Another pause, then I'm slapped hard across the face. The slap comes from the side. The gun is poked harder into my temple.

'We know yer fuckin lying. They don't bring any Tom, Dick or fuckin Harry into Paddington Green. They only bring in IRA men and touts and the only people they let go after twenty-four hours are fucking touts!' I'm slapped again this time on the other side of my face. 'I'm giving you one more chance to tell us what else you told them.'

I decide to remain calm and speak in as measured a voice as I can. I assumed, although I had no evidence of this whatsoever, that machismo in the IRA was *de riguer* and if I was to man it out, I might have a better chance of survival than if I snivelled and begged for my life. I think about the poem. *First they came. . .* Maybe I would write my version, *First they came for me and I spoke out, and then the others came for me and blew my face off.*

'I'm not a tout. I told them nothing and they beat the shit out of me. I was off work for three weeks. Mickey Peach was my best friend. I've known Harry Lagan all my life. He's our Bread Man for Christ's sake. I'm no tout. So do whatever you're going to fucking do but I'm no tout.'

I hear the safety catch click off and the hammer being drawn back. 'One more chance mate.'

I grit my teeth and clench every muscle in my body. Time is flying past but at the same time seems to be standing still. I can hear crows cawing and the sound of a tractor. The tractor is changing gear. It is far away, in some other time perhaps, in some other place? I hear another voice, and even though it's a whisper, I recognise it. It says, 'OK H Let him go!'

I'm dragged out of the door and flung into the van. The knee in my back, my face squashed into the floor the smell of sheep shit and hay. About twenty minutes later the van screeches to a halt, the doors open I'm dragged back out of the van and shoved across the road. 'Keep yer hood on until we're good and gone. Tick it aff before that and I'll fuckin shoot ye. We know where ye live in London. We'll be watching ye.'

The van drives off. I wait until I can't hear it anymore and slowly take off the hood. I'm in a pitch-dark country road. My stomach begins to contort and vibrate. I stumble into a hedge, pull my trousers down as fast as I can then vomit and shit a violent foul-smelling liquid which gushes out of me from both ends. The smell makes me wretch, my stomach turns and tightens until it can go no further. I'm in a cold sweat, my legs are trembling. I stay on all fours until I feel able to stand. I grab a handful of grass and clean myself as best I can. I can see one farmhouse with lights on. I have no idea where I am. I start walking until I reach a T junction. I squint at the road sign. It says Omagh 25 Carricktown 3. I start walking and know for a fact that I have Jackie Westwood to thank for saving my life.

Maeve asks where I've been and then says, 'As if I don't know. That vet will neuter you if he knows you're sniffing after Rosie.'

Six weeks ago this statement would have driven me insane with rage and jealously but I just smile and say, 'Rosie hasn't broken up from university yet and I wish her well with her Vet Man.'

I go to bed about half-eleven. Lenny and Maeve are still serving. It takes me a while to get to sleep. My dreams are weird but in the morning I can't remember them. The door is knocked lightly and Maeve tells me my breakfast is on the tray outside. I check the time, it's 8.45. I open the door and Fergal is standing there with an empty tray. He laughs loudly. I give him a massive hug and I really have to use every trick in the book not to cry. I mustn't cry. I pretend to laugh and wipe my eyes.

'Have you eaten my breakfast?'

'Ha! It's downstairs Emmy. What time are ye leaving?'

'I have to go in about an hour.'

'Maeve says I can come with ye to the airport. Can I Emmy?'

Jesus Christ. What was Maeve thinking? I'm sure she's doing this on purpose to break me. 'Yeah, course you can.'

Maeve tries her best to get me to stay for Christmas. 'Och go on Emmet, it's only two weeks away.'

'I have to get back Maeve. I need to go to work. You've enough people here.'

'Well you better come back for the christening in August. The baby might be born on your birthday who knows?'

Fergal is already in the taxi shooting his cap gun at me. I

give Maeve a hug and shake hands with Lenny. He makes a big, scared face, 'Can I come with you?' Maeve hits him playfully. 'Don't be a stranger you hear me?'

The taxi pulls away. When we're outside the town the taxi driver says to me. 'Can ye tell the wee fellah not to be pointing the gun out the windy. We don't want tay be target practice for the Brits.'

Fergal makes a face and points it at the back of the driver's head. I learn a lot about Fergal on the taxi journey. He tells me everything. His favourite subject is drawing. He likes Clare Fagan, but now she has braces he prefers Katie Sweeney. But Katie Sweeney likes Aidan Kelly, but Fergal thinks Aidan Kelly is a slabber. He loves the new house. He says, 'Da didn't have a bath until he found Jesus and now he baths all the time. Emmy, why do people always find Jesus, is Jesus lost all the time?'

This really makes me laugh. 'I don't know Fergal, I'm not the best person to ask.'

Fergal's knowledge of every town we pass is impressive. The kid has a very enquiring mind which I hope he never loses. He tells me, 'Magherafelt has been a town since 1425 in Irish it's Machaire Fiolta, which means Monastic house. Randalstown was founded in 1650 and was named after Randal McDonald who married Rose O'Neill of Shane's Castle. We learned all this in history class with Mrs Dunniford. She's a bit mental and has one hairy leg and one shaved leg.'

I'm convinced Fergal will become some kind of comedian. He's made me laugh for the whole trip. At the airport entrance the RUC wave us through. I tell Fergal not to point the cap gun at them. Fergal gets out and insists on getting my bag out of the boot. There is that moment of awkwardness before you say goodbye to somebody you love. I give Fergal a hug and then I give him two ten-pound notes. His eyes are on stalks.

'Fuckin Hell, Emmy, sorry, but that's twenty quid. Is that what yer givin me really?'

'It's for Christmas Fergal, don't tell Maeve, she'll make you put it in your money box.' Fergal gives me another hug.

I pat him on the head, 'See you around dude!' I walk away and when I look back the taxi has gone.

TWENTY-THREE

I spend Christmas with Sam in the flat. We buy Christmas lights and decorations. It's the first time I've ever put up decorations and surprise myself at how good I am at it. I think of Annouska and the Christmas I spent with her and Keefer, and the decorations she made herself. I take ages choosing the tree. I tell Sam the Norwegians invented the Christmas tree, and she doesn't believe me. We make love almost every night. I find out that the butterfly on her thigh isn't a Red Admiral. It's something called Rauparaha's Copper, named after Te Rauparaha, a famous Maori warrior and chief of the Ngati Toa tribe.

She says, 'I've had more sux with you Tom in the past month than I've hid in all of my life. Do you think we're overdoing it, too much of a good thing and all thit?'

I say 'No. Let's just enjoy it. There's no such thing as too much of a good thing.'

Sam's surname is Pinkerton. Her mother died of cancer when she was sixteen. She is an only child. Her dad is in his fifties and she describes him as the gentlest of gentlemen. The most laid back human being on the planet. He loves his Jazz and his fishing and his pipe. The landlord has put phone extensions in all the flats so no more running down to the

landing. Our phone is busy over Christmas. Sam speaks to
her dad but the line keeps cutting out. She gets to say, 'I
love you Dad, Merry Christmas,' but that's about it. I speak
to Maeve and Fergal and Ma and even Da comes on and
sounds normal enough. He doesn't mention Jesus once.
Reading between the lines I think things are OK and for the
first time in my life I feel free from the McCruddens. I know
I'm building something here with Sam. Something which I
hope can last. She knows I come from a family of eight, but
I haven't told her my real name is McCrudden. I will have to
tell her at some point, but since I've changed it legally, I
really do feel like Tom Joad is my real name and Emmet
McCrudden was a character I used to play in a soap opera.

Joe Eagan is still at the synagogue. Fast Eddie had a word
with him and whatever he said did the trick. The Jew-hater
hasn't said a word against them since, he also hasn't spoken
to me or anybody else. Maybe building the pork pies into
the wall has sated his hatred for now. But there is no doubt
he is building what is going to be a very impressive
synagogue. As a bricklayer I'm learning a lot from him and
eventually the pork pies will rot.

I buy the NME and see that there's a Boxing night double
bill of Dr Feelgood and the Kursaal Flyers playing at the
Nashville Rooms. This is too good to miss. The Flyers open
and are brilliant as usual. But Dr Feelgood blow the roof off
the place. Lee Brilleaux is wearing a white suit that looks
like he slept in it and Wilko is all in black. John B 'Sparko' is

playing the bass out of his skin and John Martin is the most energetic drummer I've ever seen.

I had a great night and got extremely drunk. Sam was very patient as it's not really her kind of music. We didn't have sex that night. I could just about walk. I get a postcard from Eva with something written in Russian which says *YA dumayu chto ya tebya lyublyu, Tom Joad.* The lady who works in the launderette is from the Ukraine. When I pick up my laundry I ask her what it means? She smiles at me and then laughs. 'Eeet says I theenk I love you, Tom Joad.'

Sam and I are watching The Likely Lads. I don't get it, maybe it's too English for me but Sam loves it. I find a lot of the set-ups pretty stupid. Strawbs gave me an LP last week, Solo Concert by a folk singer called Billy Connolly and it includes a routine called 'The Crucifixion', all about the lead up to the death of Jesus but set in Glasgow and all the Apostles are Glaswegians. It's the funniest thing I've ever heard. He's definitely a lapsed Catholic.

The phone rings and makes us jump. We still haven't got used to it being in the living room. Sam answers. 'Hullo.' She gives me one of her looks. 'Oh hullo Eva. How are you?.. Yes Sam, thit's right well remembered. Yes, he's here right beside me, you want a word? OK, yeah, hippy Christmas to you too.'

Sam hands me the phone. 'Hi Eva, how are you?'

'I'm fine Tom Joad. I've tried calling but no one ever answers.'

Sam is pretending to watch TV but I know she's listening.

'I've been busy working.'

'Hey listen do you want to meet up. Just go for a drink no big drama.'

I think about how I can answer this. 'I think you should know Eva that Sam and I are together now.' Sam makes a face and does a heart flutter mime with her hand against her chest.

'Oh. . . really?. . . OK, well why don't the three of us go for a drink?' I let that question hang and so does Eva.

'I don't think that's a good idea Eva. I think you and I should make a clean break.' I can hear a stifled sigh. I feel sorry for Eva. I can almost feel her rejection through the phone line.

'You did say I could call you.'Why did you say I could call?'

'I didn't know this would be my situation when I said you could call me.' There is a long silence.

'OK Tom. I get it. I won't call you again. Merry Christmas.'

'Happy Christmas Eva look after your. . .' Before I could say 'self' she had hung up.

Sam flings a cushion at me. 'I'm your bloody situation now am I?'

I grab her and tickle her feet. She squeals with laughter! I pick up the phone, 'Hallo, is that the police station? I've got a situation here, officer!'

April fifteenth is Sam's 24th birthday. I buy her the book she wanted. Took me ages to find it. Black Holes: The End of the Universe by John Taylor. I sign it with This is where my odd socks are. Love Tom xx. When Sam comes in from work I give her the book and a birthday card. But something is wrong, she is on the verge of tears.

'What is it Sam, what's wrong?' She hugs me and starts to cry. I've never seen her like this before. I sit her down on the couch and push the hair away from her face.

'What is it?'

She takes a breath and tries to speak; it comes out in a sough of tears.

'I'm preegnant Tom. I don't know how it hippened I've been so careful. I must have forgotten to take my pill and I thought I started my new dose, but I checked and I haven't opened thit packet yet.'

She stared at me accusingly. 'I knew we were having too much sux.'

I hold her close. 'Jesus Christ Sam. I thought it was bad news! I thought you were going to tell me you were ill! Or your father had died or something!'

She looks at me with what looks like pity. 'You're nineteen years old Tom. You're not ready to be a dad.'

When she says *dad,* the news that she's pregnant really hits home.'My stomach turns over. I suddenly feel deflated. I want to say something profound and adult. *I'll be twenty in four months. When the kid is born I'll be into my twenty-*

first year. Perfect age to be a dad. She wipes her nose with the back of her sleeve, something else I've never seen her do.

'This is serious Tom. This is a baby we're talking about.' I get a fluttery panic in my head which could get out of hand if I don't try and think straight. I begin to wonder if Sam has been taking me seriously these past few months. She seems to be very dismissive of me all of a sudden. The fact that I'm nineteen and not mature enough to take on any proper adult responsibility. Is that what she really thinks of me?

I sit opposite her on the armchair I feel myself bristling. Don't react, I tell myself, don't get angry. 'How does anybody know how to be a dad or a mum? It's not something anybody can teach you. You just get on with it. I looked after my little brother. I fed him, changed his nappy, played with him.'

'Yeah, then you handed him bick.' Sam takes off her coat and flings it over the back of the couch. 'If I have this baby it will be my responsibility. I'll be the one thit will have to look after it.'

I can barely speak I'm so angry. 'What's that supposed to mean Sam?'

She gets up and walks around the room. 'It will be me who will carry the baby for nine months. Me who will give birth to it. Me who will breastfeed it. Me who will watch it day and bloody night so it doesn't choke on something or have a cot death, or catch measles or whatever the hell else babies catch! It's a massive fucking scary responsibility Tom, thit's what I mean!'

I give her time to get her breath back. I know if I jump in it will become an argument. 'I know it is, Sam. I come from a family of eight. I know how it works. So where do you see me in all this? Where do I fit in?'

She sits back down on the couch and then gets up quickly. 'I'm going to bead. I want to be alone Tom, so sleep in your own bead tonight.' I decide not to argue with her over this. Let her sleep on it.'

In the morning I can hear her being sick in the bathroom. I remember this happening to my mother. We have a very quiet, tense breakfast. She leaves without kissing me. I have a bad day at work. I feel detached from myself. I can't take in information. Joe Eagan shouts at me and is pointing at something. First time he's spoken to me in weeks. 'Fuckin wall ties there and there, wake up!'

I'm expecting the worst. I knew I shouldn't have let myself get happy. I let my guard down. I wait nervously for her to come in, she's late. I hear someone on the stairs. She comes into the living room, and glares at me. I don't want to hear what she's about to say.

'Lit's go for a drink.'

Jesus. I'm so glad to hear that. But maybe she's just prolonging my agony.

We go to the Clarence. It's quite full for a Monday night. We sit on the stools at the bar. Sam orders a vodka and coke.

TOM JOAD AND ME

I have a pint of lager. The barman asks me what kind of lager I want. I say it doesn't matter. He pours me a Harp, which I hate.

Sam is silent for a long time until she says. 'I hid plans Tom. I wanted to stay in England for at least two more years. I wanted to travel to Europe and see Paris and Berlin and Madrid and Amsterdam.' She goes to take a drink of vodka but sets it back on the bar. 'How would you feel if I got rid of it?'

All my blood begins to race around my head. I try and absorb and make sense of the question. I have a feeling my mouth is hanging open. She snaps at me. 'Oh come on Tom, for fucks's sake what do you feel in your gut?'

'NO!' I shout at her. Everyone in the bar is staring at us. 'No,' I say again more quietly. 'I don't want you to get rid of it. It's half mine.'

She takes a large mouthful of the vodka. 'I've already made up my mind. . . I'm not getting rid of it. I just wanted to know how you felt about it. I'm going to have to stop drinking.' She takes another large drink of the vodka, turns around on the stool and looks at me. 'I promised Dad thit if I ever had a baby, it would be born in New Zealand and thit if I got. . . married, he would walk me up the aisle. I promised him thit and I keep my promises Tom. It's all he's ever asked of me. It would break his heart if I broke my promise to him. I can't ask you to emigrate to New Zealand. You've got friends here, family in Ireland. New Zealand is a long way away. It's the bottom of the bloody world.'

I nod as casually as I can. 'Why don't you ask me if I want to go with you to New Zealand, Sam? Why don't you start there.'

She sips her vodka. 'Would you really come all the way to New Zealand with me, Tom?'

I pretend to think about it.

'Nah I can't, I've got a lot on this week.'

She shakes her head. 'You see what I mean though Tom, you can't take anything seriously you always make a joke of it.'

'I can make a joke, and still take things seriously Sam. The Irish are good at that.' I kiss her on the lips. 'Does this mean our baby will have that stupid friggin accent?'

She smiles and hugs me. I'm so relieved to feel that hug and see her smile. 'Fraid so, bro.'

I get a package addressed to Emmet McCrudden. This really pisses me off. It's like I have a real live ghost walking beside me. I know it can't be my passport. I rip it open. It's from Maeve. She's sent me a photograph of all of us at her wedding. Mother, Father and their eight children. I stare at it. It feels like this is the first time I've really looked at these people. Everyone is smiling apart from me. Sam comes in from the kitchen.

'What's thit you've got?'

'Oh it's just a photo from Maeve's wedding.'

Sam looks at it over my shoulder. I give it to her. She studies it. 'Bloody Nora that's all your family? The bride looks gorgeous. It must be great to have such a big family. Thit's your mum and dad there yeah?'

'Yeah.'

'Your mum looks too young to have all those kids.'

'She had her first when she was just seventeen. She's still only forty.'

Sam studies it some more. 'Who's the little guy making a face?'

'Ah, that's my kid brother, Fergal.'

'He's a deedringer for you.' I take the photo and look closer at Fergal. I can't see it. I can only see me looking miserable amongst my smiling happy family.

Everything is beginning to move very fast. Sam has given in her notice. My passport has arrived. I keep staring at it. Tom Joad. This is it. I feel excited. I try and think what it will be like to live in somewhere like New Zealand. I can't imagine it. I know nothing about it. I don't have any pre-conceived ideas. This will be Tom Joad, a new man, entering a completely new country. It feels right. Sam asks me do I want to marry her? I say yes. She says I'll ask you again in the morning and then before you go to bed tonight, after that I won't ask you again. I say thanks. She asks me in the morning and before I go to bed and I say yes both times. I remember not to make a joke about it. Sam wants to be in

New Zealand by end of May and for us to marry in early June. She doesn't want her bump to show in the wedding photos. I apply for a working visa and when we're married I can apply for citizenship. She calls her father and tells him she's coming home to get married. She said he was overjoyed. I tell Fast Eddie. He thinks I'm joking. All the lads think I'm messing around. When I finally convince them I'm not, they all seem happy for me.

Crash Test says. 'I thought summit was goin on wey you two!' Although I know he didn't have a clue.

Fast Eddie says. 'You'll have to go out with a fuckin bang. I'll organise the back room in the Swan and you can try and book one of them bands you like.' This makes me laugh. It would be great to book Dr Feelgood, but I doubt that will happen.

I think about whether I should tell Maeve. I decide I'll write to her when I get to New Zealand. I don't want her to try and dissuade me not to go and if I know Maeve that's exactly what she'll do. I don't want to have that phone conversation. I need to focus and not be distracted. Not by anything. I ask Sam if she will come with me after work and visit someone.

'Visit? Visit who?'

'A friend of mine. It's not far.'

I buy a bottle of Courvoisier brandy and get the girl in the wine shop to wrap it up in nice wrapping paper. Sam is intrigued.

'Who is this person?'

I knock on Hilda's door. The gnomes are smiling at me. I nod at them. 'Alright lads?'

Hilda opens the door, she's cooking again. But it's not turtle soup. I don't recognise the smell. 'Hi Hilda, it's Tom, remember me?'

Hilda looks slyly at me. 'Oh, Tom, yes of course, do come in.'

I introduce Sam and give Hilda the bottle of brandy. She laughs. 'Oh you shouldn't have. I'll be drunk for a week now.' I tell her we're emigrating to New Zealand.

'Oh, that's a wonderful place. My first husband and I visited Auckland. I remember we drove all around Coromandel peninsula, what views, it's a heaven on earth, most beautiful country I've been to.'

Hilda is cooking something called a risotto she insists on sharing it with us. She shows us photos of all of her husbands, all of her trips. It seems that Hilda has lived ten lives. She's a real inspiration. Before we leave she hugs me and kisses my cheek, whispers in my ear, 'She's the one.'

I phone Maeve and tell her the phone in the flat is going to be disconnected. I hate lying, but I can't take the chance. I've spent four months jumping on it when it rings and I know my luck will eventually run out. She'll call and Sam will pick up and say 'Emmet? I don't know any Emmet.' I also tell her not to send anything to me by post as I'm moving flat and will give her the new address as soon as I move in. I'm just not ready to explain why I'm emigrating. Da is still off the drink and preaching the gospel to anyone who will listen. He's also taken up making headstones and the back garden of the new house in Burren Park View looks like a graveyard. Ma is working part-time in the Brewery Tap doing lunches. I feel relieved that things seem to be coming together at home, I just hope they stay that way. I know how my father can change once he gets bored with something. It would be great if Fergal could enjoy his teenage years. I will tell Sam my McCrudden saga eventually, but for now she doesn't need to know. She's got enough to deal with. Our flights are booked. We leave on Monday 6th May which is in five days' time. Fast Eddie has booked the Swan for Saturday night. I tried to book the Winkies, but they were on tour and would have cost a fortune. I end up with a band called The Crypt. I'd seen them open once for Ducks Deluxe and I thought they were great.

My going away bash was probably the best night I've ever had in my life. The Crypt were fantastic, a great covers band, they played all sorts. Stones, Zeppelin, Who, Kinks, some John Lee Hooker, Leadbelly and a great souped up version of Robert Johnson's '32/20 Blues'. The lead singer also told some very funny and outrageous jokes between songs. Sam danced with everyone. Crash Test was in tears and then fell over a chair and split his lip.

'I did that on purpus jus fir you Tum!'

At the heel of the hunt there was a lot of drunken hugging and handshaking and back slapping, and I was an emotional mess. Fast Eddie gave me a hundred quid. He said it was a present for the breadsnapper. Sam got me out of there at 2am and we taxied home. I stayed in bed the next day until noon.

TWENTY-FOUR

The furthest I've flown is 500 miles which took fifty-five minutes. Christchurch is 12,000 miles away and takes twenty-nine hours, stopping at Hong Kong and Auckland. It has cost us £280 each, this is the most money I've ever spent on anything. Thank you, Madge McGuckian. Terminal 3 was a much more emotional terminal than Terminal 1. Lots of people hugging and crying. I assumed this was because the planes flew to far flung places and the passengers were not holiday makers who would be back in two weeks. There was also a high intensity of British soldiers and police which immediately made me nervous. Sam talked non-stop, the freckles on her nose fighting for space as she laughed at something. After we checked-in our luggage we headed straight for departures. I kept feeling for my passport in my inside pocket and staring at my boarding card. SEAT NUMBER 142F. This was actually happening. I was going to New Zealand, the bottom of the bloody world with the girl I loved who was carrying our baby. I hadn't planned any of this and I thought to myself that's probably why it was all going so well. I knew this was the happiest I'd ever been in my entire life.

Arrows pointed us in the direction of PASSPORT

CONTROL. As we turned the corner I could see a security checkpoint looming, similar to the ones I'd experienced on my trips to Belfast. Two Special Branch officers in grey suits behind a large lectern with that familiar blue police logo with the two lions holding up a gate, or maybe the bars of a prison? I could feel my chest tighten, took a deep breath and told myself I now had ID. I was legit and had Sam by my side. We were almost past when I looked one of them in the eye. Always a mistake.

Suit number 1 said, 'Excuse me sir could we have a word?' There was just something about the way these people said 'sir' that turned my stomach. 'Can I see some ID please, thank you?'

I had my passport in front of his face before he'd finished the sentence. Sam had to search for hers in her handbag. Suit number 2 joined in the merry banter, 'Travelling somewhere nice?'

'Christchurch,' I replied.

My tongue felt like it was growing in my mouth. He didn't respond. All I could see behind his eyes was a determination to find something wrong, something bad. He didn't care where I was going. Suit number 1 studied my passport, studied me, then back to my passport.

'Tom Joad?' This was a question and I knew I was in trouble. 'Have you been through here before sir?'

I hesitated, something else you must never do when being questioned, but I wasn't sure if I could speak with a swollen tongue. 'No.' Sam answered for me.

Suit 2 smiled at her, handed back her passport. 'If you would like to take a seat over their Miss. . . Pinkerton. Thank you, we shouldn't be long.'

Sam stared at him. 'Why? Whit's goin on?''

This time I interrupted. 'It's OK Sam, take a seat.' Sam snorted and went and sat in a red plastic chair.

Suit number 1 looked me over again. 'It's just that I recognise you from somewhere. Could you come through sir?'

This was made to sound like a request, but I knew it was an order. I followed the suits into a small room. I turned and smiled at Sam who give me a puzzled shrug. I knew all the blood had left my face. If I wasn't blushing like a beetroot, then I was doing an impression of a sick corpse. I sat on the chair and tried to keep my hands from shaking. This wasn't lost on Suit 1.

'You alright sir?' I nodded. He looked at me again the way someone looks at you when they don't believe a word you're saying. 'You sure we haven't met before?'

'I'm fairly sure.'

He made for the door. 'Ok I've just got to check something.'

Suit 2 sat opposite me. 'We have to be thorough sir, you understand?' I nodded. He lit a cigarette. What part of Northern Ireland are you from?' Here we go. 'County Tyrone.'

'Ever been in trouble over there?''

'No.' He shook his head sadly. 'It's bad what's happening over there wouldn't you say?''

I had to agree. 'Yeah. It's bad.'

He nodded again. 'And now they have the gall to bring it to our door. . . the bastards planted a bomb in the car park last year, you must have heard about that?'

I nodded. He glared at me, a challenging look that wanted me to condemn it, to agree that they were bastards, and the poor British were being put upon for no reason by these animals. I didn't look away from his gaze. I knew I should be cleverer. This stare could affect the rest of my life but I couldn't help it. I wasn't going to play his game. I wanted to say you need a history lesson you moron. Then to my relief he suddenly changed tack.

'Christchurch eh, that's a long way. You emigrating?' The word emigrating sounded final. I wanted to say I hope so. I nodded back.

'Yeah. Sam's my girlfriend, we have a baby on the way.'

Not a flicker from this bastard. 'You been back lately. . . to Tie-rone?' It was as if he was saying it like that on purpose, like it wasn't really a proper place.'

'Yes, I've been back.'

'Holiday was it?'

'No, a wedding.'

He nodded again, 'Hmmmm.'

He stared at me for the next five minutes. I tried looking

back at him in a normal way but his expression was making me angry and I was suddenly frightened that I might say something stupid. I looked down at my shoes. Suit 1 entered smiling like he'd won the pools. It was a smug smile of triumph. He shouts across the room.

'Emmet McCrudden!'

I felt like I'd been hit by a train. I stared back at him. He lit a cigarette. Smoked it like he'd just had sex. I suddenly had a flashback of my face being rubbed in my own piss. This couldn't be happening, not when I was so close to escaping. He blew smoke at me.

'I knew I recognised you. I just been on to my old sergeant in Hammersmith. You were the bloke who broke into the station through the skylight.' He turns and laughs at Suit 2. 'Straight up he thought it was the fucking Hammersmith Palais. Yeah you give the sarge a right old laugh that night. He loaned you a pair of boots and when you brought them back wrapped in brown paper, we all thought you were planting a bomb. I was the first to jump you, threw you on the ground. Remember now?'

I was too weak to speak. I nodded and tried to smile.

'So what's with the Tom Joad passport. . . Mr McCrudden?'

I knew I had to get it together. I took another obvious deep breath. 'I changed my name by deed-poll, it's all legal.'

'Changed your name eh, so why would you want to do that? With a good Irish name like McCrudden! You running away from something?'

I suddenly felt the blood coming back into my system. I couldn't mess this up.

'I changed it because I hated it. McCrudden was a name that always seemed to get me into trouble. That's my girlfriend out there, she's pregnant. I'm going to Christchurch with her to start a new life. . .' I looked the both of them in the eye. . . 'I'm Tom Joad. OK. I'm legal and I haven't been in trouble.'

There was a silence, a long lumbering silence. I could clearly hear a loud clock ticking in my head. Suit 1 handed me back my passport. 'Have a good trip Tom Joad, and don't go breaking into any more police stations.'

I could've hugged him. I took my passport. 'Thank you.'

Sam was all over me when I came out. Her concerned hands on my face. 'You alright? Whit was thit all about you were in there for bloody ages.'

'I'm Irish. The Special Branch love talking to us.' I kissed her more passionately that I meant to. She giggled.

'Whit's got into you?'

'Come on let's go for a drink.'

We flew with New Zealand Air. The flight wasn't full so we were able to spread ourselves across three seats and get some sleep. The last leg into Auckland wasn't as good. A baby cried nearly all the way. I thought about Andre and wondered how he was? Sam slept through most of it. The last two hours was the worst. I desperately wanted to get off but comforted myself with the thought that I wasn't in a pitch-dark cell in Paddington Green Police Station.

Sam's dad was called Robby. He wore a checked shirt with the sleeves rolled up. He had a big happy sunburnt face, blue eyes and a strong jaw. I could see the resemblance straight away. He was all quick movements like he had come from working hard at something and was still in that rhythm. He hugged Sam and shook my hand warmly. He picked up two of our cases. I carried the other two. He walked quickly to the car park, talking all the time but I didn't catch all of it, my hearing had gone and I felt like I was in a dreamlike state walking in another world and I guess I was. Robby drove a big old Dodge pick-up truck which smelled of pipe smoke. There was a dog in the back tied with a rope. The dog went berserk when it saw Sam. She ran towards it and let it lick her face.

'Ollie, you beaut, you silly sausage.' Ollie the Collie I was told, was the much loved family dog. Robby laughed and shook his head. 'I niver git thit much atteention.'

We drove for about forty minutes until we reached Sumner. Sumner was Sam's home town. A beautiful little place right on the ocean. Robby says. 'I rinted a place fir you on Hardwicke Street Samo. Jus to you find sumthin else. It's gotta gardin and an apple tree. I know the bloke who owns it. He's a straight up bloke and he's geeven us a fair deal on the place.'

'Hardwicke, right beside the beach. Thit's great Dad. Thank you so much.'

'Sawright love. I opened the windows a bit jus to ear the place. Hasn't been luved in for a while.'

It made me smile the way he said 'luved' for lived. I thought the rented house on Hardwicke Street was amazing. It was all on one floor, sort of like a bungalow. The outside was newly painted, it had three bedrooms, a big living room and kitchen. It also had a wood stove. I love a wood fire. The garden was overgrown, but even the weeds looked exotic. The apple tree was heavy with fruit, some lay on the ground eaten by worms. I'd pick them first chance I got.

Sam and I slept long into the morning the next day. After a breakfast of porridge and banana, Sam suggested she give me a tour of the place. Sumner was almost perfect. The beach was a five minute walk and what a beach, soft sand that curled around for a couple of miles or so. Sumner was surrounded by hills dotted with brightly painted houses. The town itself had a little cinema that showed the latest films, a couple of cafes, one pub and two restaurants. It seemed that Sam knew everyone. We met a family called the Thomsons. Mum and Dad and eight children, two of them grown up and about my age. The Thomsons ran the grocery store and had a farm in the hills. The whole family worked in the business. Sam said they were inseparable and all lived in a massive farmhouse. The next week saw Sam and I looking for work. Sam soon found a job just outside Christchurch as a Data Scientist.

'Bloody hell listen to this, Tom, *Some of the work will*

involve interpretation of bird calls to help people engage with nature.' That made us laugh long and hard. I ran around the house shouting *Cuckoo Cuckoo!* I eventually found a job in the middle of Christchurch building a new primary school. The foreman was Sean O'Hanlon from Ennis, County Clare. Sean was lean and angular with the biggest Adam's apple I've ever seen. It looked like he'd swallowed a bird and it was trying to escape. He had been in New Zealand for twenty-five years but his accent was as strong as the day he left home.

Sam and I paid a visit to the pastor at the local church. Pastor Nigel Williams was like every vicar you ever saw in any Carry On film: buck teeth, round glasses and a smiley holy happy face. His catch phrase was *Yes yes yes very good.* I'm sure that's all he said throughout the meeting we had about our marriage. The date was set for three weeks time 14th June. *Yes yes yes very good.*

Work was so laid back compared to London. We finished at 4.30 every day and didn't work Saturdays. I was working with Tomaz from Poland and a Maori guy called Tawhiri, both nice lads. Tomaz played drums in a band at weekends. They did mostly weddings but he was hoping they'd be able to get some gigs in the city. He suggested we should go to the Ram Jam Club as that was the best place in town for live music. The Christchurch music scene would be something that I'd have to check out. I was asked could I open up on Saturday morning to let the school governors have a tour around the site. When I got home Sam had left me a note to say she had gone to visit her Dad. I decided to go for a swim. I stopped off at the Kiwi Kitchen to grab a Sausage Sizzle. This was a local delicacy. Sausage, onion and sauce between two slices of crusty white bread.

As I came out of the cafe and bit into my sandwich, I heard someone shout 'Emmet!' My heart kicked my chest like a mule! What? Emmet? Was there someone else in Sumner called Emmet? 'Emmet!' The voice rose with excitement. It was a voice that sounded familiar and then. 'Emmet McCrudden! Is that you? Oh my God. Emmet!' I drop my sandwich on the pavement.'

My first instinct was to run, but I turn around to see Mandy Patterson lolloping towards me with Jem hopping in her wake. She throws her arms around me. 'Good God Emmet! I knew that was you I could tell by your walk.' What was it about my walk that people noticed? I had changed my name and it looked like I would soon have to change my walk as well.

'Jesus Emmet, everybody has been looking for you.' Mandy and Jem are staring at me. I try to work out what Mandy's horrified expression means.

'What the hell are you doing here?'

I'm thinking the same thing about these two wandering weirdos.

'Why didn't you come home? Maeve was very upset.' I

step away from Mandy who has inched uncomfortably close to my face.

'Upset about what?'

Mandy turns to Jem, 'I don't think he knows.'

'Knows what Mandy, what are you talking about?'

Mandy's face becomes sad and sympathetic, she folds her arms and lowers her head. 'Your father's dead Emmet. He died two weeks ago.'

Jem takes my arm. 'He collapsed in the street in the middle of one of his sermons. Fatal heart attack. I know your father liked a drink Emmet, which turned him into a demon, but he was good man sober, and he died sober. So I suppose that's a blessing.'

Mandy is wiping her eyes with a tissue. 'Maeve went to London looking for you. Hoping she'd find you and bring you back for the funeral.' I was suddenly aware of a seagull swooping and squawking above my head. It was as if it was angry at me, squealing at me, chastising me. It wouldn't shut up. I wanted to strangle the fucking thing.

Jem squeezes my arm 'How long have you been here?'

'Eh, oh not long, I'm eh. . . just touring around with a friend. We're leaving in about an hour actually. Going back to London.''

Jem nods, 'Ah that's a shame we're here for two more days and then we're off to Madura in Eastern Java for the Karapan sapi, the annual bull racing. But I understand that you'll have to get back home.'

Mandy takes my hand in hers. 'We're sorry to bring you such sad news Emmet. You must come for a quick drink with us now before you go, you and your friend. We passed a nice little place just around that corner.'

'OK sure yeah, listen why don't you two wait there and I'll go get him.'

'OK. See you in a minute. Emmet McCrudden, I can't believe it.'

I walk as casually as I can, turn the corner into the bottom of Scarborough Road and run like hell. I don't stop until I get to the sea. I would have to hide for two days. That wasn't going to be easy. Sumner was a small place. I drop my swim bag on the sand and sit on a rock. I think what I feel is guilt. Not about missing my dead father's funeral but about Maeve. The thought of her searching for me in London. The seagull lands on the sand near my feet its glassy eyes staring at me. I shout at it 'What the fuck are you looking at?' It flies off, taking a shit as it does so. I breathe deeply. This was what I'd been dreaming about. A clean break. A fresh start. A new beginning. I'd used up every cliché. I ask myself am I sad? No. Am I frightened? No. Am I angry? No. Do I feel regret? No. I have Sam and a baby on the way. I have a job and a house. Happiness is waiting around the corner. I just have to forget about everything else.

The Thomsons come into view. I sit and watch them. There they all are, that big inseparable family chiacking around as Keefer would have called it. The Thomsons. My sober Daddy, his trousers rolled up kicks water at the young boy, who would be about Fergal's age. Fergal splashes him back and runs off shouting and waving. Robert and Connor are wearing bathing trunks and searching the sand for something. Noreen, Maeve and Emmet dressed in shorts and bright Hawaiian shirts are playing with a frisbee and two of the others Aisling and Sean, have a net and jam jars on a string. They trail the jam jars through the water's edge. Mum is swiping at something above her head, maybe a wasp? She tries to get away from it, this makes them all laugh. Their laughter echoes around the beach, big squeals of happy laughter. I stand and watch my family. Mum and Dad and their eight children, underneath the bright blue Sumner sky.